A PLUME BOOK

THE DOUBLE CROSS

Maria Kielar

CLARE O'DONOHUE is a freelance television writer and producer. She has worked worldwide on a variety of shows for the Food Network, the History Channel, and truTV, among others. An avid quilter, she was also a producer for HGTV's *Simply Quilts*.

ALSO BY CLARE O'DONOHUE

The Lover's Knot
A Drunkard's Path

The
Double Cross

A SOMEDAY ✂ QUILTS MYSTERY

Clare O'Donohue

A PLUME BOOK

PLUME
Published by Penguin Group
Penguin Group (USA) Inc., 375 Hudson Street, New York, New York 10014, U.S.A. •
Penguin Group (Canada), 90 Eglinton Avenue East, Suite 700, Toronto, Ontario, Canada M4P 2Y3
(a division of Pearson Penguin Canada Inc.) • Penguin Books Ltd., 80 Strand, London WC2R 0RL,
England • Penguin Ireland, 25 St. Stephen's Green, Dublin 2, Ireland (a division of Penguin Books
Ltd.) • Penguin Group (Australia), 250 Camberwell Road, Camberwell, Victoria 3124, Australia
(a division of Pearson Australia Group Pty. Ltd.) • Penguin Books India Pvt. Ltd., 11 Community
Centre, Panchsheel Park, New Delhi – 110 017, India • Penguin Books (NZ), 67 Apollo Drive,
Rosedale, North Shore 0632, New Zealand (a division of Pearson New Zealand Ltd.) • Penguin
Books (South Africa) (Pty.) Ltd., 24 Sturdee Avenue, Rosebank, Johannesburg 2196, South
Africa

Penguin Books Ltd., Registered Offices: 80 Strand, London WC2R 0RL, England

First published by Plume, a member of Penguin Group (USA) Inc.

First Printing, October 2010
10 9 8 7 6 5 4 3 2 1

 REGISTERED TRADEMARK—MARCA REGISTRADA

LIBRARY OF CONGRESS CATALOGING-IN-PUBLICATION DATA

O'Donohue, Clare.
   The double cross : a someday quilts mystery / Clare O'Donohue.
      p. cm
   ISBN 978-0-452-29642-8 (alk. paper)
   1. Quilters—Fiction. 2. Quilting—Fiction. 3. Quilts—Fiction. 4. Murder—
investigation—Fiction. I. Title.
   PS3615.D665D68 2010
   813'.6—dc22   2010014242

Printed in the United States of America
Set in Granjon
Designed by Eve L. Kirch

To Sr. Mary Madonna, Una Moran, Kathleen Sweeney, Una Smith,
and Betty Sheehan. Thank you for being such wonderful aunts,
role models, and friends.

$\mathcal{A}$CKNOWLEDGMENTS

Thanks, first of all, to the many people who have read the Someday Quilts Mysteries, and especially those who have taken the time to contact me. There have been days that a supportive e-mail kept me from hurling my computer across the room. Also thanks to my editor, Becky Cole, for her patience, support, great advice, and unwavering cheerfulness; Mary Pomponio, for her excellent, as always, publicity skills; and to all the unsung heroes in sales and marketing who get the books on the shelves. To my agent, Sharon Bowers, thanks for helping me chart a course for a, hopefully, long career. To Illinois Crime Scene Investigator Howard J. Dean, and Dr. Brian Peterson, Deputy Chief Medical Examiner for Milwaukee County, for their help with the murder part of the story, and to Debby Brown for showing me around a long arm quilting machine. While these three people provided invaluable help, I do want to say that if any of the details are wrong in the book, the fault lies with me. Thanks also to Alex Anderson, for her friendship and support, and to the folks at AccuQuilt for helping with the die-cut section of the book, and their enthusiasm for the entire Someday Quilts Mysteries series. I'd also like to thank my mother, Sheila O'Donohue, for helping with the manuscript, Jim McIntyre, for being such a good sport, and his family Peggy, Matt, and MaryKate for all the encouragement. Thanks to Maria Kielar for the photos, and Margaret Smith and Brian Mc-Donagh for the Sunday sessions. Thanks to all my friends, who have patiently listened to me talk about the series. And finally, thanks, as always, to Kevin, V, and my family—Dennis, Petra, Mikie, Mary, Jim, Connor, Grace, Jack, Cindy, and Steven.

The Double Cross

$\mathscr{P}$ROLOGUE

I crouched behind the largest tree I could find and tried to steady my breathing. It's startling how loud breathing can be when you're trying to be quiet. My hands were shaking and I didn't know how long my legs would hold, but my life depended on it. The thought made my hands shake more.

I listened. There was nothing but the sounds of a few birds. I knew it was probably pointless but I took my cell phone out of my pocket. There was one bar, so I took a chance and dialed Jesse. Just as it started to ring, the call was dropped. No signal, only the quiet of country life that my grandmother had been extolling a few days ago. I wrapped my fingers around the phone, just in case.

I heard leaves rustle. I tried to think. How close was the sound? Did I have time to run or should I just hope for the best and stay hidden behind the tree? I thought about every action movie I'd ever seen, hoping it would inspire a plan, but nothing came to me. All I could think of was Bernie's warning about going into the woods. And my unfinished journal quilt—the one that was supposed to depict my life as I hoped it would become.

My heart was pounding. I looked around for a possible escape route. I wasn't sure my feet would move even if I wanted them to, so I waited. More noise. But this wasn't birds. This was something else. Footsteps. I held my breath and prayed they would move in the other direction.

Then nothing. The noise, the footsteps, had stopped. I realized I'd caught my foot in some tangled vines and my ankle was itching. I tried to ignore it and concentrate on the footsteps. I'd have plenty of time to scratch my ankle once I got out of this. If I got out of this.

The footsteps started up again and for a moment moved toward me. I held my breath. Then, just when they seemed on top of me, they stopped and seemed to move in the other direction.

"Keep going," I thought. "Just let me get out of here and I will never stick my nose where it doesn't belong. I will live a long life making quilts and drawing pictures and staying out of trouble."

Then the footsteps were gone. Definitely gone. I stood up, took a deep breath, and ran as fast as I could in the opposite direction. I didn't care that tree branches were slapping me across the face as I ran. I didn't care that my feet were getting muddy or that I had bitten so hard into my lip that it was beginning to bleed. I just wanted to get out of the woods and back to the inn as fast as I could.

I could see the hiking trail that led back to the inn when my cell phone suddenly rang. The sound was so startling that I nearly dropped it.

"Nell?" I heard Jesse's worried voice on the other end.

"Jesse," I whispered. "I'm near where we found the body. I'm in trouble. I'm heading toward the inn."

"I'm coming to get you," he said. "And Nell, I . . ."

The signal was lost again, and with it Jesse's comforting voice. My heart sank.

"Don't let that be the last time I talk to him," I silently prayed.

Then I saw the gun.

"Jesse's on his way right now," I called out as defiantly as I could, but even I could hear the fear in my voice.

"Well, he's going to be too late," was the response.

The gun was pointed directly at me. I wasn't going to just stand there and get shot, so I turned and ran toward the trail. I'd taken ten steps when I heard a loud sound.

After that all I could feel was pain.

CHAPTER 1

Two Weeks Earlier

I t's the closest two quilters have ever come to killing each other.

"I'm not doing this to hurt you," Susanne tried to explain.

"You've betrayed me," Bernie spat back.

"You're being an old fool." Susanne sat back in her chair and looked to the rest of the group for support. The rest of us looked elsewhere.

It had started innocently enough. Just an hour earlier I'd closed up Someday Quilts for our usual Friday meeting. A small group of us met at my grandmother's quilt shop each week to work on our quilts, eat fattening foods, and catch up on gossip. To an outsider we might have appeared to be an odd group. There was me, a twenty-six-year-old aspiring artist and part-time worker at the shop; my grandmother, Eleanor Cassidy, the shop's owner; Carrie, in her midforties, a mother of two and owner of the local coffee shop; Natalie, my age and already a mom with a second child on the way; her mother, Susanne; and Bernie, the ex-hippy pharmacist and our most laid-back member—until now. The only member missing was Maggie, my grandmother's oldest friend, who was in Ohio awaiting the birth of her first great-grandchild. On the surface we had little in common, and we certainly didn't seem like a group of close friends, but we all quilted. And with that to share, the rest came easy.

Natalie, the shop's newest part-time employee, had arrived early so she and I could make the coffee and arrange the chairs. Then we set a copy of the *Winston Weekly* newspaper on each person's seat. I was expecting lots of excitement once everyone had a chance to see it, but *excitement* was hardly the right word for what I got.

"What do you want us to read?" my grandmother asked as she sat down. My grandmother, Eleanor, was part role model, part bull-dog. A wonderful quilter, a strong business owner, a loving grandma (though never one to let me get away with anything), she was the person I hoped to be one day. Even her look was worth emulating. She had let her hair turn a no-fuss gray and cut it short, but stylishly. Her clothes, a pair of dark jeans and a pink oxford shirt, created the same pretty-but-practical effect.

"We have a celebrity in our midst," I told her, to pump up the enthusiasm.

"A missing dog?" asked Eleanor. "Why is that a celebrity?"

"It's not the dog," I said.

Eleanor rolled her eyes and tossed the paper to me. I scanned it. The front-page story was about a dog that had gone missing while out on a hunt. The owner described it as a kidnapping. Apparently it was the second dog to disappear in less than a month, and the own-ers were convinced it wasn't a coincidence.

I flipped to page two, then page three. There it was. I handed the paper back to my grandmother.

Just as I did, Carrie found the article in her copy and read it to the rest of us: "'Award-winning quilter Susanne Hendrick will be teaching a class called Journal Quilting at the newly opened Patchwork Bed-and-Breakfast owned by Rita and George Olnhausen. It will be a weeklong class, beginning April second, that will encourage participants to express their thoughts in fabric and explore techniques beyond basic quilting. Beginners and advanced quilters welcome. Contact George Olnhausen for class details and enrollment.'"

"That's amazing," declared Carrie. "You're well on your way to a teaching career."

"I love teaching classes here at the shop," Susanne said to my grandmother, "but I want to do something beyond Someday Quilts. You know, stretch myself a bit."

"Yes, of course. I'm thrilled to see you taking on a new project," Eleanor told her. "And soon I'll be able to say that a world-famous quilt teacher got her start at my shop."

"I can't believe how far we've all come toward realizing our dreams." Carrie pointed out the window toward Jitters, her coffee shop across the street. "I've got my place, Natalie is five-months pregnant with baby number two, Nell is busy pursuing an art career, and now Susanne has a weeklong quilt retreat. Everyone is doing what they love."

And that was it. Bernie slammed the paper on the chair and headed toward the door. "I'm so happy for everyone," she snapped. "I guess it doesn't matter that it comes at my expense."

I had no idea what she was talking about, and looking around it was clear that neither Natalie nor Carrie did, either. But the others seemed to understand. Eleanor and Susanne jumped up to stop Bernie from leaving and to coax her back into her chair. They spoke quietly to her for several minutes, and it seemed as though the crisis would pass. Then suddenly Bernie was upset all over again, until finally Susanne seemed to give up trying to explain and just got angry. After Susanne called Bernie an "old fool," everyone was clearly at a loss for what to do.

"It's a long time ago," my grandmother said repeatedly, but it seemed to offer no comfort.

"So it doesn't matter anymore?" Bernie shouted.

"Do you regret your life?" Eleanor asked sharply.

"Parts of it. Don't you?"

Susanne and Eleanor exchanged glances; then Eleanor's expression softened. She sat next to Bernie and quietly stroked her hand.

"Bernie, what would it take for you to let this go?" Eleanor asked.

Bernie looked at my grandmother with a coldness in her eyes I'd never seen before and never knew existed in her. "It would help if they were both dead."

For a moment the rest us sat in stunned silence, afraid to look at Bernie and unable to look away. Finally Carrie looked at me, obviously hoping for answers, but I shrugged. I was new to the group, having moved to Archers Rest from New York City only seven months before. Carrie had been a member for just over two years. Whatever was going on with Bernie, it obviously predated our inclusion in the quilting circle.

I looked over at Susanne, who seemed on the verge of tears. An expert art quilter, she'd won awards, taught classes, and helped those in need. She doted on her grandson and would never hurt a friend. If anything, Susanne's biggest fault was her extreme loyalty to those she loved.

"If you don't understand why I would want to try something new . . . ," Susanne tried again.

"I understand why you want to teach. I just don't understand why you have to teach there," Bernie shouted.

"I told you." Susanne was speaking slowly but insistently. "They found *me*. That George of yours called me and asked if I'd do it. How could I turn it down?"

"Because you're my friend. That's what friends do. Everyone here understands what I'm talking about." Bernie looked at me.

I smiled weakly. "I guess I don't understand," I admitted. "Your high school boyfriend and his wife have a bed-and-breakfast in the Adirondacks, and they want to attract quilters, so they're offering classes and opening a little shop," I said, trying to piece together the story from what I'd just overheard. "But why is it wrong for Susanne to teach a class there?"

"Thank you," Susanne sang out.

Bernie sighed. "I thought if anyone would understand what it feels like to be dumped it would be you, Nell."

For lack of a better response, I smiled. Then I got up and walked to the counter to grab a cookie from the batch Natalie had baked for the meeting. Behind me, I could hear my grandmother.

"That was unnecessary, Bernadette Avallone," Eleanor said. "I really don't see how Nell's romantic issues are fair game. It's hard enough for her without you throwing it in her face."

Nell's romantic issues. That was a nice way of putting it. I'd run away from my life in the city after my fiancé took up with the woman I considered my best friend. Just the other day, I'd heard they'd become engaged. Maybe it wouldn't have bothered me so much if my most recent romance wasn't faltering. I'd been dating the town's police chief, Jesse Dewalt, until the relationship ended because, as Jesse put it, I "couldn't stop interfering in police investigations." I was 0 for 2, and I guess that translates into "romantic issues."

"Oh, Nell," Bernie sighed, finally calming down. "I know I sound crazy, but George Olnhausen? And Rita? How can anyone have anything to do with them? I just know something bad will come of it. Mark my words. I have a feeling."

Bernie was our resident, and as yet unproven, psychic. But even if her gifts were real, I had the feeling she wasn't basing her prediction on anything other than her bruised ego.

I walked over and gave her a quick hug. I looked to Susanne to join me, but she just rolled her eyes. Our quilt meeting was, as usual, about everything but quilting.

And we hadn't even told Bernie the worst part.

CHAPTER 2

"Do you have everything?" Eleanor called to me from the front porch as I packed up the car.

"Everything but you," I told her.

"Coming. We're coming." My grandmother locked the door to her large Victorian home and headed toward the car. Beside her, as always, was her golden retriever, Barney. Now twelve, he was nearly deaf and starting to be a bit absentminded, but it only strengthened the bond he shared with Eleanor. It was no surprise to me that when Eleanor got roped into joining our Adirondack adventure, Barney came along for the ride.

After Bernie had gotten over the shock that Susanne would be teaching at the inn, Eleanor firmly announced that she and I would also be going. She did it in that way only my grandmother could, leaving no room for further discussion. I waited for another outburst, another accusation of disloyalty, but none came. Bernie just nodded, wished us luck, and said good night. As far as I knew, that was the last time anyone had heard from her.

"I'm looking forward to this," Eleanor said cheerily, as she got in the car. "A week of peace and quiet in the country. I can't wait to get started. I just want to stop at the shop first."

"We have to hit the road. Susanne said she's leaving at two," I reminded her.

"Just a quick stop," Eleanor said firmly.

It would put us behind schedule, but there was no point in arguing. There was never a point in arguing with my grandmother, though on occasion I'd given it a try.

We pulled up in front of Someday Quilts at a little after two, and Eleanor and Barney went in to give last-minute instructions to Natalie about running things while we were gone. In the more than thirty years since she'd opened, Eleanor had rarely left the place in anyone else's hands. Adding to her stress, Natalie had only been officially working there for three weeks. But I knew she was more than up to the task. When I'd started I'd never worked in retail and had no idea how to quilt. Natalie had experience with both. Besides, she had an assistant of sorts. Her toddler, Jeremy, played in a little area we had set up especially for him, entertaining the customers and putting everyone in the mood to make a baby quilt.

However difficult running the business would be for Natalie, I knew it would be a breeze compared to the week Susanne was going to have, and not just because of the class. She'd never gone twenty-four hours without spending time with Jeremy. I could see that despite her insistence on being on the road by two o'clock, Susanne was inside the shop, holding tight to her grandson, as if she would never see him again.

Rather than join the excitement, I went across the street to Jitters. Though it had been open only six weeks, the coffee shop was already a town favorite. When I walked in, most of the tables were filled with teenagers hanging out, people working at their computers, and mothers looking for a little time to themselves while their babies napped in strollers. There were four people in line, so I did what I'd been doing since opening day. I walked behind the counter and poured my own coffee.

"Have Bernie and Susanne made up?" Carrie asked as I reached for a muffin.

"Not that I know of. I thought it would come to blows last week."

"Over a man." Carrie shook her head. "I still don't get it."

"I'll let you know if I ever understand love." I smiled. And as I did, I saw Jesse walk in.

I rang up my coffee and muffin, and dropped the money into the till.

"Aren't you getting anything for Eleanor?" Carrie asked. "Some tea or something?"

"She said it would mean five stops between here and Winston."

"Just in case." Carrie handed me a bottle of water. "And in exchange you have to bring me back every tiny bit of gossip."

"I would even if you didn't give me water."

Since there was a growing line, I poured coffee for the next three customers while Carrie rang them up. When it was Jesse's turn, though, I let Carrie take over. As I walked out from behind the counter, Jesse stepped out of line.

"Taking on another job?" he asked.

"No. I just serve myself."

"Another rule you don't like to follow—waiting your turn." He was smiling, but I'd heard enough from him about my inability to follow the rules to find it amusing.

"Carrie doesn't mind. *She* likes it when her friends help out."

If he understood my reference, he didn't let on. "You're a good friend." He ran his fingers down my arm. It tickled. I moved away. "And it gives us a chance to say hi to each other."

"Not this week. I'm heading to a quilt retreat with the group. Most of them, anyway."

He moved closer to me and looked into my eyes. Jesse had a perpetually serious, slightly distracted expression on his face, as if he were in the midst of solving life's biggest questions. The short dark hair and small eyeglasses, combined with crisp white shirts, only added to the sense that he had no time for anything trivial. So when he smiled—and it was a wide, expressive smile—it always surprised me. There was a professorial handsomeness to him most of the time, but when he smiled, he was beautiful.

"The town won't be the same without you," he said, his voice almost a whisper.

I smiled but took a few steps back. His hair brushed against his glasses, and I resisted the urge to move it out of the way for him. "Archers Rest will be fine," I said. "Quieter but fine." And with that I walked out of the coffee shop.

It was a weak comeback, but I couldn't think of anything to say. We'd gone on a few dates and seemed to be heading somewhere until he put the brakes on things because I took an interest in his police work—a strong interest that sometimes included chasing suspects and breaking into people's homes. He couldn't handle it. Fine. But now he was flirting. And if I responded in kind, we'd be right back where we started, wherever that was.

I understood that Jesse had someone more important than me to consider. As a widower with a six-year-old daughter, he had more than his share of challenges. He didn't need another one, and I could be, according to Jesse and my grandmother, something of a challenge.

Back at the car, Susanne was holding Jeremy while Eleanor and Natalie put fabric catalogs in the trunk. As they finished, Bernie pulled up behind them. I ran to do whatever I could to stop an all-out war, but by the time I got there I realized something entirely different was going on. Bernie was putting her suitcase into our already crowded car.

"It's the right thing to do," Eleanor counseled her. "It will help you to put it behind you."

Bernie shrugged. "It's silly to carry this around for all these years, but I just have to know," she said.

Eleanor nodded, then turned to me. "Bernie has made a last-minute decision to join us. Isn't that nice?"

"Wonderful," I said weakly. Crazy was more like it. I opened my mouth to ask why, but I could see from Eleanor's eyes that this wasn't the right time. With nothing else to do, Natalie and I glanced uncomfortably at each other.

"Have a safe trip," Natalie said as she closed the trunk. She gave each of us a quick hug and watched as we got into the car, with Eleanor uncharacteristically giving up the front seat to Bernie. Before I could get in the driver's seat, Natalie tapped my arm. "There's got to be more to this than a high school romance," she whispered. "Bernie's in her sixties. Wouldn't she be over it by now?"

"I hope so. I'd hate to think that some people are impossible to get over." I watched as Jesse walked out of Jitters and toward the police station.

Natalie shook her head. "I was hoping that by Bernie's age we'd be past making fools of ourselves for men."

As the words came out of her mouth, I saw my grandmother's . . . gentleman friend, I guess he would be, park his car across the street.

Oliver White was an acclaimed artist and art teacher. Born in England, he had a European elegance and bad-boy charm even in his seventies. But whatever his reputation had once been, he was now as loyal to my grandmother as Barney was.

He walked to the car and Eleanor got out to greet him.

"I just wanted to see you off," Oliver said. He gave my grand-mother a kiss on the cheek. "I'll miss you terribly. But I want you to have all the fun in the world, and not to get into any trouble."

He looked at me.

"It's a quilt retreat," I reminded him. "Aside from not matching our seams, I'm not sure how much trouble we can get into."

"Do some drawing while you're up there. Do something that will put my work to shame."

"Not possible," I said.

"You're an artist, Nell. You'll do lovely work. Just look beyond the ordinary."

I kissed him on the cheek. "Thanks. I promise I will."

He smiled and ran his hand lightly across Eleanor's cheek, then headed back across the street. He waved to her one last time and she waved back. Because she thought no one was looking, a smile that made her glow crept across her face. When she caught me watching, the smile was replaced by a slight look of embarrassment and then a scowl.

"Honestly, Nell, with all this standing around it will be midnight before we get up there."

"Sorry, Grandma." I smiled. "I forgot we were on a schedule."

She nodded. As she got in the car, I saw her glance in the direction of Oliver, who was about to walk into Jitters. Her scowl turned back into a wistful smile. Happy as I was that my grandmother had found someone so clearly in love with her, my happiness was mixed with a little envy.

As I looked at Bernie, I realized I wasn't alone.

CHAPTER 3

The Patchwork Bed-and-Breakfast was a good name for the place. The main building, a rambling Victorian, looked as though it had been renovated a dozen times with no particular regard for the original architecture. There were two smaller buildings on the property: one looked like it would be used for the shop, and the other for the classroom. The place had an empty, lonely feeling to it that made me wonder if it might be better suited to ghosts than quilters.

I could see Susanne grow anxious as she walked around the grounds. "Maybe this was a bad idea," she whispered to me.

"No, it wasn't," I said, more in hope than confidence. "The students will get here tonight, and the place will come alive. It will be just what you hoped."

"Found the place okay?"

I jumped at the sound of an unfamiliar voice. When I turned I saw a man walking toward us, an ax in his hand.

"I'm George. We're just thrilled to have you folks here."

I immediately looked to Bernie. She was standing, or really hiding, behind Eleanor.

When no one else spoke, I stepped forward. "I'm Nell," I volunteered. "And this is your teacher, Susanne."

George was tall, with thinning hair and a growing belly, but he had friendly eyes and a comfortable way about him. He had the sort of easygoing look that would have made me like him if he hadn't been somehow responsible for hurting Bernie. He was wearing a pair of clean moccasins, new jeans, and a red-plaid flannel shirt over a crisp white T-shirt. It looked as though the entire outfit had arrived that morning from L.L. Bean.

He walked around shaking hands with the group. I waited, as I'm sure we all did, for George to reach Bernie. When he did, he stopped and stared at her for a moment before recovering and holding out both arms.

"This can't be Bernie Keegan." He smiled. "You look seventeen."

Bernie blushed. "Good to see you, George. It's Bernie Avallone now."

"Oh, that's right. I heard you married yourself some millionaire. No surprise there. You could have gotten any man you wanted. What are you doing here?"

"I'm a friend of Susanne's," Bernie said quietly.

"Is that right? It's a small world, by God. But a wonderful one. Come in, come in. Rita is out for the moment, but she will be thrilled that you came. I can't tell you how many times we've talked about you over the years. All the good times we three had." He stopped and stared at her again. "Bernie Keegan. You make me wish I were back in high school."

I could see Bernie's eyes tearing up. Whatever her reasons for being here, I knew it took a lot of courage. It was clear that she still felt something for this man, even after all the time that had passed and all the men she'd loved since. She and George stood awkwardly next to each other, both seeming to want to speak but not knowing what to say. I could see the mixture of embarrassment, pain, and curiosity in Bernie's eyes. There was a time when she knew everything about this man, everything that happened in his life and everything he dreamed would happen. Now they were just strangers with a past.

If I ran into my ex-fiancé, or Jesse, in forty years, maybe I'd feel the same awkwardness, the same lump in my throat. I walked over to Bernie and linked my arm with hers. I could feel her sink into me, and I felt as if I were the only thing keeping her from falling down.

"Are we going inside at any point?" Eleanor looked up at George. "Or are we going to stand in the cold?"

The Patchwork B-and-B was as shabby and haphazard inside as it was outside. The front hallway was covered with the kind of embossed white wallpaper that's often found in old Victorians, though it's normally painted over. No one had gotten to that step here, even though the paper had clearly been up awhile. The edges had begun to get dirty and the texture had worn down in spots. The hallway was furnished with only a small rectangular table and two uncomfortable chairs. George had to get the guest book out of a closet to check us in. To the left of the front door, two unvarnished glass-paned doors separated the hallway from the sitting room. They were left open, and one seemed about to come off the hinges. A scratched hardwood floor connected the two. A sheet of painter's plastic covered a couch in the sitting room, though there didn't appear to be any painting going on. The few decorations were out of place for a quilt-themed inn. On one wall there was a weathered-looking deer head, and mounted above the mantelpiece was a hunting rifle and a stuffed bird.

"We're remodeling," George said. "It used to have a hunting lodge feel. The previous owner was a hunter and he left us with some of his—I guess you would call them decorations. Lots of hunters up here. But don't worry; we're going to make it nice and feminine for the quilters. We're going to paint the place as soon as Rita decides on a color. And then we're going to sand down all the wood and get it back to its original condition. A lot of the wood has twenty coats of paint on it. Shame, really, the way this place was cared for."

"Should you be holding classes when you're in the midst of remodeling?" Eleanor asked. "Paying guests might like a bit of comfort."

George's eyes hardened for a moment; then he smiled, cheery as before. "Well, we were a bit enthusiastic, but that's our way. Once we latched on to the idea of bringing you ladies up here, we figured, why not get started?" He looked at Bernie and winked. "I said to Rita, 'Quilters don't mind a little work in progress.' Am I right, ladies?"

"When will the students arrive?" Susanne asked. "I'm anxious to meet everyone."

"Tomorrow," he said.

"But surely they're spending the night." Susanne looked around, concerned. "We talked about having a little reception the night before class, so we could get to know one another. If everyone is drives up tomorrow, there could be people arriving late."

"That won't be a problem. They're all local, so they'll be here bright and early. They're looking forward to your class. We all are. And if you need anything, just let me know."

Susanne pointed to a piece of artwork hanging by the door. It was a rough collage made from old greeting cards, mementos, and photographs. Something a child might make for Mother's Day. "My eye keeps going to that piece. I wonder if I could borrow it for class. It's the same idea as a journal quilt."

"That old, ugly thing? You can have it. It's another leftover from the previous owner. I'll bring it to the classroom myself. Though I hope your students come up with something nicer than that. I expect a lot from quilters."

"When did your wife start quilting?" Eleanor asked. "Or are you the quilter?"

"Neither of us is, actually. We went to a quilt show with some neighbors of ours. They like all that craft stuff. We saw just how big it is. No idea so many people quilted. Millions and millions. Who knew? Rita's mom quilted decades ago, but I thought it had gone the way of electric typewriters and my boyish good looks." He laughed. "Anyway, we did a little research and here we are." He held his arms wide and looked around, smiling. "Or here we will be, once we get everything in place."

"Perhaps your wife will sit in on Susanne's class and take it up," Eleanor said. "Or you, of course. Lots of men are quilting these days."

"Not me," George answered. "I can't see the sense, to be honest, in cutting up perfectly good pieces of fabric and then sewing them together again, but if it keeps you ladies happy, I guess it doesn't need to make sense." He smiled widely.

I could tell that George felt he'd given the right answer, but I knew it was only my grandmother's desire to help Susanne that kept her from lecturing him on the history of quilting. There is nothing that a quilter hates more than to have a thriving art that has played an important role in women's lives for centuries treated as if it were the quaint, outdated pursuit of dotty old women and lonely spinsters.

"By the way, we don't usually allow pets in the place." He pointed toward Barney. "They tend to mess things up. But since you're friends of Bernie's, I'm sure I can get Rita to let him stay in your room." He smiled at Eleanor. "I'll just have to remember to add a 'no pets' rule to the brochure for the next group."

CHAPTER 4

"Well, I don't care if he is Bernie's first love; I don't think I like that man," Eleanor said as we settled into a small room at the top of the stairs. The room was much like the downstairs—tired looking and full of unfinished projects.

"You're just saying that because he made a joke about quilters," I said.

"I am not. I just . . ." She stopped. Rather than admit I was right, Eleanor's way of conceding a point was to change the subject, so I took it as a victory when she looked around the room and grunted. "This place is a mess."

It wasn't just a mess. There were cobwebs in the corners at the ceilings and dust on the dresser. "We're not here for them. We're here for Susanne," I reminded her, and myself.

"But I promised to help them set up their shop," she continued, whispering as though she expected the place to be bugged. "And apparently they don't know anything about quilting. How am I supposed to help when they don't know a rotary cutter from a seam ripper?"

"We'll do our best." I was feeling a little concerned myself. "I guess it takes the pressure off Susanne. I can't imagine anyone coming here will expect Rose Hughes or Ricky Tims to be teaching the class."

"I suppose not." Eleanor sighed. "But did you hear what he said about Barney? As if this run-down old shack were some kind of showplace."

We both looked toward Barney. He responded with a yawn and settled into his bed, completely oblivious to the fact that he was an unwelcome guest. Before she'd unpacked her own suitcase, Eleanor had set up a bed for him in the corner of the room. She'd brought several of the quilts she'd made especially for him and laid them one on top of another until she felt the bed was soft enough. Then she placed his two favorite chew toys, his bone, and a few of his favorite cookie treats nearby. After he settled in, Eleanor carefully unwrapped a dish of dog food and cut a vitamin into four parts, pressing them into the meat. She put the dish at Barney's paws, and he sniffed for a moment, then ate the food, carefully leaving the four pieces of vitamin untouched.

"Look at that." Eleanor pointed to the vitamin pieces, a large smile on her face. "He smelled the vitamin. I think losing his hearing has heightened his other senses."

"Or he's like every other dog and has a great sense of smell," I pointed out.

She frowned. "Not every dog. Just special dogs." She pulled up a chair next to him and patted Barney's head as and he rubbed his nose against her arm.

"When did you get so soft?" I teased her. "I don't remember you making a fuss over me like that."

"I have other grandchildren," she said, "but I just have the one Barney."

I laughed and sat down on the floor beside Barney. The three of us played with Barney's toys until we nearly forgot what we'd gotten ourselves into.

✄

I was reminded twenty minutes later, when Susanne came into the room.

"We're all settled. I'm going for takeout at a Chinese restaurant that George recommended." She sounded apologetic. "It isn't quite what we expected, is it?"

"It's lovely, dear," Eleanor said, putting the best spin on it she could. "It reminds me of when I was starting the shop. It was a bit of a mess, too, but it turned out okay."

"But Barney," Susanne said. "As if that dog ever caused a moment's trouble in his life."

"Once they get to know him . . . ," I offered.

"I suppose." Susanne stood at the door, dejected. I worried that she might decide to go home before she'd even taught the first class.

Susanne had been a beauty queen in her younger days, and though now a grandmother in her fifties, she was still one of the most beautiful women I knew. Tall, blonde, slim, and elegant, she turned heads when she entered a room. And as a quilter she was talented and versatile. But she could also be shy, nervous, and even insecure.

"How's Bernie?" I hoped a change in subject would lighten the mood. I was wrong.

Susanne sighed. "I knocked on her door and told her about the food, but she said she wasn't hungry."

"You ordered her something anyway, I hope," Eleanor said.

"Of course. Broken hearts need fattening foods."

"What is the story with that anyway?" I asked.

"High school sweethearts, broken promises. He married the best friend," Eleanor said. "At least as far as I know."

"I don't mean to be . . ." I tried to think of the right way to say it without sounding like a bratty kid who thinks her generation invented love. "It's just that it's been such a long time . . ."

"Why is a sixtysomething-year-old woman still carrying a torch for her high school sweetheart?" Eleanor finished my thought. "I don't think it's the man. It's the life that could have been."

"But she's had a good life, hasn't she?" I asked. "Why have any regrets about the road not taken?"

"Oh, I hate that," Eleanor said. "That idea that we can't have any regrets because our experiences make us who we are. That's greeting-card psychology. We all have regrets. The people we've hurt, the times fear held us back from exciting possibilities . . ."

"The weird fabric we bought and could never find a use for," I added.

Eleanor and Susanne laughed.

"Not fabric," Susanne said. "You never regret a fabric purchase, no matter how weird."

After Susanne left to get the Chinese food, I settled back on the floor, laid my head on Barney's back, and let him lick my hand. I envied his uncomplicated life of dog treats and unending love. "If she's going to have regrets anyway, what good does coming here do her?" I finally asked my grandmother.

"She needs to make her peace with them," Eleanor said. "Bernie is wondering what might have been, and she can't shake herself out of it. People get stuck like that sometimes."

She reached out and brushed a few stray hairs off my forehead, stroking my head gently. "It's like when you make a quilt," she said. "You see a pattern you like and you think you want to make something just like it for yourself. But as you find fabrics, and cut and sew, the idea becomes something else. Something real, but something different from that pattern. If you measure the success of your quilt, or your life, by what you started out to do, more often than not you will decide you've failed. But if you realize that the pattern you followed is the one you created for yourself, you will love the quilt you made, and the life you made, more than the one you thought you were supposed to make."

Twenty minutes later while I was still thinking over my grandmother's words, Susanne opened the door to the room, her hands filled with plastic bags. "This place is spooky. When I drove up, I thought I saw a light coming from the woods. Then I swear I saw something run from the back of the house."

"Probably a deer," I suggested.

"Maybe, but it didn't run like a deer. It sort of floated. I couldn't see what it was because the porch light was out. It must have burned out when I was gone."

The thought of something out there, in the dark, hovering around this broken-down inn, made me shiver, but I put it out of my mind. It was going to be a long week if I succumbed to my imagination.

"Whatever it was, it's gone," I said. "And tomorrow we'll be quilting. Nothing's going to spoil that."

CHAPTER 5

Quilt retreats are usually weekend or weeklong quilting classes where experts, often nationally known teachers, give participants a chance to immerse themselves in a new technique or pattern. During the day, the teacher instructs the class, and in the evening the students are welcome to sew on their own or wander into town. The retreats are often set in the country, so there's little to do but quilt, talk about quilting, and look at quilts. And that's just what most of us want to do anyway.

It was going to be the first retreat for the Patchwork Bed-and-Breakfast, but, instead of comforting her, this seemed to make Susanne nervous. She had piled every possible tool, book, fabric scrap, and finished and half-finished quilt she could find into her car.

I'd volunteered to work as Susanne's assistant. I wasn't sure what that would involve beyond helping set up the classroom, but it seemed to provide Susanne with some relief to know that there would be a friendly face in the room. In her mind, the class would be filled with quilters as expert as herself, and I tried to reassure her that, regardless of their skill level, every student would learn something because Susanne wasn't teaching a pattern or a technique that someone might have picked up elsewhere. She was teaching a class on how to express oneself in fabric.

Journal quilts have become popular among quilters. Generally eight inches by ten inches or smaller, they serve as a way for quilters to document their experiences, much like a page in a diary. But journal quilts use visual images as well as words and reach beyond fabrics to include found objects, paint, paper, and lots of nontraditional methods. I'd never made a journal quilt and I couldn't think of any experience important enough to document, but I was looking forward to the class anyway.

Though Susanne, like most of us, had started as a traditional quilter, she had moved toward making art quilts—a large and sometimes difficult-to-define category that my grandmother described as quilts made, not for use, but solely for visual effect. And Susanne's quilts certainly had visual effect. She made landscapes, variations on traditional patterns, pictorial quilts of her grandson, and vibrant abstract quilts. Every quilt was free and open, and unconcerned with what quilters laughingly call "the quilt police"—the rules or rule enforcers that insist a quilt should have matching seams and perfect corners and the like. Every time I looked at a quilt of Susanne's, I sensed the rebel in her that I rarely saw in real life.

I knew there was a lot I could learn from her. And that, as much as a friend's desire to show support, was why I had offered my services.

"I'm Susanne Hendrick. And I'm very excited to be sharing the art of quilting with all of you." Susanne smiled nervously at the start of class. "Journal quilts, like a written journal, are private expressions. You shouldn't worry about what others will think, only what you wish to say. Use symbols, images, and objects that matter to you, even if they mean nothing to the rest of us. In my own quilts, I have found that I sometimes express quite private thoughts without meaning to, and I am always glad I did. I hope you'll get caught up enough in your work that you'll do the same. We will be making several small quilts this week. We'll start with a quilt that expresses your view of what's around you. To do this, you'll go into the woods around the inn and look for inspiration. The second quilt will show something of your life now. And finally you'll make a quilt that tells us a dream, a goal, or even a fantasy you have for your future."

When she stopped talking, I waited for the class to show some excitement, but there was only silence. Susanne looked at me, concerned. I nodded to her to continue, looking as encouraging as I could.

"Each quilt will focus on a different technique," she said, "but each will build on what we've learned. The point is to experiment and have fun. And by the end of the week, you will have not only a few quilts, but a whole new way of looking at quilting. Is everyone ready to get started?"

I looked out at the group of students that had been assembled. It wasn't promising. Susanne seemed frozen by their lack of enthusiasm.

"Why don't you introduce yourselves?" I suggested.

"I'm Helen," a dark-haired woman of about fifty said. "I've tried my hand at quilting a few times but I don't like to follow patterns."

"You won't have to follow them here," Susanne said hopefully.

"Well, I like to buy crafts more than to make them, but I'll try. George and Rita spoke very highly of you, and it would be nice to know if all those quilts I see at art fairs are really worth the price they charge for them."

"And hopefully you'll enjoy yourself," Susanne said meekly. "And you are?" She turned to the attractive, middle-aged man sitting next to Helen.

"Frank Ackerman. Helen's husband. I'm semiretired. I was the town druggist before that big-box store opened ten miles from here and stole my business," he said. "George and I played poker last week and I lost. Said if I came to the class, I wouldn't have to pay my debt."

"Oh good God!" Susanne blurted out and turned to the two women at the next table.

"We're Alysse and Alice," one fortysomething, brown-haired woman said as she pointed to the identical woman standing next to her, identically dressed in blue jeans and a yellow shirt. "We're twins. Both quilters."

"Quilters for years. Traditional Quilts," said her twin.

"We don't much like the arty stuff but we'll try it," said the first.

I could see panic creep into Susanne's eyes. She said nothing though. She just turned up the corners of her mouth in what, I assumed, she hoped would look like a smile. I waited for a moment, but when it was clear that Susanne was going to remain silent, I jumped in.

"What's your favorite quilt pattern?" I asked.

The first twin shrugged. "All of them. All the normal ones that you see."

I nodded. This was going to be a lot more work than I had imagined. "The great thing about Susanne's techniques is you can take something traditional and add your own spin to it," I said.

I pulled out a couple of Susanne's sample quilts. One was a six-foot-square double cross—a seemingly complicated quilt pattern made up of squares and half-square triangles. The quilt, made in a variety of reds and whites, was actually Bernie's, but Susanne had borrowed it to explain how it could be used as inspiration for an art piece. The second double cross was a variation Susanne had made, which included batik fabrics and was equally beautiful.

"See," I said. "Tradition meets art quilt."

"We have a quilt just like that."

I turned to see George at the back of the room.

"I'm sorry to interrupt your class, but I wanted to stop in and see if anyone needed anything," he said.

"You have quilts?" I asked. "Where did you get them?"

"I found them," he said. "They were up in the attic. One is just like that red one you have there, only it's mostly greens and blues. A bit stained but a nice quilt."

"I'd love to see them sometime," Susanne said.

"What are they worth?" one of the twins asked. "They are so lovely. They must be expensive."

"Quilts sell for as little as fifty dollars and as much as five hundred thousand," Susanne explained. "It depends on their age, the workmanship, the condition. But that's really not what this class is about."

"What about a quilt like that double cross?" one of the twins asked.

Susanne shrugged. "I don't know. I made it a couple of years ago. Maybe a couple of hundred. If I were selling it." Susanne turned back to George. "Did you remember to bring the collage from the entryway? I was going to show it to the students."

George looked around. "I brought it here last night," he said. "Left it right on your table."

Susanne and I searched her table, at the front of the room, and the other students did the same at theirs, but nothing was found.

"Raccoons must have taken it. They'll take anything, the little bandits." George smiled. "Lot of them around here. Sorry about that." He took a seat behind Helen and Frank. "I'm just going to watch, if that's okay."

Susanne nodded, then turned to the last person in the class, a man of about sixty. "Are you a quilter?"

"No, ma'am. But I'm a carpenter, so I am good with my hands. And I live next door, so I'll be in class on time," he said. He was sandy haired with a strong jaw and the look of a man who worked outdoors. "I'm Pete. I'll probably be very bad at this, but I'll do my best if you're patient with me."

"You'll be fine, Pete," George chimed in.

Pete laughed. "If it's so easy, you join the class."

The two men made a few jokes at each other's expense, which Susanne and I enjoyed, but the twins sat stiff, Helen sighed, and, instead of joining in, Frank just seemed annoyed.

Susanne waited for them to stop joking, then smiled, quietly taking back control of the class. "The wonderful thing about this process is that there is no right or wrong. We're just playing. All I ask is that you don't focus on creating a masterpiece but instead focus on learning something new. There are many wonderful patterns out there, traditional patterns," she nodded toward the twins, "but too often we rely on the patterns that others have made. They are tested. We know they will work. So I understand why it's easy to want to follow them. What we neglect when we do, though, are the patterns we can create for ourselves. This class is a chance to do, not what we know we're good at, but what we don't know. It might be a bit scary, but I promise it's a lot more fun."

I looked around the room. I could see that the twins, Helen, Pete, and even George were all nodding their heads in agreement. Only Frank seemed unswayed. He checked his watch.

Susanne gave each student a small sketch pad and a pencil, and told them to go outside to look for something that might inspire them.

"Our first quilt is to express your feelings about the world around you. I find it helps to think small—walk outside and take a fresh look at things you pass every day. When you find something you like, draw it. Don't worry about getting a lot of detail, just make a simple sketch," she said. "Organic items are better than buildings for this purpose because the lines will not be straight. And if you want to draw a tree, for example, don't stand far away. Don't worry about getting the whole tree. Walk up to it, look up, look down. Find an interesting angle. Then draw what you see. And don't worry if you think you can't draw. The drawing is just a reference."

"Why can't we just bring cameras and work from photographs?" Frank asked. "I'm sure George has a digital camera I could borrow. Save the trouble of sketching."

"You can. Of course you can work from photos," Susanne said. "But I find that if people are nervous about their quilting skills, it helps to work from a sketch. If you work from a photo, you might be tempted to try and translate it too literally to fabric. But if you work from a sketch, you have already taken a step away from reality and it's easier to take a second step as you move to fabric. Once you are more experienced, obviously you can save yourself the trouble of a sketch, if you prefer."

As Susanne talked, I could see her relax. Good students or not, they were *her* students and she was going to teach them what she could. The only question was whether anyone in this odd group wanted to learn.

CHAPTER 6

As the class dispersed, I stood outside and enjoyed the quiet. On the path leading to the woods, I could see Frank and George engaged in what seemed to be a serious discussion, but I couldn't hear what they were saying. Helen sat on a rock about ten feet from the men, and as I watched her, it seemed she was purposely staying close. When the men moved, she moved, but always keeping some distance. After a few minutes, George glanced over and saw me watching him. He moved back from Frank and loudly said something about the New York Yankees, then walked into the house. Frank turned toward the woods, walking right past his wife without acknowledging her. I felt a little bad for Helen, but I didn't know her and for once my curiosity was not going to get the better of me. With nothing more to see outside, I headed back to the classroom to help Susanne set up for the next step.

"Have you seen the postcards I brought?" Susanne was searching her tote bag.

"The old-fashioned ones? They were by the ribbons."

After an exhaustive search, we gave up. "They were antiques," Susanne said. "It's so strange."

"Maybe the raccoons that took the collage took them," I suggested. "Or maybe it's ghosts."

"I wouldn't be a bit surprised if this old place was haunted."

⊱

After about forty minutes, the students began trickling back in. Alysse or Alice—I couldn't tell which—had made two sketches and her sister had made three. Like everything else about them, their sketches looked alike, yet they fussed about which sketch would make the best quilt and demanded Susanne's attention. I floated around, and looked at what the others had drawn, until Susanne could pry herself away and explain the next step.

"The next thing is to take a piece of black felt," Susanne said. "Everyone has a piece that's twelve inches square. The felt will give your quilt some weight and be strong enough to hold the embellishments we'll add later. Lay it flat on your table. Then, using your sketch as a guide, choose fabric that loosely represents the background in your sketch. Start with a few pieces and audition them, play with them, and if you like the fabrics, you can begin cutting them to represent the sky or grass or water in your sketch. Focus only on the background, and once we've done that, we'll go on to the next part of the process."

I admired the way Susanne explained the process. I'd made quilts with her before and knew she was a patient teacher, but she was also a very good one. She slowly broke down a very intimidating idea—making an art quilt—into steps that took the fear out of the process. She also walked around offering suggestions, praise, and encouragement, which gave me hope that even this group could be transformed into art quilters.

The students chose fabric to play with and they each set themselves up at a workstation. Perhaps *workstation* is too kind a word. Each person had a plastic folding table that was too low to be comfortable if they were standing and too high if they were sitting on one of the metal folding chairs. There were only two cutting mats and one rotary cutter, so I spent the morning running back and forth to Susanne's car, where she had stored several of everything. Her overabundance of caution was now looking like good sense.

The twins seemed the most tentative about their projects. They took turns asking for Susanne's advice, and one of them went back outside to make a new sketch after she'd decided she didn't like anything she'd already drawn.

Helen, on the other hand, took to the process quite naturally. Her sketch of a tree next to a stream just a few yards from the classroom was quite detailed, but she seemed to be having an easy time as she turned the sketch into cloth.

"Doing okay?" I asked, though I could see that she was.

"I hope so," she said. "This is really fun." She moved several pieces of fabric over the felt, laying them flat, then pleating them, then discarding them and trying another. "I don't often get much of a chance to focus on myself. I have six grandchildren."

"That must keep you busy," I offered.

I sensed that she wanted to tell me all about them, and I was right. After explaining why each child was special, she smiled. "They don't get it from me."

"Don't say that. I'm sure you have lots of talents. You're already a pretty good artist." I pointed to the sketch that lay next to her pile of fabrics.

"If I do alright, maybe I'll start making quilts for the church auction. I'm very active in the community. Keeps me busy."

"And it helps others."

She nodded. "I do what I can."

Message received. Helen was a giving, yet humble, member of the Winston community, and she wanted to be praised without seeming to want it. There were dozens like her in Archers Rest.

"I'm not sure I have the right blue for the sky." She scrunched up her face as if she was intensely staring at the three blue silks before her, but I could see that she was watching her husband out of the corner of her eye.

Frank, who was only a few feet away from us, had cornered Susanne, asking more questions about her than about quilting. Susanne kept pointing toward his sketch of a rock formation and suggesting dark greens and purples as perfect colors to represent the rocks, but Frank had no interest in her ideas. Instead he stood uncomfortably close to her, smiling in a way that suggested he had mistaken the classroom for a singles bar. But the only man Susanne was interested in, other than her husband, was her grandson. Frank, no matter his charm, was out of luck.

"I saw a deer when I was walking," Frank told her. "I like deer."

"Yes, they're beautiful animals," Susanne agreed. "You can add one in if you like."

"To hunt," Frank corrected her. "Not to look at. Ever do any hunting?"

"No. My husband and I are not hunters."

It was the fourth time in five minutes that Susanne had mentioned her husband, but Frank wasn't getting the hint. Of course, any man who would flirt so openly just a few feet from his wife wouldn't let a small detail like a husband get in his way.

"People up here like to get out in the open, enjoy nature. You enjoy nature, don't you?" Frank moved closer to Susanne, who was trapped against one of the worktables.

"Enjoying the class?" I interrupted, much to Susanne's relief. She quickly moved on to the twins, while I stayed with Frank. "Your wife is doing some amazing work. Take a look."

Frank's smile faded. We were in a standoff, but I held my ground.

He struck me as a man who used his charisma to get what he wanted, and when that didn't work, he tried intimidation. "Not this time," I tried to say with my eyes. He held my gaze for what seemed like an eternity; then he blinked. I smiled and turned away. I left Frank with nothing to do but work on his quilt and talk to his wife. I moved on to Pete. He had no real talent for the art, but he was earnest and seemed to be enjoying himself.

"He's a piece of work," Pete said, nodding toward Frank. Frank caught Pete and I looking at him and scowled back.

"Not friends, I take it," I said.

"Let's just say we have a different way of looking at women." He blushed a little. "Of course, he's still married, and my wife just left me, so maybe my way is wrong."

"I doubt it," I said as I glanced back toward Frank.

"That's why I'm here. Rita thought I should get out of the house and maybe use the class as an opportunity to meet someone new." He nodded over to the twins. "Not what I had in mind though."

"What's your type?"

"Why? Do you know someone?"

I shrugged. I did think that, maybe, he might be a good match for Bernie. They were about the same age and had the same laid-back quality about them. I didn't know if she would think so. But, then, I didn't even know where she was. Eleanor had agreed to spend the day helping Rita set up the shop, but I couldn't picture Bernie being anxious to offer her services. Maybe I needed to get her into the class-room for a casual introduction to Pete.

"I'm open to any woman who has the patience to put up with me." He smiled and held up two pieces of fabric. "Now, what exactly am I supposed to do with this?"

"This would be a good color for the sky," I suggested. I pointed to a hand-painted fabric that had streaks of pink and blue across it.

"I'll take your word for it." He cut a four-inch strip and laid it across the top of his felt square. "Looks good," he admitted. "Like a sunset." He grabbed a piece of dark navy dupioni silk. "I could put a small strip of this below it, as if it were the ground for the woods. It gets quite dark in there. Very spooky, really."

"I'll keep that in mind if I ever take a walk in the woods at night," I said. "I think you're getting the hang of this."

"It's actually a lot of fun," he said. "I've lived in the area most of my life and I don't think I've ever looked at the trees in quite the same way as I did today. I was kind of dreading this, to tell you the truth. Figured I'd be looking for the exit the whole time. But this is cool."

"When my grandmother offered to teach me to quilt, I felt the same way; then I fell in love with it. And the way Susanne teaches, you can do whatever you like."

"My wife would say that I've been doing what I like for thirty years," he said. "So maybe that's why this class is so appealing."

"Her loss, Pete," I said, and I meant it. I was glad to see that Susanne was already winning over students and that someone new was finding out how enjoyable it could be to make a quilt. But I was also getting quite stuck on the idea of reminding Bernie that there were nice men in the world. Nice, single men that didn't own broken-down inns or condescend to quilters.

For a moment I thought maybe I shouldn't focus so heavily on Bernie's romantic problems and should instead spend a little time on my own, but that made me think of Jesse. And that made me think that he'd be pleased to see me spending my time on quilting and romance, and not, as he put it, getting myself into dangerous situations. And that made me think that maybe he should trust my ability to get out of dangerous situations—and I realized that in ten seconds I'd gone from missing Jesse to being mad at him. "That's why," I told myself, "I should focus on Bernie's love life. Less chance I'll get emotional whiplash."

That was the thing about Jesse. He thought that just by staying away from crime scenes and criminals I was staying out of trouble. He had no idea how dangerous romance could be.

CHAPTER 7

We all gathered for dinner in the B-and-B's mismatched dining room. Having skipped the traditional first-night "welcome to the quilt retreat" celebration, George and Rita put together lasagna and salad for the whole group after the first day of class was over.

Normally I'm against all forms of forced socializing, but I was glad of the dinner because it would give me a chance to finally see Rita. For the moment, though, the only Olnhausen in the room was George, holding an armful of quilts and looking for a place to set them down. When he saw me and Susanne standing near the buffet, he rushed over.

"I want to show you these. These are the quilts I was talking about," he said.

He laid them out on a table, and Susanne, Eleanor, and I starting going through them.

"I would say they're all quite old. Maybe a hundred years," Eleanor said. "They're all classic patterns: hunter's star, log cabin, double cross. Really lovely workmanship."

"Are they valuable?" Helen had moved closer to get a good view, as did one of the twins, Frank, and Pete. George moved aside to let Helen get a better view, and as he did, I noticed the way she smiled at him. It was a loving smile. But George didn't pay attention. He was looking at my grandmother, and she was looking at the quilts.

"They aren't in the best condition," Eleanor said. "I'm not sure what they would be worth, but they are beautiful."

"Whatever they're worth, we'll find a place for them once we're done with the remodeling," George said. "Nice to have something from the house to showcase."

The twin started refolding the quilts. "You should store them somewhere safe," she said. "I can put them away for you if you like."

"That's very nice of you, miss." George directed her to an armoire in the corner of the dining room, and we all watched her lovingly place each quilt inside it. "Everyone's so helpful," he said as he headed back toward the kitchen.

I noticed that Bernie was the only one who hadn't come to look at the quilts. I sat next to her, and we smiled, but she didn't seem to want to talk, so I dug into my dinner instead.

"Thanks again for today." Pete was behind me with a plate of lasagna.

"Join us." I gestured to an empty chair across from me. "This is Bernie Avallone. Bernie, this is Pete . . ."

"Pete Carson." He shook her hand then smiled at me. "You're the last of the ladies who came up to help. Nell was telling me about you. About all of you."

"It sounds like you're having a nice time in the class."

"Better than I thought."

"Maybe Pete can show you around town," I suggested.

Bernie looked at me. "I'm sure he has better things to do."

"Not really," Pete said, smiling.

As I looked for a way to make myself scarce, a woman walked into the room.

She had to be Rita, though she was not at all what I'd pictured. She was tall and model thin, with chic razor-short blonde hair. She wore black pants with a black turtleneck, a zebra-print belt, and high-heeled boots. A sparkly diamond bracelet hung from her wrist, and her diamond ring seemed larger than her finger. She looked like one of those women who wander Beverly Hills with dogs in their purses. Of all of us, she seemed the least likely to own a tear-down B-and-B in the mountains.

"She has not changed one bit," Bernie said. "Not one bit. Can you believe it? How does someone not age in forty-five years?"

"You are every bit as beautiful," I told Bernie, and I meant it. Bernie might not have Rita's Paris-runway fashion sense, but she had warmth and kindness and a smile that made everyone who saw it feel happier.

Pete looked at Bernie. "You know Rita?"

"Old friends," I said.

"Ex-friends," Bernie corrected me.

Pete looked at me for answers, but I just made a face that I hoped would convey that, however dramatic Bernie's statement seemed, it was a minor thing that should not detract in any way from his interest in her. It was a lot to say with a smile, but Pete smiled back and seemed to go along.

"She's a bit much sometimes," he offered, in a supportive way that made me like him more. "She's always disappearing on George. I was actually kind of surprised when they told me about opening the place as an inn. Seemed like more work than Rita, or really either of them, would enjoy."

"Then why are they doing it?" I asked.

Pete shrugged. "Maybe they wanted a project. They retired early, and instead of the good life they got bored."

"They probably had no idea how much work it would require," I said. "They seem a bit in over their heads, with the condition of this place."

Bernie put her head on my shoulder. "I suppose I can't avoid her anymore."

"You haven't seen her yet?" I asked. "What did you do today?"

"I borrowed Eleanor's car, went into town, and shopped. I couldn't face it. I don't know what I was thinking by coming here."

It looked for a moment like Bernie might run from the room, but Rita glanced our way and all chance for escape was lost. We sat and watched her walk across the room, coming closer to us with each step. I could feel the tension rising in Bernie, so I took her hand under the table.

"Bernadette," Rita called out. She grabbed Bernie and pulled her up, forcing her to let go of my hand. She hugged her close until Bernie managed to get free. "I have thought of you so often over the years. I've missed you terribly."

"This is Nell," was Bernie's reply. "She's Eleanor's granddaughter."

Rita held out a perfectly manicured hand. "Your grandmother is a lifesaver. I've never met anyone who knows as much about anything as your grandmother does about quilting."

"And she's happy to share it," I said. "Did you get inspired?"

Rita sat next to Bernie. "I can't wait to get started. I feel like it's just the thing I've needed—an outlet for my creativity and a stress reliever in one. Now I understand why you've quilted all these years, Bernie." She smiled. "Honestly, I was shocked when George said you were here. It was such a wonderful surprise."

"It was a last-minute decision."

"I want to know everything you've been doing," Rita said. "I know it's a lot of years to catch up on, but I want to hear about every one of them."

Bernie nodded and looked to me for help. I assumed that Bernie had been picturing this moment, but now that she was facing Rita, she looked desperate to end it. I knew the conversation couldn't go on much longer.

"Bernie, I'm sorry to ask you this, but could you check on Barney?" I said. "I'm still eating and . . ."

"Absolutely." Bernie jumped up from the table. People flee a murder scene more slowly than Bernie left that room.

"Maybe you can help her," I said to Pete, who took the hint and went after Bernie. If I could get Bernie to have even a slight interest in Pete, it might water down the discomfort she felt and maybe even lead to new romance for two deserving people. And then there was my third motive for getting rid of Pete: I wanted answers.

"So you knew Bernie in high school," I said to Rita as soon as Bernie and Pete were gone. I was determined to get the whole story and figure out why, after all these years, this woman could so intimidate my usually confident friend.

"We were the closest of friends," Rita told me. "The absolute closest. We knew each other all through grade school and high school. We smoked our first cigarette together, drank our first cocktail." She laughed. "We even had our first kisses at the same party."

"Was George your first kiss?"

Rita smiled. But it wasn't a real smile. A real smile is as much in a person's eyes as in their lips, and Rita's eyes were cold. "No. He was actually Bernadette's first kiss. They were sweethearts for a time. Nothing serious, you understand, just high school stuff."

"So how did you end up together?" I looked across the room and saw George still sitting with Eleanor.

"After they broke up," Rita told me, "Bernie went off to college. She got involved with that Avallone boy. Johnny, I think, was his first name. Cute. I only met him once but I remember he was cute. George was devastated." She smiled. "I guess I was his rebound."

"Seemed to work out," I offered.

"Yes. Happily married for nearly forty-two years."

"Any children?"

"A daughter. She . . ." Rita's voice trailed off. "She doesn't live close." She looked toward her husband, and for a moment, I thought she might go over to him and leave me with more questions.

"You must have lots of stories about Bernie," I said quickly.

Rita turned back to me. She smiled, this time warmly. "I don't know how we lost touch. I suppose . . ." She paused. "I suppose she was a bit surprised about George and me, but she was married and pregnant when we got engaged so I didn't think it would bother her. I hope she was happily married for years and years."

"Eighteen years," I said. "She moved to Archers Rest when he died."

"They didn't divorce?"

"That was her second marriage."

"Oh. I didn't realize. How many times has she been married?"

Suddenly I felt like I was betraying Bernie by giving Rita too much information. Though I knew the answer was three husbands—the third one died after only a year—I told Rita that I'd only known Bernie a little while and wasn't sure I was getting my facts straight.

"But she has kids, right?" Rita pressed on. "She was pregnant the last time I heard anything about her."

I nodded. "As I said, I've only known her a few months. She can give you all the details next time you talk."

"I'm so looking forward to a nice long chat," she said, more to herself than to me.

There are some people you meet and, without having a good reason, immediately like. Rita was the opposite. I couldn't put my finger on it, but there was something about the way she sat just a little too close to me, the way she stared at me so intently, and the way she made me feel slightly inferior to her by waving her jewelry in my face. And yet, she seemed genuinely interested in reconnecting with her old friend, and that made me want to like her.

I thanked her for the dinner, which apparently George had cooked, then walked out of the dining room. As I did I caught Eleanor's eye. It was clear that she had something she wanted to tell me, so I gestured toward the bedrooms. She nodded slightly, the way they do in spy movies, and turned back to her conversation with George.

CHAPTER 8

"I don't think I can last another five days," Susanne said, an hour later, as we gathered in the bedroom I was sharing with Eleanor. "I never should have agreed to do a whole week."

Eleanor sat on my bed, and I sat on the floor with Barney. Susanne just paced. We had barely settled in when there was a knock at the door.

"It's me," I heard Bernie say. "Can I come in?"

"Of course," Eleanor said. "Susanne is worried about teaching her class. Tell her it's going to be fine."

"It's going to be fine. At least for you," Bernie said. "I feel like a fool for coming here."

"Why did you?" I asked. I could see Eleanor give me the eye but I ignored it.

And Bernie ignored me. "Anyone still hungry?" She was carrying paper cups, a small cardboard dispenser of coffee, and a bag of doughnuts.

"Where did you get that?" I asked.

"After dinner I went back to a bakery I found in town this afternoon. I figured we deserved a treat after that awful dinner."

The dinner was actually pretty good, but out of solidarity we all agreed. We sat, drank our coffee, and ate our doughnuts while Susanne and I filled the others in on the students.

"It would be one thing if we had the right kind of classroom, with the right equipment, or if the students were really motivated. I think Rita and George just grabbed a few friends and neighbors and forced them to take the class," Susanne said. "It's not really a retreat. We're the only ones actually staying here. I feel like such a fraud."

"Look at this place. Can you blame them for not wanting to stay here?" Bernie asked. "I tried to take a shower this morning and there was no hot water."

"Hot water is the least of our problems," Eleanor said. "I woke up in the middle of the night and I swear I heard squeaking on the stairs. The place is probably filled with mice."

Susanne looked about ready to cry. "Not one person really wants to be in that class."

"But they are learning," I pointed out, "and so am I. I'm excited to make a quilt based on one of my sketches." As an art student, I had a million sketches, most of which would end up in a landfill. Translating a few to quilts would give a couple of good ideas a place to live.

"They're just such an odd group. I don't think Helen and Frank spoke to each other all day," Susanne said. "And Pete is a charming but he's all thumbs. And the two sisters, the twins, there's something off about them. I can't figure out what they're doing here. The others are all friends of the Olnhausens, but I don't think they know them."

"They probably saw the ad in the *Winston Weekly*," Bernie suggested.

"I don't think so," Susanne said. "Alysse, or the other one, said something about how they *had* to take the class. As if they were forced to."

"Well, they're learning, whatever their reason for being here," I said. "And in their own strange way, they all seem to be enjoying the class."

"I suppose." But Susanne didn't seem satisfied with my observation.

"At least you accomplished something," Eleanor said. "I spent the day just trying to explain the basics of owning a shop to that woman. She has never run a business. She's never quilted. They've had this house, this land, for ten years—inherited it from her father. She said it was their summer place for years and years. And now she's decided to turn it into an inn. Almost on a whim, it seems to me."

"She inherited it from her father?" Bernie looked at Eleanor. "I know I haven't seen her in years, but she didn't have this place when we were growing up. Her father was unemployed half the time. The kind of guy who would work a job for three weeks and then stop showing up. He was always getting fired, and they would end up with their electricity shut off or their car repossessed. It really embarrassed Rita as a teenager. I can't imagine he ever put together enough money to buy a meal, let alone this place."

"Isn't that interesting," Eleanor said. "She painted an entirely different picture of her life. She did tell me that she and George had been working hard for so many years, dreaming of this place . . ."

"Doing what?" I asked.

"She was a little vague about exactly what they did. She did tell me that a year ago they decided to retire and turn it into a bed-and-breakfast and live out the rest of their lives . . . How did she put it? To get out of the chaos and instead be surrounded by beauty and peace."

"What's wrong with that?" I asked.

"It's nonsense," Eleanor said. "I've been helping people open shops for years. I've seen plenty of weekend quilters get romantic dreams about opening a little business because they imagine they'll spend all day making quilts and playing with fabric. And a few times I've been approached by nonquilters who want to know if there's a lot of money in opening a shop."

"And you explain that there isn't," Bernie cut in.

"Exactly. But I've never had someone like Rita want to have her own quilt shop. She doesn't give a hoot about business or about quilts. So why this shop? Why now? To my mind, there's something else going on."

"Especially with how run down this place is," I agreed. "You would think they'd put their money into fixing it up rather than buying inventory for a store. They seem like pretty reasonable people, so I can't figure out why they were in such a hurry to get this place open."

"They were both dreamers when I knew them," Bernie said. "Rita was always coming up with money-making schemes. Maybe she still is."

Eleanor sighed. "I wish we had Internet access up here. I'd Google the two of them and see if I could find out the real story."

"We should call Natalie and see what she can find out," Susanne suggested.

"And have Carrie check their financials," Bernie added. Carrie still had connections with bankers from her days in finance. She could get a complete financial history.

"We can't dig into these people's lives just because we're curious," I pointed out. "Maybe all they're doing is padding their life story a bit to impress Bernie. George said they went to a quilt show and couldn't believe that there are millions of quilters out there. Maybe they saw this place as a way to cash in on that, and now they're running out of money and a bit desperate."

It was rare that I was the voice of restraint in the group, but there was no good reason to invade their privacy. In a week we would be back to our lives, and this mess would be a distant memory.

"She wants the names of my distributors, my favorite fabric designers, teachers, and book publishers," Eleanor said. "She's going to be spreading my name at every wholesale market and quilt show. I've spent years building a good reputation and I want to keep it."

I gave in. I grabbed my cell phone to call Carrie's coffee shop, more anxious to hear how things were in Archers Rest than to investigate the Olnhausens. Maybe see if anyone missed me. But I couldn't get a connection.

"No service," I said. "I think it's pretty hit or miss in the mountains."

"And there are no phones in the rooms." Eleanor looked around.

"The only one I saw is in the front hallway," I told her. "I'll run down and give Natalie a call."

I left the women in the room and ran down the stairs. The students were gone, and the hallway was dark. The only light came from under the kitchen door. I knew the phone was in the entryway, but instead I walked toward the kitchen. Maybe I had no good reason to eavesdrop, but that had never stopped me before, so I stood at the door and listened.

"This isn't working," I heard Rita say.

"I'm taking care of it," was George's reply. "I'll get Bernie to understand."

"And the others? That Eleanor woman thinks I've lost my mind, opening the quilt shop."

"So what? We have to stay focused, Rita. We're so close to getting everything we want."

Behind me I heard a thud. I knew George heard it too, because he moved toward the kitchen door. I ducked into the dark dining room, hoping to hide there, but it didn't work. George walked into the room and turned on the light. I stood there, feeling suddenly vulnerable.

"I heard a noise," I said, hoping to distract him from the fact that he found me standing in the dark.

He looked around the room. "I heard it too. There are a lot of strange noises in this house. I swore I heard footsteps a week before you came. Scared Rita so much I changed the locks."

I took the opportunity to move away from the wall where I had been hiding. When I did, I noticed something odd about the armoire. It was empty.

"You moved the quilts," I said.

George walked to the cabinet and examined it so carefully it seemed as though he was looking for a needle rather than three large quilts.

"Rita must have done something with them," he finally said.

He walked me back toward the stairs in a way that suggested he didn't like me lingering on the first floor. I looked toward the phone, but there didn't seem any chance I could use it without George listening in, so I headed back toward my room.

When I got there, Eleanor and the others were waiting. I told them what I'd overheard, and my grandmother took it as confirmation that the Olnhausens were not to be trusted.

"Bernie and I can go into town in the morning and make some calls," I suggested, "if Susanne doesn't need me in class."

"I'll be fine," Susanne said, more relaxed than she had been before. "I think most of them are in there for free. Not exactly what I'd imagined for my first quilt retreat, but I suppose it takes the pressure off."

"But it does beg the question," Eleanor said. "If there weren't people interested in taking your class, why did they go through with it? They could have canceled. Instead they're paying you to teach a weeklong class to a group of people who don't want to be there. Why drag you up here for no good reason?"

"Maybe they have a good reason," I said.

"That's what we have to find out," Eleanor said, with a determination in her voice that made me remember my promise to Oliver that we would stay out of trouble. Maybe the only way to do that was to find out who George and Rita really were.

CHAPTER 9

The next morning I waited for Bernie by the car. I watched as Helen, Frank, Susanne, and the twins each made their way into the classroom. Eleanor offered a few reminders about what information I should get, before joining Rita in the shop. Barney sniffed at the trees, and I looked at my watch. Fifteen minutes late.

Finally I saw Bernie coming from a wooded area quite a ways from the house. Behind her, Pete scrambled up to the walkway and headed into class. As she reached the car, Bernie caught my eye.

"Don't look at me like that." Bernie jumped into the passenger seat.

I shouted to Barney, who paid no attention until I grabbed him by the collar.

"Backseat." I pointed to the seat, and he jumped in the back; then I climbed into the driver's seat and tried hard not to smile.

"I suppose we could go back to the bakery you saw in town yesterday," I said.

"Honestly, Nell, you get so many ideas into your head."

"About what? Baked goods?"

Bernie laughed. "Okay. Maybe I'm a little sensitive. I came down early this morning. Didn't feel like breakfast. I saw Pete walking, and we took a little stroll together."

"That's nice."

"It's not what you think. I wanted to grill him about Rita and George."

"It could be both," I suggested.

"Well, it isn't."

"So what did you learn?"

Bernie shifted in her seat so she could face me. "Pete said he and his wife, Siobhan, just moved into their house about six months ago. Rita and George owned the place already, but it was just sitting there empty. He didn't know anything about Rita's dad, but if he did own it, he must have bought it after I knew Rita, because I'm certain they didn't have this place when we were kids." She took a breath. "Pete said they tried to sell it once but they must not have been able to get a decent offer, because they pulled it off the market. He said there are a lot of old places for sale in this area."

"So maybe they need money," I said.

"They have to, considering the way that place looks."

"But they must have had money at one point," I pointed out. "Look at the way they dress."

"Pete didn't know what they'd been doing before or where they'd been living. He said they were always fuzzy about the details of their earlier lives. He said they kept to themselves until recently. Pete hadn't even been inside the house until last night. One day last week, Rita showed up on Pete's doorstep and suggested he take the class."

"They have a daughter," I said. "Does she ever come up to visit?"

Bernie seemed upset by that news. "He didn't mention her."

"There's some rift there, so he may not have known she existed."

"Pete said Rita and George aren't getting along, but they seem okay to me."

"They barely speak to each other," I pointed out. "Have you ever seen them talking or eating together?"

"I didn't want them to be happy," Bernie said, turning back to face the windshield.

"Then you seem to have gotten your wish."

"I guess," she said. Then she just stared ahead.

There was a pay phone just outside the bakery. Bernie went in to get us coffee while I made some calls: first to Natalie, for news of the shop and Jeremy, then Carrie, to see if she could get info on Rita and George's financial situation.

I filled Natalie in on the class, the Olnhausens, and the condition of the bed-and-breakfast. I asked her to do an Internet search on George and Rita and she asked me to pass her good wishes on to Bernie and Susanne. Everything at the shop was fine, she told me, though Jeremy missed his grandmother. Then she hesitated.

"I have something to tell you," she said, sounding as though the world had fallen apart.

"Then tell me."

"It's about Jesse. He went on a date last night. Carrie saw them."

It took a moment to process. "I don't know how to respond," I admitted.

"Well, it's lousy of him."

"Yeah," I said. "It is." The great thing about girlfriends is that you don't have to pretend to be okay when you're not. "I guess he's moving on."

"Maybe not. I can find out details if you want. All I know is that they were at DeNallo's for dinner. She's got red hair, and Carrie had never seen her before, so she must not be from town. We figured you had a right to know."

"Thanks. I actually have to call Carrie," I said, and after a few more reassurances from Natalie that Jesse's date probably meant nothing, I hung up.

Bernie was beside me, holding two paper cups of coffee. "Everything okay?"

"No," I admitted. "Nothing too serious, but Jesse has a girlfriend."

"That can't be." Bernie handed me one of the cups.

"Carrie saw him on a date with someone."

"A date isn't a relationship."

"Maybe not," I admitted, "but it's usually how things start."

"If Jesse doesn't realize what a wonderful woman you are, to heck with him. You're better off without such a stupid man."

"I could say the same to you."

Bernie smiled. "I'm better at fixing other people's lives than fixing my own. Call Carrie or we'll get in trouble with Eleanor."

I dialed Carrie's number and gave her as many details about Rita and George as I knew. She offered to do a title search on their land and see where it led, and she repeated what Natalie had already told me.

"They didn't look right together," she said.

"Okay." I wanted to talk about it for hours, and I didn't want to talk about it at all. I decided on the latter. "Cell service is spotty up here, so I will call you tomorrow," I told her.

Though it was a chilly April morning, Bernie and I sat at one of the outdoor tables to drink our coffee. I'd eaten breakfast, but Bernie dove into an egg-and-bacon sandwich while Barney salivated.

"At least he still has his sense of smell," Bernie said.

"That's what Eleanor says." I patted the dog's head. "Poor guy, he hates being away from his routine. I think it confuses him."

"He's not the only one who's confused."

"Confused about what?"

Bernie shrugged. "Why I came, I guess. It's just been so long. Maybe too long."

"Did you keep in touch with George and Rita at all after high school?" I asked.

"No. I heard things. We're all originally from Long Island. I moved into New York City with Johnny. They moved to California for a time. Then I'd heard they'd come back east maybe fifteen years ago."

"But you don't know what they did for a living?"

"The last time I really wanted to know anything about them was so long ago. We were all kids. Everyone changed jobs. George wanted to be an actor, which seemed, when we were teenagers, like a really romantic thing to do. He said he wanted to make movies until he made enough money that we could travel the world." She sipped her coffee and stared off at the distance. "At one point I heard he sold office supplies."

"Doesn't that make you feel better in a way, to know that he didn't end up living the perfect life?"

She shrugged. "No one lives the perfect life. I made T-shirts when I first got married. Johnny worked at one of those free newspapers, drawing cartoons. Then when the kids came along, he worked at a greeting-card company, and I got a job behind the counter at a drugstore. When he died, I went back to school and became a pharmacist. It was a struggle but that's life. It's scary sometimes when you don't know what's going to happen next, but that's what makes it fun."

"That's what Susanne says about making an art quilt."

Bernie laughed. "She's a wise woman."

"And a good friend," I said.

Bernie nodded. "She always has been. I guess I was a little rough on her. I think I was just embarrassed by how hard it hit me, hearing those names again." She waved her hand as if to dismiss the topic. "We should get back."

I was beginning to realize that something about Bernie's story didn't make sense. "George said Johnny was a millionaire."

Bernie laughed. "His family had money, something to do with the insurance business. I never really knew much about them, because his father thought Johnny was a hippy, throwing his life away on some girl from nowhere. He cut Johnny out of his will. We never saw them after we were married. They never even met their grandchildren."

"Does George know that?"

Bernie frowned. "Why would he care?"

"Maybe he thinks you can help. They're obviously in over their heads at the bed-and-breakfast."

"That's crazy, Nell. Even if I could, I wouldn't be so foolish as to invest money in a broken-down inn in the middle of nowhere."

"It makes you wonder why they did."

"Well, if you're worried that they're hoping to get some cash from me, rest easy. Johnny didn't leave me anything but memories."

I nodded. "Good memories, I hope."

"Very good memories."

I hesitated but I said it anyway. "Rita told me you were already married by the time she and George got together."

"Did she? Well, I guess time plays tricks on some memories." She got up and threw the rest of her sandwich away.

"Not so fast, Bernie," I said as she walked toward the car. As I spoke a police car, lights flashing, pulled up next to me.

CHAPTER 10

"Hello there." A large man in his sixties got out of the police car.

"Is something wrong?" I asked.

"Maria just took some scones out of the oven. She always calls me when she has fresh ones."

"You had your lights on," I said.

He blushed. "I never have reason to use them, so once in a while I fire 'em up. Everyone in town knows it means there are fresh scones." He looked at Bernie and me. "On your way through town?"

"We're staying at the Patchwork B-and-B," I said.

He nodded. "Quilt classes. They threw it together so quickly, I didn't think they had time to find any folks looking to learn. Glad to see I was wrong."

"We're not taking the class," Bernie explained. "We're here to help the teacher."

"Well, nice to have you here either way. I'm Jim McIntyre. I'm the chief of police, so if you ever need anything . . ." He started to walk away then stopped. "Can you ladies wait a moment? I'll be right back."

As he walked into the bakery, Bernie leaned in and whispered. "I feel like we should make a run for it."

"Why? Have we done something?"

"Why else would he ask us to wait?"

We found out a minute later, when Chief McIntyre emerged with two warm cranberry scones and a dog biscuit for Barney.

"If you ever need me, my office is one street over," he said. "But you're more likely to find me here."

"The hope is that we won't need you at all," I said. "Unless Maria makes another batch of scones."

We watched him get back in his car and drive up the street, not so much because we were interested in the chief, but because the scones were so good that we couldn't move until they were finished.

When we returned to the bed-and-breakfast, Bernie went straight to her room, saying she was in the middle of a good book she had to finish. I stuck my head into the class and saw that everyone was working away and Susanne seemed very much at ease. I stayed in the back, but Barney wandered the class, greeting everyone and being his usual welcome distraction.

The students had translated their sketches to fabric and were now adding details that expressed their point of view. One of the twins was carefully removing small twigs from a plastic bag and placing them on her quilt, while the other was adding words to her quilt in longhand. Frank had also added words, but he had printed them onto fabric, using Susanne's computer, and was fusing them to his quilt top. The others were adding beads and drawings. Everyone seemed busy and focused on their work.

Susanne held up several antique postcards, smiling.

"They're back," I said.

"I must have dropped them or something. Helen found them on the floor near my desk this morning."

"But we looked there," I said.

Susanne just shrugged. Things seemed to be going better for her today, so I sat in the back of the class, taking notes on a small sketch pad and thinking about what kind of journal quilt I would make, until the group noticed I was there and began coming over to say hi. Rather than interrupt their work any further, I took Barney and headed toward the other small building, the one intended to house the quilt shop.

>%

"What do you call this?" I heard Rita asking, as I opened the door.

"It's a walking foot," Eleanor told her. By the way she said it, I guessed it was not the first time. "You use it on your sewing machine when you machine quilt."

"I thought you used the other one."

"The darning foot is for free-motion quilting," Eleanor said. "The walking foot is for straight-line quilting."

Rita looked up at me and wrinkled her nose at the sight of Barney, who had trotted over to say hello. Poor thing. Since he liked everyone, it never occurred to him that someone might not like him.

"Can he wait outside?" Rita looked at me.

"He knows his way around a quilt shop," Eleanor said. Though the words *better than you* were not spoken, no one missed her meaning.

Before Rita had a chance to take offense, though, Eleanor put the two quilting feet on a table and sighed.

"When you finish with your quilt top, you layer it, baste it, and quilt it," Eleanor said. "If you're just using straight-line quilting, you use the walking foot because it grips the top layer of the fabric and helps move the quilt evenly under the needle. But if you're free-motion quilting, the kind where you want to move the quilt up, down, left, or right without any restrictions, you lower the feed dogs—the little teeth that move the bottom of the fabric—and you use a darning foot." Eleanor paused, waiting to see if Rita understood, but apparently finding no lightbulb over Rita's head she went on. "This really would be easier if we made a quilt together. Instead of being abstract ideas, they would be practical pieces of information. Quilters really expect an expert when they come into a store like this," Eleanor said, the frustration evident in her voice. "Much of my day is spent offering advice or troubleshooting for folks. It helps that I'm familiar with the various feet available for machine quilting."

"Well, it doesn't matter because I have that." Rita pointed to an object the size of a dining room table that was covered with layers of plastic.

"You have what?" I asked.

"She bought a long-arm machine and is going to let people use it," Eleanor told me.

"It's for quilting," Rita said.

"Yes, I've seen them," I said. "They have frames, sort of like the hand-quilting frames people think of when they think of quilting, but instead you use them with a specially designed machine that allows you to quilt an entire piece in no time."

"And this one is all computerized," Rita explained. "You can set it to a preprogrammed pattern and it will do all the quilting for you."

"Cool." I walked over to get a better look. "We should get one of these for Someday Quilts. We have the room."

"We don't know how to use it," Eleanor pointed out.

"So we learn."

"I saw it demonstrated by a woman in Lake George," Rita said. "She's an expert at the squiggly lines quilting."

"Stippling," Eleanor said, with a tired sigh that obviously came from hours of explaining her passion to a disinterested party.

"I'd love to learn this," I said. "I'm terrible at machine quilting. I think it's because you have to shove half the quilt under the machine and it only has, like, twelve inches of clearance. It's hard to move a big quilt around. But with one of these babies . . ."

"They're nearly the price of a car," Eleanor said.

"But if you quilt for other people, or rent time on it, I'll bet it pays for itself."

I could see Rita smiling. Clearly she'd already had the same conversation with Eleanor and lost. Now she'd found an ally, a role I was uncomfortable playing. I backed off from the long-arm machine.

"It's quite an investment for your shop," I said, trying to add a neutral comment to counteract my enthusiasm. But it didn't work.

"If you like that, you should see all the other gadgets she's bought." Eleanor pointed to a pile of boxes near the back of the shop.

"I went to a quilt show where they sell just to shops . . . ," Rita started.

"Quilt market," Eleanor and I said together.

"Yes, and they had amazing things that I knew quilters would love."

"How do you know what quilters will love if you don't quilt?" Eleanor was no longer even trying to hide her annoyance.

"I may not know anything about quilting, but I know how to shop," Rita said, a slight snap in her voice. "And obviously the younger generation of quilter agrees with me."

"I'm not an expert," I pointed out.

"But you're open to new things, and that's what this shop will be all about. The latest and coolest things in quilting. I don't want any old, stuffy shop." She glanced toward Eleanor, who rolled her eyes at the snub. "I want something cutting-edge."

"In the Adirondacks?" It came out of my mouth without thinking. I could see that it hurt Rita, but Eleanor was smiling ear to ear.

CHAPTER 11

The Adirondacks is a national forest and a popular destination for hiking and boating in the summer, skiing in the winter. With the southern tip only four hours north of New York City, and the top just to the south of Canada, it's large enough to sustain enormous tourist trade while still leaving some towns untouched.

Winston was one of those untouched towns. Or maybe *forgotten* would be a better word. It wasn't near the places likely to draw large numbers of visitors, like Lake Placid or Lake George. And it wasn't near the major highways, where anyone on their way to somewhere else, like Montreal, would be likely to stop for a quick look around.

Though quilters are an adventurous bunch, going on organized cruises to Alaska or on tours of China, I doubted many would venture to the Patchwork Bed-and-Breakfast or its quilt shop. The whole thing seemed like a waste of time. Eleanor, who lived to pass on her love of quilting, clearly felt drained. Susanne was teaching a ragtag bunch of conscripted students. Bernie was reliving a painful chapter from her past. And while I was stuck up here, Jesse was in Archers Rest, dating redheads.

"Let it go," I said out loud, once I'd walked outside and into the woods. "Focus on the beauty around you."

I looked around. The trees were pretty. The sky was darkening, but the air was fresh and there was a lot to explore. Barney and I headed toward a hiking trail that led from the main road into a patch of forest. It was an isolated area, with sparse foliage and a few fallen and rotting trees. There was something haunting and, I had to admit, beautiful about the place—once you got away from the inn.

I sat on a rock and took out my small sketch pad. Susanne was right. Keeping a small drawing pad and pencil with you at all times led to the most interesting discoveries. I tried to remember Oliver's advice about getting out of my own way and seeing beyond the ordinary. While Barney sniffed at a patch of earth nearby, I sketched a pile of branches that had fallen a few feet away. I was feeling peaceful for the first time since arriving at the retreat, and even when drops of rain began hitting my head, I didn't want to leave.

"What are you doing there?"

I jumped up and spun around, startled by the sudden presence of another person, but I relaxed when I saw that it was only Pete walking toward me.

"Is class out already?" I asked.

"Lunch." He patted Barney on the head. "I thought I'd head home for a bit rather than eat with that crowd." He turned a little red. "I mean, Susanne is nice, and the class is actually quite enjoyable, but the other students . . ."

"You don't have to explain. But I would have thought you knew the others from town."

"I know Helen and Fred. Don't know the twins. Don't want to know the twins." Pete picked up a branch, showed it to Barney, and then threw it down the road. Rather than chase it, Barney looked at me, then went back to sniffing the earth.

"Hey, guy," Pete called to Barney. "Go chase the stick."

"He gets a little confused sometimes," I explained. "And he's nearly deaf."

"That's all right. He's loyal, looks like, and that's all you need in a dog. Though around here he could step into a mess pretty easy. Lots of old vines, a few half-dead raccoons, even some old traps. You want to steer clear of that stuff, don't you boy?" He patted Barney's head and Barney wagged back. "Besides, a lot of folks up here aren't keen on people or dogs tramping on their land. You need to be careful."

"I don't think George or Rita will care," I pointed out.

"They own everything up till the woods start. The owner of this land is a grumpy old guy with an antisocial streak." He smiled widely while he watched me guess.

"You?"

"Too obvious a description." He laughed.

"Exactly the opposite. You're the nicest guy in the class." It took me a second to realize what I'd said. "Well, Frank isn't exactly competition. But you're not grumpy or antisocial."

"Just old," he teased.

I laughed. "I don't want to get in trouble for trespassing."

"I'm just giving you a hard time. People trample through here once in a while, but very few stop to sketch it."

"It's quite pretty here," I said.

He nodded. "This has been my dream my whole life. I wanted a nice piece of land close to where I could hunt and fish. It took everything I had to get this place. I love it."

"I can see why."

"Just be careful. Don't want to see your dog get himself in a mess."

"I guess I should get him back before my grandmother misses him too much."

"She's a nice lady, your grandmother. You're all nice women," he said. "Especially that Bernadette. She seems like a nice, old-fashioned lady." Then he turned and walked farther into the woods.

I stood watching him. Old-fashioned wasn't exactly the description I would use for Bernie, but maybe something good would come of this trip after all. There was a little bounce in my step as Barney and I headed back toward the house, until a flash of light and a crash of thunder turned my nice stroll into an all-out run for safety.

Barney and I were soaking wet by the time we got back to the Patchwork, and I knew that Rita would flip out if there was a wet dog tramping through her premises, so I left him in the entryway and headed to the kitchen, in search of paper towels.

As I opened the kitchen door, I caught sight of a familiar figure. I took a step in to say hi, then realized that if I did I would be interrupting something, so I stepped back and listened. Walking away would have been the polite thing to do, but I didn't do it. I couldn't do it. My friend was making a big mistake, and I wanted to be nearby to stop it if I could.

On the other side of the door, Bernie and George were talking in muffled tones, broken up by long silences. I knew what those silences were. She had clearly reconnected with her high school love.

"Looking for something?" Rita was coming up behind me.

"Paper towels," I said loudly. "Barney got wet. I figured I could get something to dry him before I took him upstairs."

"I have some old towels in the basement," Rita said. She turned into a dark hall and disappeared down some stairs.

I coughed and headed into the kitchen, hoping I'd given them enough warning. I had. Almost. Bernie and George were standing several feet apart, but they both had a flushed, embarrassed look that would have been unmistakable to Rita had she seen it.

"Is it still lunchtime?" I asked. "Can I get something? I just got back from doing some sketches in the woods." I knew I was explaining way too much, but it gave me time to watch their faces for signs of guilt.

George's voice was calm. "It's a buffet. Sandwiches and soup," he said. "I think everything you'll need is out there."

"I could use some company. Bernie, you want to sit with me?"

Bernie nodded and walked out of the kitchen ahead of me. I stayed behind and almost said something to George. I just didn't know what to say. It was none of my business, but if you see someone walking into traffic, you call out to stop them. And from where I was standing, it looked like Bernie was walking straight in front of a truck.

"Not a word to anyone," Bernie said, as we filled our bowls with cream of asparagus soup.

"Is there something to tell?"

"No." She hesitated, and then, just as she was about to say something more, Susanne called out.

"There you are, Bernie," Susanne said. "I thought you were going to spend the whole day in your room."

"You're in a good mood," I said to Susanne as Bernie and I took seats at her table.

"I think they're finally enjoying the class." She smiled. "It proves my theory: Everyone has an artist in them. They just need a safe place to play."

"There are no safe places," Bernie muttered, giving me a sideways glance I pretended not to see.

"I ran into Pete," I said. "He seemed to be enjoying the class."

"He's a carpenter by trade," Susanne said. "He brings a builder's perspective to his quilting. Very interesting stuff." She leaned forward. "Bernie, maybe you don't want to hear this, but he asked about you."

"Me?" Bernie seemed confused at the idea.

"He mentioned you to me too," I volunteered. "I think he likes you."

"I can't imagine why. I barely know the man." Bernie sounded defensive, and I could see that Susanne was about to question it. The two women were just making peace, and I didn't want a new argument starting again, so I jumped in with a new topic.

"I talked to Natalie," I said. "She's fine. Jeremy is fine. I meant to tell you, Susanne, but I got caught up with other things."

"Oh that's okay. I talked to her a few minutes ago."

"How?"

"I got a signal. Only for a couple of minutes, but long enough for Natalie to tell me she was fine. She also said she had some news for you."

I waited, but Susanne took a bite of her sandwich.

"What news, Susanne?"

"Don't know. Lost the signal. If you walk around by the classroom, you might get through to someone."

"She must know something about George and Rita," I suggested. "She must have found out something on the Internet."

"Why wouldn't she tell Susanne that? Why wait to talk to you?" Bernie asked. "It has to be the other thing."

"What other thing?" Susanne looked up.

I sighed. I hadn't really wanted the whole group to know. Not because anyone would be dismissive of my feelings. Quite the opposite. I knew that once Susanne and, especially, Eleanor realized that Jesse had found someone else, they would align themselves with me against him. Even though it would be out of love for me, I didn't really want anyone against him.

"Jesse went on a date, that's all," I said.

"What kind of a date?" Susanne sounded alarmed.

"The kind with a girl," Bernie said.

"It won't come to anything," Susanne said confidently. "That man loves you. Even if he is too stubborn to admit it." Susanne put down her soupspoon and looked at me. "He wants to be with you. I know it."

"And if he is who you want to be with," Bernie added, "then don't let anyone get in your way."

As she spoke, I glanced up and saw Rita hovering by the door.

CHAPTER 12

After lunch I wandered the grounds in search of a signal. In the war between modern technology and Mother Nature, technology was clearly losing. As I walked into a clearing, I got one bar on my cell, but when I dialed Natalie's number, the signal disappeared again.

"I give up," I said to no one.

Then as I put my phone in my pocket, it rang. I grabbed it before I even looked at the name of the caller.

"What's your news?" In my excitement at getting through to civilization I assumed it was Natalie.

"Nell. It's Jesse."

That required a deep breath and a change to a less frantic tone. "Hi, Jesse. How are things?"

"Boring. We haven't issued so much as a traffic ticket in over a week."

"That's good, isn't it? I mean, it's what you want." Jesse hadn't cared for the excitement I brought to the place, so he should be happy, right?

"I suppose. How are things at the retreat? Are you all having a good time?"

"It's okay." I hesitated, then found myself explaining about the unusual students, the dilapidated house, the conversation I'd over-heard the night before, and the fact that neither Rita nor George seemed to know, or care, anything about quilting, even though they were trying to turn their inn into a destination for quilters. All I left out was the situation that might be developing between Bernie and George, and the group's decision to look into the Olnhausens' back-ground. That, I knew, would not go over well.

But much to my surprise, the Olnhausens were exactly what Jesse wanted to talk about. "What do you think is their angle?"

"I have no idea."

"It's just weird," he said. "They don't know anything about quilting . . ."

"They think they can make a few bucks off a growing trend. But you don't become an instant millionaire from a bed-and-breakfast or a quilt shop, and it sounds like they need money now." Since he was asking, I told him what I suspected. "George said something about Bernie marrying a millionaire, which she didn't, but . . . It's a long story. The point is that maybe they think they can get Bernie to give them some money."

"That makes sense," he said. "It might be what they were talking about in the kitchen. It does seem like a hell of a coincidence that they hired one of Bernie's closest friends for their first quilt retreat."

Now that I thought about it, it did. "I don't know what's going on but I don't want Bernie getting in deeper."

"Nell, I'm going to . . ."

The line went dead. I walked around in circles for nearly a half hour, trying to get the signal back, but no luck.

I was about to go inside when something in the house caught my eye. I could see an odd scene playing out near a window of the third floor. Someone was grabbing the curtains as if they were trying to hold themselves up. As the person moved, I saw blonde hair and knew it was Rita. There was too much distance to see her expression, but the arm that wasn't holding the curtain was waving frantically. She seemed to be signaling for help. Just as I was about to run to see what was the trouble, another figure appeared in the window. It was George. He pulled her away from the curtain, and as he did, he looked down. I knew he could see me watching him. Then he closed the curtain.

I might have witnessed nothing more than a couple arguing, but it didn't feel that way. I ran into the house and took the steps two at a time until I'd reached the third floor. There were three rooms off the landing. Two of the doors were open and led to empty spaces. The third door was closed. I knocked, but without waiting, I also tried the knob. The door was locked. I listened but could hear nothing. I knocked again. Nothing.

I was sure something was going on. True, all I had to go on were hunches and suspicions, but there were starting to be too many of those to ignore. I could stand by the door and wait, but what good would that do? I needed to talk to someone with a generally more level head than mine. Since I couldn't get Jesse on the phone, I would talk to Eleanor.

When I got to the shop, though, it was empty. And it hardly looked the way I'd seen it earlier. Instead of boxes in the midst of being neatly unpacked and inventoried, rulers, scissors, rotary cutters, and packets of needles were strewn all over the place. It looked as if the room had been ransacked.

I didn't quite know what to do. The adrenaline of a few minutes before was giving way to confusion and frustration. I walked back to the bed-and-breakfast and looked around the dining room. Empty. As I was walked back into the entryway, I ran into one of the twins.

"The bathroom in the classroom is unusable," she sniffed.

"The place is a bit rustic," I agreed. "Not what you would like in a quilt retreat, I'm sure."

"My sister and I adapt to circumstances, regardless of our preferences."

As she turned and walked out the front door, I felt as though I'd been scolded for the condition of inn. But there wasn't time to worry about Alysse/Alice. I had better reasons to be angry.

I walked upstairs to the guest bedrooms and checked each one. No one, not even Bernie, was around.

I went back downstairs, to the only room I hadn't checked. The kitchen.

"Hi."

I bumped into George.

"Is everything . . ." I hesitated. "Is Rita okay? I thought she looked upset." There was no point in pretending I hadn't seen.

"She's fine. She's going out." George was flustered. His hands were shaking.

"She didn't seem fine," I pressed. "Can I help?"

He took a deep breath. "No. She's fine. I think we're just a little overwhelmed. I didn't think it would turn out like this. I thought . . ." He hesitated. "I guess I thought it would all be okay if I just believed it would be okay."

"What would be okay?"

George stared down at his shaking hands. "I guess I wasn't cut out to be an innkeeper," he said quietly.

"Running an inn and opening a shop. It's a lot to take on for someone without experience. You don't have hotel experience, do you?"

George stared at me. Finally he seemed to recognize that he hadn't answered. "No hotel experience," he said.

"Is that what you were fighting about?"

George looked at me. There was a flash of anger, then a blank expression that frightened me more than the anger. "Did you want something?" he asked.

I needed a reason to be in the kitchen, so I said the first thing that came to me. "I'm thirsty."

George smiled and slowly took a pitcher of lemonade from the table and poured it into a glass; then he got up and opened the freezer door. I waited as I heard the sound of ice cubes being dropped into the glass.

"Here you go," he said. He leaned against the counter and crossed his arms so that his hands were hidden. "How's Susanne's class coming?"

"Great. Thanks." I gulped down the lemonade. "I should head back."

"Get a sweater," he said. "It's getting a bit chilly out there, and the classroom isn't as well heated as I would like."

I nodded and headed upstairs to my room. Anything to get away from him. I checked my cell phone, just in case there was a signal and I could try Jesse again. Nothing. I went back to my room and flopped on the bed. As I did I noticed a large spider dangling from the ceiling. It spun its elaborate web right above my head, twirling in and out of its delicate creation, waiting for an unsuspecting fly to get caught. That's what we were, I thought: unsuspecting flies. But not anymore. Whatever was going on, we would find out the truth. Hopefully.

"It can't get any worse," I said.

As I spoke, the spider dropped onto the pillow.

CHAPTER 13

"Nell."

I opened my eyes to see a figure standing above me.

"Nell."

I looked up. The figure was becoming clearer but it still felt far away. I wondered for a moment if I was still dreaming, until I felt hands on my shoulders and realized that someone was shaking me.

"Nell." The voice was more insistent.

I blinked hard and looked into the face. "Jesse? What are you doing here?"

"Are you okay?"

"Yeah. I guess. I must have fallen asleep." I forced myself to get out of bed. "Have you seen my grandmother?"

"She went into town."

I shook the sleep off me. I was confused. I stood up to give myself half a chance at staying awake. "I fell asleep."

"You said that."

I looked down at the bed, my head still in a fog. "There was a spider on the pillow."

Jesse ran his hand along the pillow and the bedcover. "It's gone."

"No. You don't understand. There was a spider on the bed pillow, and I fell asleep."

"So? You were tired. Based on what you told me on the phone, this whole trip has been pretty stressful."

"But there was a spider."

"Okay." His voice was calm and reassuring. "There isn't one now. And you're not exactly squeamish about spiders, are you?"

"No," I admitted, "but I don't want to nap with one either." I looked up at him, as it finally sunk in that he was there. "Something's wrong," I muttered.

"It's okay. It's going to be okay. You must have had a bad dream."

Against my better judgment, and all the rules of playing it cool, I lay my head on his chest. He wrapped his arms around me, and I found myself drifting off again.

I pulled back, if only to keep myself awake. "It wasn't a dream. I think I was drugged."

✁

Though it wasn't yet night, the sky was dark. It wasn't windy but it was cold. There was a sudden flash of light followed quickly by a loud clap. Maybe it was the fog in my brain, but everything about this place was beginning to seem unreal.

Jesse wrapped one arm around my waist and held my hand with the other one. As I was coming down the stairs, I'd felt unsteady, but now with the cold air hitting me, I was finally waking up. Still, I leaned into Jesse as we walked toward Susanne's class.

"Where are we going?" I asked.

"I want to get you away from here."

"I'm fine," I said, but I felt woozy and a little scared. "Where's my grandmother?"

"Susanne thought Eleanor must have gone somewhere with the lady who owns this place, but she doesn't know where," he said. "She also said the husband is supposed to be around here somewhere, but the place is deserted. Where is everyone?"

"I have no idea. I thought Eleanor would be unpacking in the shop, but no one was there when I went by a few hours ago."

"No one is there now either," he said. "Bernie isn't around. Susanne and a few other people are in that building." He pointed toward the classroom. "She looked as though she was finishing up for the day."

"We have to find my grandmother," I said. "And Bernie." I looked around as panic began to rise in me. "And Barney."

"Barney's fine," Jesse said. "He's got to be with Eleanor."

I shook my head. "Not if Rita had anything to say about it. She hates him."

Jesse wrinkled his brow. "She hates Barney? What kind of people are they?"

✄

Susanne's class let out as Jesse and I discussed what we should do. The twins eyed us suspiciously but walked away without saying a word. Pete came over and introduced himself, and beckoned for Frank and Helen to do the same.

"Couldn't live a whole week without Nell," Pete said once he realized who Jesse was. "I can't blame you. These are the nicest ladies I've met in a while."

"That Susanne is one hell of a teacher," Frank chimed in. "I enjoy every moment I'm in class."

Helen rolled her eyes. "We missed you today," she said to me. "Were you helping Rita or George?"

There was an edge to her voice that took me by surprise.

"Neither," I said. Before there were more questions I didn't know how to answer, I walked away.

I went into the classroom, where Susanne was refolding fabrics. "I may actually be making some progress," she said. "People found some really interesting objects to add to their quilts."

She pointed toward a pile of items, among them some twigs, a few leaves, a bottle cap, and a feather.

"When did they get these?" I asked.

"I sent them off after lunch. I was expecting everyone to come back in ten minutes with whatever they could find around the building. I guess I didn't have much faith in their enthusiasm. But they were gone for nearly an hour." Susanne grabbed a half yard of fabric and folded it, placing it carefully on a pile. Then she looked around. "Did you happen to take some of my quilts back to the room? I brought five large quilts and now I can only find four. I know the other one was here this morning."

I shook my head. Missing quilts were the least of my problems. "Susanne, something is going on here. I think George drugged me. I have no idea why. But Bernie and Eleanor are missing. And so is Barney. Jesse is here, and we're going to have to do something. I'm getting worried."

Susanne was the easiest of the group to frighten, so I felt momentarily guilty about adding to her stress, but there was no point in shielding her from possible danger.

Without saying a word, she dropped the fabrics she was folding and followed me out of the classroom, while a bolt of lightning flashed overhead and a steady rain began to fall on all of us.

CHAPTER 14

"I just got off the phone with the police chief, a guy named McIntyre," Jesse said as he met us on the inn's veranda. "He said he'd look around town and ask if anyone knows where Mrs. Olnhausen is. He also told me that there are very few strangers in town this time of year, so Eleanor should be easy to spot."

Everyone but the twins had stayed to talk with Susanne and myself, and seemed equally concerned about the disappearances, which made me feel closer to each of them.

"I thought you were helping your grandmother," Susanne said.

There was no accusation in her voice, but I felt somehow responsible that some of our group was now missing.

"I fell asleep," I said meekly.

"She was drugged," Jesse corrected me. "Look at her eyes—they're glassy. Something's going on here."

The waiting had finally gotten to me. "I'm going to walk toward the hiking trails," I said. "Barney and I were there this morning. Maybe he wandered back. He was sniffing at something, so he might have gone back to check it out. At least it would be something he's familiar with."

"I can go with you," Pete volunteered.

"Helen and I are heading back toward town anyway," Frank said. "Why don't I drive around and see if I can spot Eleanor?"

"Cell service is really bad around here," I warned Frank. "Call the inn if you have any news."

"Someone stay by the phone."

"I'll do that," Susanne volunteered. "Jesse, you should go with Nell and Pete. I don't like the idea of Barney wandering around in the woods with this storm going on."

Jesse, Pete, and I retraced the steps of my earlier walk. The rain had started to come down hard, but I was determined to find Barney. I just couldn't understand why he would wander off. I knew he was starting to be forgetful, but he was also pretty lazy. At home he might halfheartedly chase an occasional squirrel, but he wouldn't wander in the rain when there was a soft bed and a cookie waiting for him. When I found him, I had every intention of giving him a piece of my mind—one I knew he wouldn't hear or pay attention to. But when I finally located the patch of dirt that had interested him earlier, there was no one there.

"He's not here," I shouted to Jesse and Pete, who had wandered several feet away from me. Now worry was being overtaken by anger. If not for Rita, Barney would be at Eleanor's side, and I would know that both of them were safe. But because of this ridiculous charade of a quilt retreat, they were both gone. Maybe it was too early to be so afraid, but if George had drugged me, and I was certain he had, what might he have done to the others?

Suddenly I heard a rustling in the trees in the direction Jesse had walked. I heard Jesse and Pete talking in soft tones for several minutes before Jesse called out, "I've got him."

I walked over and saw Barney digging at a patch of ground. I grabbed at his collar, but he was too intently focused on his task to notice that I was there.

"What's he doing?" I asked.

Jesse pointed to the ground near Barney's nose. I saw a lifeless dark brown paw sticking out of the ground.

"Is it a deer?" I asked.

"I don't think so," Pete said. "It was buried here. No one buries a deer."

"Maybe it's a dog." I peered closer at the uncovered leg and the smell of decay made me feel sick.

Jesse nodded. "That must be it. Someone probably buried their dog in a shallow grave, and the rain is washing away the dirt."

Pete shook his head. "It's my land, but it's not my dog. I'm not sure how I feel about someone doing that, but at least Barney is safe."

"There was something in the paper about missing hunting dogs," I said. "Do you think someone is killing dogs?"

Jesse took my hand. "It's probably nothing, but let's get back to the house."

"You're worried."

"I'm not worried. But we have Barney now, and the others will be on their way back. There's no point in standing in the rain because of dead dog."

For once I agreed with Jesse that curiosity wasn't a good enough reason to stick around in the pouring rain. I pulled on Barney's leash to get him away from the dog's grave and reached back for Jesse's hand. But it wasn't there.

I looked around and realized that Jesse had taken several steps away from me, with Pete following close behind him.

"Jesse, the house is the other way," I pointed out.

He nodded and kept walking.

"Jesse." I was suddenly nervous. "I really don't feel like standing around in the rain when we don't know if Eleanor and Bernie are okay."

"Jesse," Pete added. "Nell's right. We have the dog. That's what we came for. Let's get back to the inn and see if we can find the others."

"I'm coming," he finally answered. "I just thought I saw . . ."

Jesse didn't finish. He was looking toward a cluster of trees off to the left. I followed his eyes and realized what he was seeing. The red and white double cross quilt was lying on the ground under a tree. But not directly on the ground. Something was under it.

"Stay here," Jesse directed me.

"Fat chance."

Jesse, Pete, and I walked to the quilt, and as we got closer, I could see a deep red stain near the top of it. Either the rain was spreading the stain or it was what I feared: something under the quilt had bled badly. I held tight to Barney's collar as Jesse kneeled beside the quilt, picked up a corner, and pulled it back.

Barney tried to pull away from me, apparently desperate to sniff what we had uncovered. I held him back as best I could but my hands were shaking.

"Do you know who this is?" he asked.

I looked down at the eyes that were staring ahead but seeing nothing. The shock of a dead body was nothing compared to the shock of whose body it was.

"It's George Olnhausen," Pete told him quietly. "He's the owner of the bed-and-breakfast."

George was lying on his back, with a small hole in the center of his chest and blood, which still looked wet, forming a circle around the wound.

I took a deep breath and looked closer. "Is he dead?"

Jesse felt for a pulse. Seconds passed before he nodded. "I'd guess a gunshot through the heart, by the looks of it. I don't see any powder burns on his shirt so probably not close range. Good shot though."

Jesse tilted George's body slightly up. "His wallet is still there." He let the body return to its original spot.

"Do you think someone tried to rob him? In the woods?" Pete asked.

Jesse shrugged. "This guy owned the inn?"

I nodded.

"Then this is the guy who drugged you."

"I guess he had bigger problems than trying to get rid of me."

"Maybe." Jesse locked eyes with me. "I don't think he's been dead long. He's still warm."

I looked at the trees surrounding us, closing out the daylight and leaving lots of hiding places for someone with a gun.

"So the killer could still be here," Pete said. As the words came out of his mouth, I thought I heard a rustle in the trees behind me, but I told myself it was probably a trick of my nerves.

Jesse let go of the quilt and looked around. "Should have brought my gun," he muttered. "Pete, you better come back with us. But let's do it now, and quickly."

Then Jesse grabbed my hand, and the three of us ran down the hiking trail in the direction of the inn, with Barney running alongside us as if we were racing for the fun of it.

CHAPTER 15

"Everything's okay," Susanne called to us as we walked into the entryway. "Frank found Eleanor. She had driven into town. She's on her way back."

"Call the police chief," Jesse said. "We have a dead body out there."

Without waiting for her to dial, Jesse grabbed the phone. Barney shook himself violently, drying himself but getting everything around him wet. Then he scratched at the door to go out again. Pete stood at the entrance as though he were guarding it. I was shaking. The rain, the dead dog, and the sight of George's lifeless eyes had made me very cold, and all I wanted to think about was getting out of my wet clothes and into something warm and comforting. I started up the stairs to the bedroom.

But Susanne stopped me. "What is he talking about? Is he talking about a person? There's a person dead in the woods?" Susanne reached down to Barney, holding him close, as if to protect him.

"It's George. He's dead," I said.

"What do you mean, dead? How could he be dead? He was the picture of health this morning."

"I don't know," I said. I was trying to cushion the blow, but there didn't seem much point. "It looks like murder."

Susanne looked at me as if she were waiting for the punch line of a very bad joke. When she saw that none was coming, she just shook her head and moved back, leaning against the wall. "That can't be. He was with Bernie," she said, then clasped one hand over her mouth.

Bernie was now the only one of our group not accounted for. "Where is she?" I asked urgently.

"Where's who?" I turned to see Bernie walking down the steps from the bedrooms.

"Where were you?"

"Upstairs, taking a nap." Bernie pointed up the steps. Her face was flushed and her eyes were red. I wondered for a second if she too had been drugged, but she didn't give me a chance to ask. She walked past as if I wasn't there. "What are you doing here, Jesse?"

Jesse hung up the phone and moved in close. "Bernie, where were you just now?"

"I was upstairs." For the second time she pointed up the stairs.

"Nell looked upstairs," Jesse said.

I shook my head. "Before I fell asleep. She could have come in afterward. We didn't check the rooms. We came straight downstairs."

"What time did you go to your room, Bernie?" Jesse leaned closer to Bernie, who stared at him. I could see that she was about to cry, and when she looked to me for help, I grabbed Jesse's arm and forced him back a few steps.

"Give her a minute," I said.

"We don't have a minute. McIntyre's on his way."

Bernie looked from Jesse to me. "What's going on?" she asked. Her voice was raised and shaking. I wanted to bring her into the living room and have her sit down, but Jesse shook me off. He moved closer to Bernie and blocked my access to her.

"Were you with George today?" he asked.

"Yes, earlier. We went for a walk."

"Where?" Jesse moved closer.

"In the woods."

"What time?"

I could see fear spread across Bernie's face, and I could see that it was Jesse's doing. He was going into full police-chief mode. But this wasn't his town, and she wasn't his suspect. I pushed back toward Bernie.

"Don't answer that," I said. I grabbed her arm, ignoring the look of annoyance from Jesse, and took her into the kitchen.

Bernie resisted my pushing, but I didn't let up. Once we were alone, I let go of her arm.

"What are you dragging me in here for?" she asked.

"I just need you to take a deep breath and tell me everything that happened this afternoon. And quickly, before the police arrive."

"The police are coming?"

"What were you doing with George this afternoon?" I asked.

Something changed in Bernie's face. The fear and confusion left her and she seemed, instead, to be offended. "Look, I know you guys think I'm crazy, but he's an old friend and I will do what I like."

"What time did you leave him?"

"Nell, I'm a grown woman. I don't have to account to anyone for my time."

"Humor me."

"Maybe two or three hours ago."

"And you went to your room right after you last saw George?"

"Yes. What is going on?"

"That isn't true, Bernie. I went into everyone's room a couple of hours ago, and you weren't in yours."

"I was . . ." She stopped. "What are you asking me, Nell?"

"I want to know where you were this afternoon."

"Why?"

I took a deep breath and said as calmly as I could, "George is dead."

Bernie froze. Finally she said, softly, "That's not possible. He was fine an hour ago."

"Is that the last time you saw him?"

She didn't seem to hear me. I waited for an answer. Instead I got a question.

"How?" she finally asked, her voice so soft it was almost a whisper.

"Jesse thinks he was shot."

Her eyes widened and she seemed about to collapse. I reached out to her, but she waved me off and, instead of getting support from me, leaned against the kitchen counter. "You think I had something to do with it?"

"I don't know what to think. All I know is that we found him in the woods, just off the hiking trail. He was covered with one of the quilts Susanne brought."

"The double cross."

I took a deep breath and asked a question I didn't want to ask. "How do you know that?"

"We took it from the studio. George asked me to go for a walk and he'd brought a bottle of wine and some food. I thought he wanted to have a picnic, so I grabbed the quilt. It is mine, and I figured Susanne was done showing it to the class. It was harmless. Just two old friends."

"Having a romantic picnic?"

"Something like that."

"Bernie, he's someone else's husband."

The door opened behind me.

"Not anymore, he's not." I recognized the voice as belonging to Jim McIntyre, the local police chief. "Ma'am," he said to Bernie, "would you mind answering some questions for me?"

CHAPTER 16

The storm was over. It was, strangely enough, a beautiful spring night, with thousands of stars stretching out across a deep blue sky. Eleanor arrived back, and after hearing the news, she did what any practical woman would do: she set to work on dinner. Susanne took her lead and, despite being very shaken, set the tables.

Pete had gone home to get out of his wet clothes but had promised to check in on us later. I think he was more shocked than the rest of us that Bernie had spent the day picnicking with a married man. I assured him that, no matter what it looked like, Bernie hadn't done anything wrong. He didn't seem convinced, but, then, he didn't know Bernie. Of course, neither did Chief McIntyre, and he was alone with her, asking questions. After pacing the living room floor for half an hour, I went outside and waited nervously for McIntyre's interrogation to end.

"What are you doing out here?"

I looked over at Jesse, who handed me a hot cup of tea. "I was trying to make sense of it."

"It's too early for that. There are too many questions."

"There's one very big one," I pointed out. "Where's Rita?"

Jesse nodded. "McIntyre said she was upstairs, resting. I asked him how she sounded and he said 'not normal.'"

"What does that mean?"

"I'm not sure. Either she didn't sound normal because her husband has been murdered, or she didn't sound the way a woman whose husband was murdered should sound."

"I don't know if he's up for this kind of thing. Solving a homicide," I said. "He seems every bit the small-town cop."

Jesse smiled. "That's what I am too."

"You were a police officer in New York City before you came back to Archers Rest."

Eleanor once told me that Jesse had worked in New York City for several years before his wife, Lizzy, was diagnosed with cancer. He and Lizzy returned to Archers Rest, their hometown, so their families could be nearby to help with their daughter during Lizzy's illness and, eventually, after she died. Jesse didn't often talk about his days in the big city, and I always wondered if he missed them.

"Detective," Jesse said. "I was a detective in vice."

"Why didn't you tell me that before?"

He shrugged. "Never came up. Not a lot of vice in Archers Rest."

"Isn't that a shame?" I smiled.

He blushed.

"Maybe you could help McIntyre," I said. "I have the feeling he thinks Bernie is involved."

"*I* think Bernie is involved. And so do you."

I wondered if we were talking about the same thing. "I think," I said carefully, "that she may be involved in a way, but I am sure she didn't kill him and I don't want to see her railroaded for something she didn't do."

"Then tell me what you know."

I took a breath. "If I tell you, you have to promise not to share anything I say with McIntyre. I don't want him getting the wrong idea."

"I won't say a word. Mostly because I trust your instincts."

That made me smile. "And the other reason?"

"I agree with you."

Jesse leaned against a fence and looked up at the sky before turning his gaze to me. His voice was quiet, and his expression had the same earnest seriousness I'd seen the night we first met, but there was a strength to his face and a kindness in his eyes that I'd only recently come to see. Standing there, I realized how much I liked that face.

"Bernie wouldn't kill anyone," Jesse continued. "I've known her for years. She plays cards with my mom every week and babysits for Allie when my mom can't. I wouldn't trust her with my daughter if I thought for a moment she had an ounce of violence in her."

"Okay," I said. "I'll tell you everything."

"If we're going to find out who the killer is, then you have to."

I smiled. "We?"

He nodded. "We."

So I told him about seeing Bernie and George in the kitchen. Even as I spoke, I knew how it would sound. The picnic, the kitchen, and George's comments about Bernie marrying a millionaire—it added up to a pretty good motive. A lonely woman reconnects with her lost love only to find out his sole interest is her back account. Angry and hurt, she shoots him. A lazy or inexperienced cop would have her arrested in the time it takes for a batch of scones to come out of the oven.

I could tell by the expression on Jesse's face that he thought the motive was pretty compelling, but instead of saying so he shrugged his shoulders. "It's going to be fine," he said quietly.

I smiled. I was glad, for once, to be on the same side of an investigation as Jesse. I'd gotten used to getting help from the other members of the quilt club, and I knew they would be willing to do anything, but knowing Jesse was there as well almost made me confident that we would find the killer. Almost, because I had the odd and uncomfortable feeling that I had lost a normally reliable ally in Bernie. From the moment George's name was brought up back in Archers Rest, she had become unusually secretive, and without her telling the whole truth, I wasn't sure there was anything we could do to help.

✄

We ate dinner in silence. Once McIntyre had finished with Bernie, she sat at a table by herself, nursing a glass of wine. Any attempt to comfort her was brushed off, and after we all had failed, we gave her the space she seemed to want. I watched her for any hint of, I don't know, guilt, remorse—anything that would tag her as the killer—but all I saw was the blank expression of shock. As we ate, Rita walked downstairs but went straight into the kitchen with McIntyre, without even looking toward us. There was no guilt on her face either. Just tiredness and tears.

Halfway through dinner the silence turned from awkward to unbearable, but none of us seemed to be able to figure out what to say. Susanne started to say something about the class, and then stopped. The only words my grandmother spoke were to Barney, who sat at her feet. Jesse and I watched the kitchen door for any sign of Chief McIntyre.

As soon as I finished eating, I used my dirty dish as an excuse to interrupt. Not that there was much to walk in on. Rita stood by the sink, drinking a glass of lemonade, while the police chief sat at the small table on the other side of the room.

"I hope it's okay to come in here," I said as I placed my dish on the counter. I waited for a moment to see if their conversation, whatever it had been, would continue, but neither Rita nor McIntyre spoke.

"I'm so sorry, Rita. We all are," I eventually said. "If there's anything we can do." I looked for a reaction, but she wouldn't look at me. "Maybe it would be best if we cleared out. Since the rest of the week is canceled . . ."

"Why?" Rita's head swiveled and her eyes met mine.

I was taken aback. "Because you must want to be with your friends and with your daughter. You can't want strangers in your house."

"My daughter won't come," she said.

Even though I didn't like Rita, I found it hard to imagine what she could have done that would keep her daughter away at a time like this. But this wasn't the moment to ask.

"I'm sure you don't want us here," I said, even though I didn't want to leave the inn. More than anything I wanted to stay and find out who had killed George, but I needed to get Bernie away from this mess.

"I don't care if you stay." Rita's face was blank. She raised one of her perfectly manicured hands to her face and wound a flyaway strand of hair behind her ear. "In fact, I see no reason why the class shouldn't continue. People signed up to take it, and you have driven all this way. I really would prefer it if it went forward."

"If I have a vote, and I hope I do, I'd rather none of you ladies left," McIntyre said. "I'd like to keep everyone here until I get full statements, and that may take a day or two."

"None of us knows a thing about why this happened," I said firmly. "We barely knew him."

"That isn't true for all of you," he countered.

"Bernie hasn't seen him since high school," I shot back. "She hadn't a reason in the world to want George dead." I was proud of just how certain I sounded, even though I knew it wasn't entirely true.

"He was her sweetheart at one point. Broken heart, I believe."

I rolled my eyes to emphasize the ridiculousness of this motive. "Forty-five years ago. I imagine she's over it by now." My voice dripped with sarcasm, but McIntyre seemed unfazed. I tried a new tactic. "Even if she was still upset, and that's ridiculous, Bernie doesn't have a gun."

"A gun is missing from above the fireplace. A hunting rifle, which is probably what killed George."

"That would mean someone had to take the rifle, hide it from others, probably load it," I said, "then follow George into the woods and shoot him."

"Unless George brought the gun with him," McIntyre suggested. "Some hunters like to carry their guns with them, just in case."

I shrugged off each of his ideas. "In any case," I said, "a high school romance is hardly enough motive to do all that. You need to look closer to home."

At that Rita broke down in sobs, hysterical, uncontrollable sobs. In my attempt to deflect suspicion from Bernie, I'd laid George's murder at the feet of his widow, and right in front of her. Tact was clearly not my strong point. Thankfully, it brought Jesse and Eleanor into the kitchen to find out what was the matter.

"Why don't you call it a night, Mrs. Olnhausen," McIntyre said in a casual manner, but one that implied it wasn't a suggestion. "I'm going to talk to these good folks for a while, and in the morning we'll call someone to come over and sit with you."

That stopped her crying. "I don't need a sitter," she snapped, and left the room.

Eleanor watched her leave, then turned to the rest of us. "Interesting woman."

CHAPTER 17

"I think you have a pretty good suspect in Rita," I said to McIntyre.

"Maybe."

"They seemed to have some money problems."

"How can you tell?" McIntyre leaned back in his char.

"Look around you," I said. "The place is falling apart."

McIntyre nodded. "Could be. Lot of people have money problems and live to tell about it though."

"He might have had life insurance," Jesse jumped in. "Money problems and life insurance make a pretty strong recipe for murder."

McIntyre nodded. "Something to check on, for sure."

"And Rita had access to the gun and knew the woods better than any of us," I added. "She could have found him easily."

"Your friend Bernadette didn't need to find George. She was with him," McIntyre pointed out.

"What better reason to kill your husband than finding him with an old girlfriend?" Jesse said.

"And there's something else," I said, and then told him about what I'd seen in the window of the third floor earlier in the day.

"You weren't close enough to really know what was going on," he pointed out.

"I know they weren't having a good time. Whatever was going on up there, they wanted to keep me from seeing it."

"Well, it was none of your business," McIntyre said as he got up from the table. "I appreciate the ideas. It's certainly nice to have an opportunity to throw around a few ideas with good people like you. It's nice when we're all working together. Much more interesting conversation than my usual partner, my dog Russ."

He smiled cheerfully at me and I smiled back, but I suspect my face showed more concern than friendliness. Not that McIntyre seemed to care. He shook Jesse's hand and said something about being glad that a police chief from a "big town" would be around for the investigation, murders being so scarce in Winston.

Then McIntyre nodded to the rest of us and wished us a good night's sleep. "You folks will all be here in the morning. Maybe we can hash out the case then. Sometimes it helps to let the brain work on a problem. Maybe we'll get lucky and some idea will come to one of us tonight." He turned to Eleanor. "If you make coffee, I'll bring something from the bakery. Maria bakes up some pretty tasty muffins. I think you'll really enjoy them." Then he walked out of the kitchen, leaving us all standing there trying to decide whether to laugh or be alarmed.

"He seems to think the whole thing is just an excuse to get together for brunch." Eleanor said, once McIntyre had left the room.

"It's like he's made up his mind it's Bernie," I said.

"He's talking it out, that's all," Jesse offered. "And even if he has made up his mind, he needs proof. And since Bernie is innocent, he won't be able to get it."

Eleanor smiled at Jesse, but when she turned to me, I could see she was worried. She wasn't the only one. If Bernie had lied to McIntyre the way she'd lied to me, he would have more reason than motive to suspect her.

✂

After I helped Jesse settle into a room across from the one Eleanor and I were in, I took Barney out for one last walk. I knew Eleanor and Susanne were waiting upstairs to talk about everything that had happened, but I needed a moment to think. Barney seemed to have had enough adventure for one day though. I could barely get him off the porch, so I sat on the steps while he sniffed at some nearby flowers.

As I stood up, I saw a strange light going on and off in the woods. It must have been the same light Susanne saw the first night. I waited for movement, but there was none. In case it was a signal, I walked around the entire house, but there was nothing out of the ordinary. The ghosts or deer or whatever had scared Susanne seemed to be lying low for the night. Just as I returned to the front porch where Barney had remained, I heard a noise behind me.

I turned to see a car pulling up and watched as Helen and Frank got out.

"We heard there were police at the inn," Frank said. "We got worried after what went on this afternoon. Everything okay in there?"

"No, I'm afraid not. There was a . . ." I struggled for the right word. "There's some sad news."

Even in the moonlight, Frank seemed pale. "I'm so sorry," he said.

"What happened?" Helen stepped forward.

"George was found in the woods. Jesse, Pete, and I found him in the woods. He'd been shot."

Helen gasped. "He's dead?"

"Are you sure?" Frank didn't wait for my answer. He ran up the steps to the house and went inside.

"Why don't I get you some water?" I said to the shaken Helen.

She nodded, and we went inside to the kitchen. Frank wasn't on the first floor, so I assumed he must have gone up to Rita's room.

"I don't understand why," Helen kept saying.

"I know it's a great shock."

"He didn't have to . . ." She stopped and took a deep breath. "I never imagined this would happen."

"Of course not," I said. "It will be a great comfort to Rita that she has such good friends here right now. I feel a bit like an intruder, but she's asked us not to leave. She wants the class to continue."

"That can't happen," Helen said firmly. "It would be completely inappropriate."

"She's right," Eleanor said twenty minutes later, when I sat on my bed and related the story to her and Susanne.

Helen and I had sat in the kitchen with very little to say since there was very little information. Even if there had been, after her initial outburst Helen seemed unwilling to talk. She just stared at the glass of water I'd gotten for her. Once Frank returned I'd grabbed Barney and headed toward my room, leaving them to see themselves out. Frank didn't tell me if he'd spoken to Rita, but I assumed he had because I couldn't think of where else he would have disappeared to.

"Rita is the one who wants the class to continue," I said to my grandmother.

"That's another odd thing about that woman." Eleanor shook her finger at me. "Her husband is dead. Even if she didn't like the man, shouldn't she close down her business until she's put him in the ground?"

"Maybe she can't," I offered. "They wanted us up here. It obviously wasn't to teach a quilting retreat."

Susanne had been pacing the floor, but she stopped and said quietly, "I've been wondering what he was doing under the quilt. Don't you sit on top of a quilt when you go on a picnic?"

"If he was lying under it, maybe the killer didn't intend to kill George," I said. "Maybe the killer didn't even see who he was shooting."

"Who would they *want* to kill?" Susanne asked.

We all stopped for a moment. The answer just hung there, but no one seemed willing to say it.

Finally Eleanor spoke up. "No one would want to kill Bernie," she said.

"Except maybe Rita," I offered.

"But if Rita killed George, thinking it was Bernie, what would Bernie have been doing under the blanket?" Susanne asked.

"She might have been under it with George," I suggested. "They might have been—"

"We know what they might have been doing," Eleanor interrupted, "and it's ridiculous."

"The ground is cold and damp," I agreed. "Whatever they might have been doing, they would have done it on the quilt, not under it."

"Okay, so why was George lying under the quilt?" Eleanor asked. "If he and Bernie were having their picnic and sitting on the quilt, someone must have come upon them and shot him."

"And then what?" Susanne took up the thought. "Maybe Bernie ran once George was shot. Maybe she knows the killer."

"Then she would have told McIntyre," I pointed out. "And I don't remember seeing any picnic items there. If the killer caught them together, then there would have been food or wine. I don't think Bernie would have grabbed the picnic supplies as she ran from a killer."

"What did it look like when you and Jesse found George's body?" Susanne asked.

I searched my memory for the crime scene as I first saw it. Something stood out. "I don't think there was a hole in the quilt," I said. "George must not have been lying under it when he was shot. The person who killed him might have covered him with it."

"Why?" Eleanor seemed suddenly confused. "It would hardly make him less noticeable. The quilt was red and white. You could see it a mile away."

"Maybe she panicked," Susanne said.

We all looked at her. A long stretch of silence followed as the word hung in the air.

"She?" Eleanor finally said.

We turned to Susanne. "We can't ignore the facts," Susanne said. "She did it."

CHAPTER 18

"How can you say that?" Eleanor seemed ready to burst. "I know you two have been at odds lately, but that hardly . . ."

Susanne turned bright red. "Rita. I think it was Rita. Good heavens, Eleanor, I wouldn't for a minute suspect Bernie."

We all took a relieved breath.

"Susanne is right. It had to be Rita. How can we prove she did it?" Eleanor looked at me. "We need to find out her motive, right?"

"Just because a person has a motive doesn't mean they will kill someone, and people are killed with no logical motive at all," I said, as if I were an expert on the subject. But it seemed to me that finding motive wouldn't get us very far until we had first sorted out a few other things.

"What we need to do is figure out where everybody was this afternoon," I said. "Who had access to the gun? Who knew where George was going to be? Who can't be accounted for? That's going to help us eliminate people."

"So we talk to everybody," Susanne said. "We can find out where they were this afternoon, what they saw."

"But they were in class," Eleanor said. "That means none of them could have done it."

Susanne shook her head. "I sent them all out to find embellishments for their quilts."

"So they could have been in the woods around the time of the murder," I said. "And they all knew George."

"I'll talk to Rita," Eleanor said. "If she doesn't call a friend, she will need someone to talk to, and I've spent a lot of time with her already, so maybe she'll talk to me."

"But she was with you, wasn't she?" Susanne asked. "This morning didn't you go off with Rita somewhere? The last time I saw George, he said you and Rita were going out."

Eleanor shook her head. "She was supposed to meet me in town, but she went into the house at lunch and that was the last I saw of her until tonight."

"Where were you?" I asked.

"I went to the library to check my e-mail. I have a shipment due at the shop early next week. I was also going to try to find a little background on this property."

"Why would Rita be with you for that?" I asked.

"She wouldn't be. But I did ask her to meet me later, so I could show her some Web sites to attract quilters to her shop. I guess she didn't care enough about it to join me."

"I'm not sure that was the reason." I reminded them about what I'd witnessed in the window of the third floor and filled them in on my conversation with George in the kitchen.

"All the more motive for her to kill him," Eleanor said. "They were fighting and one thing led to another."

"There were several hours in between," I pointed out.

"Maybe that picnic with Bernie was the last straw."

"Maybe," I said. "I think that may be what Jesse believes."

"What's he doing up here anyway?" Susanne asked.

"I'm not sure. I guess he was worried and he came to see if everything was okay."

"Good thing he did," Eleanor said. "I wouldn't feel comfortable leaving Bernie's fate up to a stranger."

"I'm not too comfortable leaving any of our fates up to that man," Susanne said. "If Rita is a killer, then we are all sleeping under her roof, and if the killing has something to do with George and Bernie, isn't Bernie at risk as long as she's still in this house?"

It wasn't a comforting thought. "What about this place?" I asked. "Did the library have any information?

"Oh, heavens! I nearly forgot about that in all the excitement." Eleanor leaned forward. "It's better than just information on the inn. Much better. I didn't find anything really on the Internet, but I got into a friendly conversation with the librarian. She gave me some very good information."

"What information?" The buildup was killing me.

"Well," Eleanor continued, "you remember how Rita and George told us she had inherited the place from her father?" Susanne and I nodded. "Not a bit of truth to it. This place was owned by a local man until about two years ago, when he passed on. He was said to have been quite an eccentric. The rumor is that he amassed quite a fortune and hid it somewhere in the house. He had one heir, a nephew, who tore up the place looking for the money and finally, in frustration, sold it."

"To Rita and George," I said.

"Yes." Eleanor smiled. "And they paid cash for it. The house was torn apart, and the nephew was desperate to sell, but the Olnhausens paid his asking price without any negotiations. Then they opened an account in town. Deposited nearly a hundred thousand dollars. Haven't touched it as far as the librarian knows."

"Is she sure?"

"She's married to the president of the bank," Eleanor said, "so she would know."

"We couldn't get better inside information in Archers Rest." Susanne smiled.

I looked up at my grandmother. "But it means they aren't short of money after all. If they weren't interested in conning Bernie out of her money so they could fix up the place, why did they want us here?"

CHAPTER 19

"If the librarian knows, so does McIntyre," Jesse said the next morning. He had barely finished dressing, but I couldn't wait and had barged into his room. "That's why he didn't see money as a motive."

"And that makes Bernie look even more guilty."

"Not necessarily. Rita could have been jealous of a renewed relationship between her husband and his first love." Jesse put on his watch and looked at me. An amused look, clearly at my expense, spread across his face. "I would love to have seen Eleanor questioning the librarian and looking for clues."

"She was just asking around." I wasn't sure the idea of my grandmother helping to find George's killer was as funny as Jesse found it.

"You've turned the entire quilt group into an amateur detective agency, haven't you?"

"Not the entire group." I was thinking about how Maggie was out of state, and we had left Bernie out of our most recent discussion.

"Right, Natalie, Maggie, and Carrie are clear on this one."

"Carrie is looking into financials, and Natalie is checking to see if she can find anything about them online," I said before I could stop myself.

He nodded. "You don't have access to the Internet in the inn, I guess." His smile widened. "How does Carrie get financial information? You've got to have a social security number for that."

"Rita asked to open an account with a fabric supplier, using Eleanor as a reference. Eleanor's known the owner for years and she's a great customer, so I'm sure he would have been happy to extend any credit Rita or George wanted. Natalie told him Eleanor wanted to read the application and cosign it to smooth the process. She asked him to fax her a copy to give to Eleanor."

"Which he did, because people will do anything for your grandmother."

"I also told her to promise him one of Eleanor's rhubarb pies."

"Nice touch." He sat on the bed. "And the form had their social security numbers on it." He shook his head and started laughing.

"I amuse you now, since it's not your jurisdiction."

"I guess. It's nice to be in on the caper for a change."

"Happy to include you."

"You're kind of cute when you're masterminding an end run around a police investigation. I'm surprised I never noticed it before."

"So am I. Do you think George engineered this whole quilt retreat to get reintroduced to Bernie?" I asked.

"Okay, boss, I guess we're back to the case." He was having a little too much fun at my expense. "I have a question. Was Rita surprised to see her?"

I tried to remember. "I guess. It's hard to tell with Rita. I haven't spent much time with her. She's always in town or shopping or something. It seemed to me that George did most of the work."

"Okay, then that's another contributing factor. George had some *Green Acres* fantasy of a backwoods home. He bought this place and put all his energy into turning it into a quaint inn. But Rita, who is every bit a city girl, saw herself as stuck here. Then add their argu-

The Double Cross ◆ 109

ment and the fact that maybe George was shopping around for a better fit to his dream, and you have a pretty strong motive."

"Except, how did he know Bernie would be here? I didn't even know Bernie would come until she put her suitcase in the car. Being friends with Susanne was certainly no guarantee that she would come with us."

Jesse shrugged. "No idea. He had roped two of Susanne's friends into helping. Maybe he just hoped Bernie would be the third."

I nodded, but that seemed like too much for George to hope. He tracks down a woman he hasn't seen in over forty years, a woman he may have dumped for his wife, because he wants to leave his wife for her? I guess crazier things have happened. But after all that, rather than contact his lost love directly he sets up an elaborate ruse to get her friends to visit his country inn, hoping that she will just happen to be among them? That was a little too rose-colored glasses, even for a guy with no quilting experience who thought he could run an inn designed especially for quilters.

But for the moment the explanation seemed to satisfy Jesse. As he tied his gym shoes, I got momentarily distracted by the length of his legs and the muscle in his arms and hint of neck that appeared between his shirt collar and his hair.

"This is how it all starts," I silently reminded myself. "A moment of distraction becomes a romance, then a broken heart, and then what? Maybe in George's case it turned into a murder."

Much as I was glad that Jesse and I were unofficially in this investigation together, I didn't feel ready to share the nagging feeling eating away at me. Especially when I might find myself getting lost in the way he smiled at me or, worse, being more a source of enjoyment than an equal partner in our hunt for George's killer.

I promised myself I'd share my suspicion with Jesse. But only when I'd gotten to the truth myself.

CHAPTER 20

"Yes, I talked to him," Bernie said as she poured herself some coffee.

"When?"

She sighed. "The day before we came. He tracked me down at the pharmacy and left a message, and I called him back on his cell."

"So it wasn't Eleanor who talked you into coming?"

"No. Though she was right. I had been carrying around a lot of old baggage and I needed to figure out if I could let it go. I needed to come here and I'm glad I did, or I was until yesterday."

"And that whole 'Bernie Keegan, small world' thing that George did when we arrived . . ."

"It was because he didn't want anyone to know we had talked."

"What did you talk about?"

"Nell, I know you're trying to help, but some things are private."

"This isn't one of those things, Bernie. A man is dead. And as far as I can tell, you were the last one to see him before the killer. What you and George said to each other is important, and I'm not the only one who's going to think so."

She seemed about to cry but held it together. I led her to the kitchen table, and we sat awhile before she spoke.

"It was strange. When I heard his message, I almost dropped the phone. I didn't think I would ever want to talk to him again, but I couldn't help myself. I suppose curiosity got the better of me."

"Just curiosity?"

"Maybe a little nostalgia. I got out a box I keep in the attic, filled with photos of me and George and Rita when we were all kids together. And other things. Movie stubs, a postcard he'd sent me when his family took a vacation in Florida. Dumb stuff. I hadn't looked at it in years, but for some reason, I never threw it out. It's just stuff you keep when something or someone is important to you, you know?"

I nodded. "It made you miss him."

"It made me wonder what happened. We had so many wonderful times. The three of us used to go to the drive-in every Wednesday. We'd sneak Rita in because she never had money for a ticket." Bernie laughed at the memory. "Then we'd go for pizza or get a bottle of wine out of my parents' house and drink it in the yard. I thought we'd always be together. Me and George. And Rita too. The three of us were so close, and then it was just him and Rita. He never even told me. I had to find out . . ." She took a deep breath. "He never told me why."

"So you asked him that in the call?"

"No. I chickened out. He seemed nervous. I felt stupid for even calling. So I just let him talk. He told me about the inn and about the quilt shop. He told me that he thought about me often. He asked if I ever thought about him."

"What did you say?"

"I reminded him that when we were kids, he told me he wanted to die in my arms. He was romantic like that," she sniffed. "So I said, 'George, you'll die in Rita's arms. That's your choice.' And he said he didn't think that would happen."

"So the marriage was in trouble?"

"He didn't say so in those words. He just asked me to come up.

Begged me, really. He sounded so sad, so defeated. And once I got here and saw the place, I thought I knew why. I thought he was at a place in his life where he was wondering if he should have made different choices. Not that I would have gone along with him, I swear to it Nell. I'm not that kind of person."

"I know." I put my hand on hers. She looked so tired. The take-no-prisoners Bernie I knew in Archers Rest seemed to be gone, and I missed her terribly.

"I just wanted to know why he'd chosen Rita over me. Maybe a part of me wanted to hear him say he'd made a mistake. Dumb as that sounds, I really thought that was why he wanted me here. That is, until you thought maybe he had lured me up here to take the money he thought I'd inherited from Johnny."

"Did you tell Chief McIntyre about the calls?"

"No," she stuttered. "I told him I came up with my friends and talked to George for the first time when he greeted us the other day. I didn't think it was any of his business. And I figured it would only hurt Rita, and, believe it or not, I really didn't want to do that."

I took a deep breath. I wanted to shout but instead I tried to be as quiet and calm as possible. I knew that Bernie was fragile and I didn't want to make things worse, but, considering how she had handled the matter, I wasn't sure they could possibly be worse.

"McIntyre will check phone records. He'll find out the two of you were talking and that you lied about it. And if you lied about that, he'll start to wonder what else you lied about."

Bernie put her head in her hands and cried for several minutes. "I didn't kill George," she said over and over.

"I know." I hesitated, but it had to be asked. "What *did* you do with George?"

CHAPTER 21

After a frustrating attempt to get answers from Bernie, who refused to admit that anything was going on with George—she said I "misunderstood" the scene in the kitchen, and was "mistaken" about George drugging me—I headed out, thinking it might be possible to search the crime scene for myself.

But something else caught my eye. Helen, Alice, and Alysse were huddled together outside the classroom.

"Rita called us this morning and told us about George," one of the twins said. "She said we should come anyway."

"We want to do what's right," the other twin added.

"I'm sure Rita will be glad you're here," I said

"Ladies." We turned around to see Pete coming from the direction of his house. "Rita called me about coming to class."

Helen leaned toward him. "I certainly don't want to criticize, but I'm not comfortable continuing under the circumstances."

He nodded. "She's grieving. She doesn't want to be alone. Why don't we stick close for today? Helen, remember how you brought a tuna casserole over to me after Siobhan left? It meant the world to me that you did that. I bet if you made one for Rita, she would be very grateful."

He walked toward the house, leaving Helen and the twins to discuss what meals they could cook and whether there was adequate space in the kitchen to make them at the inn, so they could be close if Rita needed them.

I walked into the woods, letting my feet take me in the general direction of the crime scene. When I got there, I was surprised to realize that I wasn't exactly sure which tree George had died under. I had expected to see crime-scene tape cordoning it off from hikers and helping with the collection of evidence, but aside from a few small bloodstains on the tree trunk, which took me nearly twenty minutes to find, there was nothing to distinguish it from the rest of the woods.

If McIntyre was right about the weapon being a hunting rifle, the killer could have been several hundred yards away. But even at a distance, it seemed unlikely that the killer could have mistaken George for a deer. George was tall, over six feet. Though my experience of deer is limited to occasionally spotting one in the woods near Archers Rest, and a traumatizing viewing of *Bambi* when I was six, I knew that deer average only about three or three and a half feet in height. Whoever shot that rifle knew a person was on the other end of it.

It seemed pointless, but I began walking the circumference of the tree, making a wider circle each time. If the police in Winston were careless enough to let the crime scene be open to anyone, they might have missed a shell casing or something that could lead to the real killer and away from Bernie. At least I hoped so. But there was nothing on the ground but leaves, twigs, and dirt.

Just as I was about to give up, I saw something shiny in the dirt. I crouched down to get a better look and realized it was exactly what I thought it was: a seam ripper, a little metal tool with a blade that looks like a hook on one side and usually has a plastic grip on the other. The grips come in different colors and thicknesses depending on the brand and price. In this case the plastic was thin and medium blue, about the cheapest seam ripper around. Since a seam ripper is used to undo sewing mistakes without ripping into the fabric, it's an essential tool for any quilter, the sort of standard sewing item we might carry in our pockets and forget about. Or that might fall out of them during a romantic rendezvous. Or a struggle.

I picked up the tool and examined it closely. The only thing that distinguished it from the millions of others just like it was a spot of shiny red paint, but that wasn't much help. If George was planning to paint the house, like he said when we arrived, maybe he had red paint. How it got on a seam ripper was something I couldn't even guess. Obviously the police had been through the scene and missed what could be an important piece of evidence—another reason why I wouldn't entrust Bernie's fate to McIntyre.

On my way back to the inn, I got a little lost. I'm no Girl Scout, and one tree looks pretty much the same as the other, so it wasn't difficult. At one point I thought I was taking a shortcut but I ended up in an unfamiliar area. There was another hiking path that I followed for a while. I could see a house in the distance, and I wondered if it was Pete's, but I wasn't sure if I had been walking toward his house or in another direction entirely. Whoever the house belonged to, I reasoned, they would probably know the way back to the Patchwork Bed-and-Breakfast, so I started toward it.

As I walked I saw an open basket near a tree. There was no one around, so I went over and checked it out. A half-empty bottle of wine, a few glasses, and the bones of what had probably been a chicken leg were lying on the ground nearby. Whatever food had been in the basket was pretty much eaten by animals. It might have been the one Bernie used, making it another piece of missed evidence. I wasn't going to help McIntyre with anything that might strengthen his case against Bernie, so I left it there and walked on.

Then I heard a shot. I gasped and whirled around.

"I could have blown your head off," Frank said to me. "What are you doing in the woods?"

"Me?" I yelled back. "Shouldn't you be with your wife?"

"I'm looking for found objects for my quilt, just in case we have class today."

"With a gun?"

He shrugged. "I keep it in my car. I'm no good sitting around being sad, and that is what the women will do today, so I thought I could bag a deer."

As Frank was talking, I stared at this gun. He wasn't exactly pointing it at me, but he wasn't pointing toward the ground either.

"I should get back," I said.

Frank looked at his gun. "This make you nervous?"

"I just should get back."

He grabbed my arm. "Don't go anywhere."

I pulled back anyway and was prepared to run, but Frank handed me the gun.

"Hold the butt under your right arm, just under your armpit, and rest your left hand under the rifle and your right hand on the trigger. Aim it toward that tree over there." He pointed toward a tree about thirty feet away.

I did as I was told.

"Look through the sight."

I did. "It seems closer," I said.

"Makes it easier to hit your mark," he said. "Now pull the trigger."

I did. And as I did, I fell back on the ground.

"Sorry. I should have mentioned that. You need to have solid footing if you're going to shoot a big gun like that."

I handed him back the gun and walked toward my target. Sure enough, there was a hole in the tree trunk just where I had aimed.

"It's important to have a healthy respect for a weapon," he said, "not a fear of it."

I suppose that was true enough, but it was the way he said it that made me shudder. I looked back at the tree trunk, and the hole I'd just put into it, and wondered if it had been that easy to shoot George.

Chapter 22

There was a lot of activity when I returned to the house. A pickup truck with paint cans and rollers in the back was parked outside. Several cars I didn't recognize were parked behind it.

As I was about to go into the house, Pete walked out to the truck and grabbed a paint can.

"This morning Rita said that she and George dreamed of fixing this place up and now she was afraid that dream would die," he told me. "So Helen and I and the other ladies, the twins, called a few neighbors and we're going to get started."

"That's incredibly nice of you."

"As much as we enjoyed Susanne's class, we figured it would be better to do something for Rita. She insisted we all stay, and all of you stay. She seemed to want activity at the inn, so we're giving her plenty of that."

"I should find my grandmother and tell her."

He smiled. "It was her idea."

I could hear voices inside the shop before I'd even opened the door. When I did, Eleanor, Susanne, and Bernie were standing at a large metal machine, turning a handle. It didn't seem nearly as exciting to me as it did to them.

"What's up?" I asked.

"Nell, look at this. It's a die cutter for quilts," Eleanor said.

She showed me a piece of foam-backed wood. It looked like a giant rubber stamp, except that instead of images embossed on the foam, there were squares cut into it. She put the die on a metal tray and covered it with a layer of fabric, then put a piece of plastic over that and rolled the whole thing through the fabric cutter. She lifted up the plastic to reveal a dozen perfectly cut two-inch squares.

"Cool, huh?" she said. "You can cut ten layers of fabric at a time."

I had to agree. "It would make pretty fast work for a quilt that needed lots of squares."

"Oh, there are lots of other shapes." Eleanor sounded like an old pro. "I'm just demonstrating this one for you. I don't know how I lived without it. I can cut a whole quilt in ten minutes."

I laughed. "This is one of those hip gadgets that Rita talked about, isn't it?"

"I'm not anti-gadget. I just think it takes a little more than the latest tools to be a quilter."

"So I get to play with it?" I asked. "And the long-arm machine?"

Eleanor looked back at the large quilting machine and table that took up nearly half the shop. "I suppose it's worth a try."

"Pete told me that you suggested helping Rita fix up the inn. So what are you guys doing hiding in here when there's painting to be done?"

"Hiding?" Susanne laughed. "We've dug into the fabrics Rita bought and made three quilt tops already." She held up a top made completely with squares in soothing blues and greens. "We're going to make a different quilt for every bed at the inn."

"And a few to hang on the wall," Bernie added. "Cheer up the place once it's painted."

Not to be left out, I uncovered the long-arm machine, and Bernie and I carefully read the instructions, then crossed our fingers and pinned one of the quilt tops to the bracers.

A long-arm sewing machine is like a traditional quilt frame in many ways, with the quilt layered with the batting and backing, pinned at the edges, and then rolled up to allow for about eighteen inches of quilting space at a time. The difference, of course, is that a sewing machine makes the work much faster than the hand sewing done on a traditional frame. Long arms have a large throat, which is the space between the needle and the arm of the machine, and instead of quilting from the side of the machine you quilt from the front. The selling point is that quilters no longer have to roll, or shove, large quilts through their machines and can therefore quilt them faster and even be more creative. As I looked at the machine, it looked easy, and the instructions made it seem easy, but I was a bit intimidated.

I grabbed the handles, which looked like bull horns coming out on either side, and with Bernie reading the instructions, I slowly moved the machine. First I zigzagged along the edges to secure them. Then I stitched in the ditch, a quilter's term for quilting along the sewing lines. It doesn't add much to the design of the quilt, but it does secure the three layers together and is the easiest way I've found to quilt in a hurry.

"This is pretty easy," I said, excited to have taken to it so quickly.

I got more adventurous as I quilted, making free-motion circles on the second quilt and simple flowers on the third. I was having fun.

Within a few hours, we had made five quilt tops and three fin-ished quilts. Though they were all simple in design, they were beau-tiful. I hoped it would bring Rita some comfort to see that we were all trying to help, but even if it didn't, it felt good to see Bernie happy and confident, at least for the moment.

I'd forgotten about what was going on outside the shop, but when I looked up, I realized that we had not been forgotten.

Rita was at the door. "What's going on in here?"

She looked fragile, but when the three of us rushed over to sug-gest she sit down, she waved us off.

"I'm perfectly capable of looking after myself," she said briskly. "I'm just trying to understand what everyone is doing."

"Would you rather we stopped?" I asked. "We don't want to dis-turb you."

"I didn't ask you to stop. I asked what you were doing."

I watched Bernie as she took a deep breath then seemed to make a decision. She walked over to her childhood friend and gave her a hug.

"I'm sorry about George."

Rita seemed more shocked by the display than anything. "It's very sad," Rita muttered. She moved past Bernie to Eleanor. "What are you doing?"

"We're making quilts for the inn. If you're going to cater to quil-ters, then you should have quilts on the beds and a few on the walls. Plus you'll need samples in the shop."

"You're making them for me?"

"Yes."

Rita blinked slowly. She looked around. "I was thinking about expanding the place to include other hobbies. Knitting, doll making, maybe ceramics. I could go into town and make some inquires about getting that started."

"Now?" I asked, a little too loudly. I pulled back a little on the tone of my voice. "Don't you want to concentrate on funeral arrangements?"

Rita looked at me, a slightly annoyed expression on her face, as though I didn't have my priorities straight. "It's really more important than ever that we get this place up and running."

Eleanor stepped forward. "I'm sure it's what George would have wanted . . . ," she started.

"It's what I want," Rita interrupted her. "I appreciate the work you're doing. Can you make ten quilts? I think I'll need ten."

And with that she walked out of the shop.

"I am sorry about her husband. I really am," Susanne said. "But that woman is just unpleasant."

"She certainly has an interesting way of mourning," my grandmother agreed.

I would have commented, but something caught my eye near the back of the shop. There was an open box of seam rippers dumped on a cutting table a few feet from the front door. There must have been a hundred of them. And every one was exactly the same: a little metal hook with a medium blue plastic handle.

I looked for Bernie, back at the long-arm machine, quietly working on the next quilt. I didn't want to share with her what I had found in the woods, because talk of her relationship with George seemed to make her defensive. But I felt better. These seam rippers meant that anyone with access to the quilt shop, and that could pretty much mean anyone, since Rita didn't seem to lock the door, could have dropped that tool near the crime scene, either by accident or on purpose.

Rita's visit and the seam rippers had brought the murder back to the forefront. Even though we were now, I suppose, directed to make ten quilts, I left the work to the others and walked out of the shop, hoping to find out who else might have left a seam ripper in the woods.

CHAPTER 23

As I walked out into the daylight, I saw McIntyre and Jesse talk-ing with Fred. The three men seemed engaged in a pretty se-rious conversation, and when I came closer, I got a stern look from Jesse. It was clear that I was not welcome to join them. I walked away. If we were going to be on the same side in this investigation, I had to trust that Jesse would share the information with me as soon as he could. Instead I walked into the classroom to see if there was a chance I could find any clues the students had left behind.

On a back table were flowers and cards that had been brought by members of the community to offer their condolences to Rita. The classroom was empty, and most of the students seemed to have cleaned up after themselves at the end of yesterday's class. Only some fabrics, a packet of needles, and a handful of seam rippers had been left out on the tables, and it was hard to tell who their owners were.

I found myself drifting toward the front of the classroom, where the group's first quilts were displayed. Each student had made some-thing unique, and it was easy to see who had made which quilt. Helen's was an orderly and nearly literal translation of a tree, with a trunk of brown corduroy and pieces of green velvet cut into dozens of tiny leaves. It was beautiful but restrained and careful. If I were judging Helen by her quilt, I'd say she didn't like to take any chances. Frank's quilt, on the other hand, was a mess. I doubt it had been his intention to make it abstract, but it had sort of turned out that way. It was a whirl of fabrics and trim and small metal buttons. He'd used the computer to print the words MY WORLD and fused them to the top. There was none of the charm he had tried to display on the first day. This quilt was all force. It must be hard for Helen to have her orderly world connected to his chaos.

I walked closer to the next quilt to see the details. It had to be Pete's, I decided. He'd used the sky fabrics we'd picked out together and added so many trees that they nearly blocked out the light. There was a dark circle in the corner, made of deep brown silk with a spray of brightly colored ribbons coming from it.

"You like it?"

I turned to see Pete at the entrance of the classroom.

"I do," I said. "Are these flowers?"

He blushed a little. "It's supposed to mean that even in the darkest places good things can grow."

"Well, it does," I said. "It's nice."

"It's not as cool as her quilt." He nodded toward one of the twins.

I looked at the quilt next to Pete's and saw a quilt that was almost black, with small blue triangles around the edges. It was as strange and inexplicable as the woman herself. But as I got closer, my nose almost touching the quilt, I realized that it was an extreme close-up of a crow, almost blocking out the sky behind it. The word PROM-ISES written over and over and over, in tiny lettering, covered each wing completely. In tiny letters in the corner was the maker's name: Alysse. I stepped back.

"That's really interesting. I wonder what it means."

"I was thinking broken engagement," Pete offered.

"Probably. This must be Alice's quilt," I said about the one next to it.

It was also a close-up image, this time of a leaf, with small green beads decorating the edges. A considerably lighter and happier image.

I turned away from the quilts. "How's the remodeling going?"

Pete smiled. "We've got the living room painted and we're working on the dining room. Helen and the twins have made lunch, if you're hungry. I told your grandmother and the others."

"And you were looking for me?"

"You always seem to be off on your own somewhere."

"Do I?" I'd thought I spent most of my time with the group, but maybe he was right. I did tend to wander off.

"I hear you like looking into things," he said. "Like what happened to George."

"I want to see justice, same as everybody else."

He nodded. "I just think a nice lady like you would rather help with the quilting than get involved in something as messy as someone's murder. Especially with your friend Jesse and Chief McIntyre around."

"I like to help." I pointed to a paint stain on his shirt. "Just like you."

I didn't want to get into a discussion about some of Pete's rather old-fashioned ideas about what women and men should do with their time, not unless it had something to do with the murder.

With me in the lead, Pete and I passed Jesse and the others, who were still in conversation. We walked into the inn, and it was obvious that in just a few hours a lot of work had been done. The textured wallpaper in the entryway had been primed; the furniture in the living room was still covered, but the walls had gone from a drab and dirty white to a warm taupe; and as I entered the dining room,

I saw that a coat of a light moss green had already been applied to three of the walls. Even though the room was under construction, a few people from town, Alice and Alysse, Bernie, Susanne, and my grandmother were eating and a buffet-style lunch had been set up along the unpainted wall. I grabbed a plate of fried chicken and potato salad, and sat across from the twins.

"I was just in the classroom," I said. "I really like your quilts. The basic idea is the same—you know, the extreme close-up of an object—but you've taken them in such different directions."

"Alysse's is very dark," Alice said. "She thinks she's profound. I think it's unhealthy. Especially now."

It was an unexpected and welcome opening. "With George dead, you mean."

"Such a terrible shame," Alysse said. "A good man cut down in his prime. A dear person. I'll miss him."

"You were friends? I didn't know that."

Alysse's face whitened. "Not friends. But since we started the class, we saw him around."

"So you didn't know him?"

"No," her sister said quickly.

"So how did you find out about the class? The others are all friends of the Olnhausens."

"We met Rita at a church function. She mentioned the class and so we came."

"Which church?"

"The one in town," Alysse said. "I'm sorry, but I promised Helen I would help with dessert. We made chocolate cake."

"Of course."

Both sisters got up from the table and left me sitting alone. I could see Susanne trying to catch my eye so I motioned to her, and she came to sit with me.

"How's it going?" I whispered to her. "Any admissions of guilt during lunch?"

Susanne grimaced. "I think Helen wants to talk. She's been hiding in the kitchen this whole time, but I don't think I'm good at interrogating, especially when I'm trying not to seem like I'm interrogating. You go and see what you can find out."

Once I saw the twins return, with chocolate cake and plates, I headed toward the kitchen where Helen was washing dishes.

"Can I help?"

"I'm fine."

"Are you sure?" I pressed. "I guess I need a distraction from everything that's going on. It must be especially hard for you."

"Why especially?" She took a step back.

"You're friends with the Olnhausens. You and Frank."

"Oh, yes," she said. "We knew them as well as anyone in town I suppose."

I leaned in and quietly said, "Rita seems so brave. I've hardly seen her cry, but, then, I don't really know her. She must be more expressive with her grief around you."

Helen's eyes darted in the direction of door, then back to me. "She hasn't said anything to me. She hasn't even thanked me for the Bundt cake I brought this morning. Not that I expect thanks."

I smiled. This was going to be easier than I thought. "Rita seems, well, I don't know how to say it but she's . . ." I hesitated.

"A bit hard?" Just as I expected, Helen finished my sentence. Now it was her turn to lean in and whisper. "She had George wrapped around her little finger, and I have no idea why. He did all the work for this place. He roped everyone into taking this class." She stopped. "Not that it hasn't turned out to be quite fun."

"Of course. But you had no way of knowing that when George asked you—"

"Asked!" Her voice rose an octave, then quickly lowered. "He insisted. Made it seem life-or-death. But that was George about everything concerning Rita. If she wanted something, he would move heaven and earth to get it for her."

"I guess that's true love."

"I guess. Seems to me that she could have done more for him. Marriage is a two-way street, but, of course, everyone has to find their own balance. If it worked for them, then I say fine. I just worried that he would end up with a heart attack, that's all." She shook her head. "Poor man."

"I wish I'd known George as well as you," I offered. "You seem like a good judge of character and you obviously felt a great deal of affection for him."

Her eyes filled with tears. "You'll have to excuse me," she said. Then she turned her back to me and walked slowly out of the room.

CHAPTER 24

I finished the dishes and left the kitchen to look for Jesse, in the hopes of finding out about his conversation with Frank and telling him about mine with Helen. I didn't find him. Instead I ran into Rita, who looked tired and pale. She was sitting alone in the half-finished living room, staring into space, car keys in her hand.

"Are you okay? Can I get you anything?" I asked.

She shook her head.

"They've painted the living room," she said quietly.

"It's a nice color." I stood for a moment, unsure of what to say.

"I need a ride into town." She handed me the keys to her car without waiting for a reply. She seemed to be struggling to get up, so I bent over to try to help her, but she waved her hand at me. "I'm not an invalid," she snapped. "I'm a widow. I can get off the couch by myself."

"If you would rather drive yourself," I found myself snapping back.

Rita immediately weakened. She seemed ready to cry, and she took a slow breath to calm herself. "I'm not up to it. Maybe I could drive there, but not back. George used to . . ."

I felt like a jerk. "It's fine. Of course I'll take you wherever you need to go."

✄

We walked to her car, a late-model BMW, and headed toward town without talking.

As much as I preferred the silence, eventually I had to speak up. "I don't know where I'm going."

Whatever weakness she had expressed back at the inn was gone. "Just drop me off at the police station," she said dismissively.

"But I think McIntyre is at the inn. I saw him earlier, talking to Frank."

"I don't want to talk to McIntyre."

"Then why do you want to go to the police station?"

"I can't imagine why that would matter to you."

"Man, you are an unpleasant person," I wanted to say. But instead I said, "Helen seemed pretty upset about George."

Rita shrugged. "People liked him. They liked him more than me."

"I'm sure that's not the case. George just seems to have gotten out more."

Rita stared at me. "Have you been asking around?"

I could feel my cheeks turning a little red but I ignored it. "When someone dies, people like to talk about him."

She turned away from me and slouched in her chair. "I suppose. Not that any of them knew him, especially that Helen woman."

"I don't know her very well but I think she's quite nice."

"As you say, you don't know her very well."

Okay. New subject. "Which church do you go to?"

"I don't attend church. I'm not religious."

"But George's burial . . ."

"George won't be buried. He'll be cremated." She glared at me. "This is hardly a topic I wish to discuss at the moment."

As she spoke we pulled up in front of the police station.

"Would you like me to wait for you?"

"No." The answer was firm. "You can come back for me in an hour. Just drop me off and go to the bakery for some coffee. Everyone goes there. Then come back in an hour to pick me up."

In Rita's world, it seemed, I wasn't someone helping her. I was the help. I changed the subject.

"I know I've said this before, but I'm so sorry about George. He seemed like a man without an enemy in the world."

"That is clearly not the case."

"So you have some ideas about who might have done it?"

"I do not. All I know is that George is dead. Shot through the heart." She took a deep breath and said the words again. "Shot through the heart. Nothing changes that."

"But you want to find his killer?"

"I want peace. That's why we came here. To finally have peace in our lives. Maybe George is at peace. I hope so. I envy him in a way." She pointed out the window. "Drop me here. Come back in an hour."

She got out of the car and walked toward the police station. I waited for her to enter, and after a moment's hesitation, she did. As I started to pull away, I glanced in my rearview mirror and saw her walk out and head in the opposite direction. As quickly as I could, I drove around the block, but Rita was gone. If she ducked into a building, it could have been any one of several small shops, restaurants, or offices. I drove slowly down the street. I considered for a moment going door-to-door to look for her but I didn't want Rita to know that I was investigating. Instead I took her suggestion and drove the one block to the bakery.

When I parked the car, I did my best to go through it, looking for evidence. I wasn't sure what cops did when they searched vehicles, but

I looked under the seats, in the trunk, and in every compartment I could find, including the cup holders. I didn't find any guns or blood. There was nothing in the glove compartment except a car manual, a flashlight, and a gas receipt for a station in Saratoga Springs.

But the trip wasn't a waste, I told myself. Even though I didn't know which building Rita had entered, I knew something for sure. Her husband had been dead for less than twenty-four hours and she was using the cover of a grieving widow to hide something.

And I was going to figure out what it was.

CHAPTER 24

"Why did she ask you to drive her?"

"I don't know," I said.

I had gone back to the pay phone in front of the bakery to call Carrie and find out what she'd learned about the Olnhausens. Instead she kept asking me questions about the murder.

"If she was really trying to hide something, she would have driven herself," Carrie said. "Maybe she wanted you to see her."

"Then why go to all the trouble of walking into the police station? Why not just ask me to drop her off in front of whatever building she went into?"

I could hear Carrie sigh. "No idea," she said. "Boy, I wish I were up there. Natalie is going crazy without her mom's help, and I'm swamped at the shop. I had no idea one town could drink so much coffee. Plus I promised my daughter I'd make her a new quilt, and I'll never have time."

"We'll be back in a few days. We'll all help. But in the meantime . . ."

"I'm just saying that you guys are having all the fun."

"Dead guy, Carrie, remember? Plus I was drugged."

"Does the police chief know about that?"

"No," I said. "If I tell him that George drugged me, it just gives me a motive to kill him. And we want him to focus where he should, on Rita."

"Right. But I don't think Rita had a motive. At least not a financial one. I found out that they have assets of over two million dollars and low life-insurance policies, only about twenty thousand dollars each—nothing that would make Rita kill him over money. In fact, they seem like really good people."

"You can tell that from a few financial records?"

"I also found that they've made substantial donations to several charities, most of them over a hundred thousand dollars."

"What charities? Could you find out?"

"Already know. An organization that sponsors free art classes, a heart-disease research center, a group that helps families displaced by foreclosure, and a support organization for Alzheimer's patients and families," she said. "See what I mean? Rita's a good person."

"I'm not sure you would feel that way if you met her," I said. "Is that all you have?"

"No. You would be very proud of Natalie. She tracked down a name and address you're going to want. Their daughter. She lives in Saratoga Springs."

After she gave me the information on Rita's daughter, Carrie filled me in on some of the gossip in Archers Rest. Apparently Jesse had left town so fast that he'd only called his deputies when he was already on the road, and his mother had to cancel a dentist appointment to pick up Jesse's daughter from school.

"He must be crazy about you," she said.

"I guess." It had just started to occur to me that maybe Jesse overreacted in rushing up to Winston, and Jesse wasn't really the type to overreact. When he arrived in town, nothing had happened yet, at least nothing he knew about. I guess I'd been so glad he'd come that I didn't want to ask why.

"Have you asked him about the redhead?"

"No," I told her. "I'm not going to. I have to focus on me, not on him, and on getting Bernie out of this mess. I don't care about any redheads."

As I hung up, I wondered if that was true.

Inside Maria's Bakery I bought a coffee and an apple-cider dough-nut. Maria was a large woman, the sort who clearly enjoys her own baking and life in general. She already knew about the quilt classes, the murder, and the sudden arrival of a good-looking police officer from Archers Rest. She knew so much that I was hoping she'd be able to tell me the name of the killer, but no luck.

"You know the Olnhausens?" I asked her, as I sipped the last of my coffee.

"Know them? I bake organic bread and scones for the B-and-B every week. Lovely people," she said. "So in love."

"Why do you say that?"

"Just the way they looked at each other. I could tell."

Could you? I thought. "Did they come into the bakery together?"

She shook her head. "I drop the bread off at the inn. George came in on his own a few times, but mostly I've seen them at the inn. I go by there on my way home and visit for a few minutes."

"I haven't seen you since we've been there," I said. I was wonder-ing why Rita hadn't been sharing the baked goods with us.

"George came by and picked up his order the day before yester-day. And he got two oatmeal cookies. Said they were Rita's favorites."

Her voice choked with emotion. "She must be beside herself without him."

I nodded. "She must be." I couldn't figure out who the Rita and George were that she was talking about, because they bore no resemblance to the people I knew. "No rumors about other people?" I asked.

"You mean that woman they knew in high school? There's nothing there."

"You know about Bernie?"

"Didn't know her name. I just knew that they went to high school with her, and she came back up with you folks. Nice chance for a reunion. Turned sad, of course, but I suppose it was good that the woman, Bernie, had a chance to see George before he passed."

"Do you get your information from McIntyre?" I had to ask. "I know the chief is in here all the time."

She laughed. "Jimmy? He wouldn't share a cookie, let alone a piece of juicy gossip. I just hear things."

"If you hear anything else, let me know," I said.

She nodded. "Back at ya." She grabbed a pastry box and started filling it with cookies. "Bring this to your friends at the inn."

She seemed friendly enough and definitely plugged into the goings-on in town, but she couldn't be right about Rita and George. I'd hadn't seen a hint of love pass between them. And since he'd died, Rita certainly hadn't been acting like a woman who had lost her true love.

I checked my watch. I had just enough time to get into position and maybe find out something Maria didn't know.

✄

I parked the car in front of the police station and walked down the block. Aside from two restaurants, neither of which opened until dinner, a nail salon, a dry cleaner, a boarded-up children's store, and a tiny storefront labeled PSYCHIC with a large hand-painted sign, there wasn't much to Main Street. With one exception. In the middle of the block was a three-story building that seemed to contain a variety of offices— doctors, dentists, lawyers, accountants, a private investigator, and several that were just names without a description. Rita had to be in there somewhere, since the nail salon had only one customer and the psychic didn't appear to be in. But knowing what building Rita was in didn't narrow the possibilities much. She could be checking with her lawyer, getting her teeth cleaned, or meeting with any one of the half-dozen people whose nameplates didn't specify their profession.

It had almost been an hour since I dropped Rita off, so I crossed the street and ducked into the dry cleaner. The large picture window had just enough signage to cover me but enough clear space so I got a good view of the building.

"Can I help you?"

I turned and saw a slight man in a gray vest, standing behind the counter.

"Oh, yes. I'm picking up the dry cleaning for the Olnhausens at the Patchwork Bed-and-Breakfast." I glanced back at the window, but no Rita.

"You have the ticket?"

"No. I'm just helping the family," I improvised.

"I heard about George. Sad thing. Didn't know him well, but he could bring his dry cleaning anywhere and he brought it here, so I liked him."

"Are there many dry cleaners in town?"

"Just mine. Why?"

I shook my head. "I think it's great that he supported local businesses."

"I'll see what they have here," he said, and disappeared into the back room.

I looked out the window again and saw Rita walk out of the office building, just as I had expected. But what I hadn't expected was that she wouldn't be alone. Next to her was a man about her age, wearing a dress shirt and tie and standing too close to be an acquaintance. She kept leaning into him, not quite touching but close. At one point she started to shake her head, and he took her hand, then reached his arm around her.

"I have three shirts and a skirt." The dry cleaner was back. "No chemicals, just like they want it."

"Great," I turned to him. "Do you know that man standing with Rita?"

"Who is Rita?"

"George's wife. You've never met her?"

"Only George."

The dry cleaner walked over to me, but just as he was getting to the window the man ducked back into the building. The dry cleaner stared out the window at Rita as she walked in the direction of the police station. "She's a pretty woman. Too thin for my taste, but pretty. A lot of the city ladies are too thin. Are you from the city?"

I involuntarily sucked in my stomach. Sad. "No. Archers Rest. It's south of here, on the Hudson."

He nodded. "That'll be $18.50."

I paid for the dry cleaning and headed back toward the car. Rita was standing at the curb, checking her watch and seeming very put out by having to wait. If I hadn't known she had been at the car for less than twenty seconds, I'd have almost felt guilty.

"I picked up some things you had left at the cleaners," I said cheerfully. There was no point in hiding it and no way to explain it.

"Why would you do that?"

I was afraid she would ask that. "I just wanted to help," I said.

She stared at me. "You are odd. You're all odd," she said as she got in the passenger seat.

CHAPTER 25

"Odd?"

I told Eleanor about my trip into town as soon as I returned Rita to the inn. We retreated to our little room, and as Barney napped, I told Eleanor everything—the call to Carrie, Rita's mysterious trip to the office building, the man Rita was talking to, and the fact that I was out $18.50 so I could be called odd instead of thanked.

"What kind of a woman would call you odd?"

"In all fairness I did pick up her dry cleaning without her asking," I said. "That is kind of odd."

"It was sweet of you."

"I didn't pick it up to be sweet. I picked it up because I was spying on her and I had no choice."

"She doesn't know that. If she had an ounce of humanity in her, she would think it was a kind gesture from a concerned acquaintance." Eleanor scrunched up her face in disgust.

"Well, she thinks we're all odd."

"Pot calling the kettle, I'd say." Eleanor tapped her fingers on her blue jeans as if she were considering whether to jump up and give Rita a piece of her mind.

"But at least I got some good information out of it," I said, to distract her from whatever plan she was forming. "She's hiding something. Maybe an affair."

"They were well suited to each other, George and Rita," my usually charitable grandmother said. "I wonder what their daughter is like."

"We're about to find out. I'm going right now," I said.

"Do you think Rita has even bothered to tell her that George is dead?"

"If she had, wouldn't the daughter have come? I don't care how estranged they are, she would have come home to be with her mother at a time like this. She only lives about an hour away."

"I walked around the house today, looking for clues. I noticed there were no personal items anywhere so . . ." Eleanor paused. "I peeked into Rita's room. The sitting room actually. The door to what I assume was a bedroom was locked."

"What if she had found you?"

"She was with you."

I laughed. "You're sneakier than I give you credit for. Did you find anything?"

"It's what I didn't find that's interesting. There was a framed photo of Rita and George when they were younger, with a little girl of about five. That's it. Then just photos of George and Rita in Paris, in Greece, in China."

"But no daughter in those photos."

"I guess they left her at home."

I tapped my fingers on the bed, thinking, until I realized I had unintentionally imitated my grandmother. "You said the bedroom door was locked."

She nodded. "As you know, their room is the on the third floor. They seem to have the whole floor to themselves. There's an empty room on the left, and on the right there is a door. It was slightly open so I walked in. That was the sitting room. There was another door at the back of the room. That one that was locked."

"Why lock the bedroom but not the door to the suite?"

"No idea. Yet." Eleanor smiled. "This is kind of fun, isn't it."

I laughed and hugged her. "I'm glad you finally see that I'm right to interfere in police investigations."

"I didn't say that," she said. "I just said that sometimes doing the wrong thing for the right reason is a little fun."

"If you were a man, I'd marry you."

"I think you're already spoken for," she said. "Any man who drives all the way up here to see you must feel something."

"Maybe he just felt the need to get away."

"Nell Fitzgerald, for someone so good at solving mysteries it's amazing you can't solve a puzzle when the answer is so apparent."

She was the second person in two hours to suggest that Jesse's sudden appearance in Winston was a declaration of love. But I wasn't convinced. It wasn't that Jesse didn't care about me. Even I could figure that out. It was just this nagging feeling that he had come for some other reason, that he was keeping something from me.

A few short months ago, I was the kind of woman who would have devoted all my time to discussing, analyzing, and debating each of Jesse's actions in the hope that it would bring me the fairy-tale ending I was supposed to want. But I had quilts to make, a murder to solve, and a friend to help. Realizing I wasn't waiting for Prince Charming to complete me was the first time anything had made sense all day.

"I'm going to Saratoga Springs to find the daughter."

"You can't go this evening. It's a long drive, and Jesse is looking for you. He said he wants to discuss something important." She smiled. "I wonder what that could be."

"I think he wants to tell me about his conversation with McIntyre and Frank."

"That's progress, isn't it? Keeping you in the loop on an investigation."

"I guess so, except it isn't his investigation."

She smiled. "Maybe he likes doing the wrong thing for the right reason too."

At that Barney woke from his nap and walked to the bedroom door, whining the whole way.

CHAPTER 26

I passed the activity in the dining room, walked Barney out the inn's front door, and waited while he found the perfect spot. For a dog that had appeared to be in such a hurry to relieve himself, he seemed pretty picky about where he would do the deed. The afternoon had turned cool, and I wasn't sure I felt like standing outside while I waited for him, so I drifted back toward the house. But before I could walk in, Frank stormed out. I was glad to see, especially considering his mood, that this time he wasn't armed.

"I have had it with that woman," he shouted to no one in particular.

"Everything okay?"

He spun around and glared at me, then took a deep breath. In seconds his face changed from anger to smiling.

"I didn't expect to see you," he said. "I thought you were helping your grandmother or that boyfriend of yours."

"I was in town with Rita."

He stared at me for a moment. "Rita? What did you ladies do, have lunch or something?"

"Or something."

"Did you two have a nice talk?"

"Does anyone have a nice talk with Rita?" I wondered. "I just gave her a ride into town," I said. "You said you've had it with that woman. Were you talking about Helen?"

He blinked slowly. I could feel him watching me, and it felt uncomfortable. "I may have overreacted," he said. "I'm an emotional guy."

"I can see that," I said. "What made you so emotional?"

"I'd have thought that would appeal to a woman like you." Frank moved closer.

"How so?" I turned and saw Barney sniffing at some flowers. I loved that Barney was a gentle soul, but at the moment I wished he were an attack dog.

"I thought you modern women liked a man who could talk about his feelings."

"You were shouting," I pointed out.

He took a step away from me. "I just don't like the way she's getting all upset about George."

"I thought he was a friend of yours."

"Rita is his widow, not Helen. That's my whole point."

"Rita doesn't seem too upset."

I thought I'd throw that in to see Frank's reaction, but I wasn't expecting what I got.

"That woman is wonderful." Frank seemed on the verge of tears. "A true beauty and a fine spirit. You shouldn't disparage her."

"I wasn't," I said. Well, I was but I wasn't about to admit it to Frank. "You obviously like Rita very much."

He moved a few steps toward me, and as he did, I saw coins drop from his trousers.

"Looks like have a hole in your pocket," I said.

He bent down, frustrated. "That's what Helen should be doing. Mending my clothes, not crying over George. I think there's a hole in nearly every one of my trousers, but do you think she cares?"

"You could sew them yourself."

He stared at me, and I didn't like how intimidated I felt by it. "You like to butt into people's business. That's what I hear about you. You like to help," he said the word as sarcastically as possible, "but you are just interfering. That can get a person in trouble, especially when you go around saying bad things about good people like Rita . . . and George."

He turned his back on me and walked toward the inn, banging the door as he walked in.

"He sure told you."

I turned and saw Jesse walking from the woods.

"Apparently Rita has a fan," I said. "So far that makes one."

"A pretty unstable one," Jesse said. "I'd stay clear of him."

I looked toward my—whatever he was—my friend, I guess. He looked concerned. Barney looked up from his flowers and saw Jesse, then ran toward him, tail wagging. Wanting to lighten the moment, I called out, "Get him, Barney. Knock him down!" Much to my surprise, Barney did just as he was told. Coincidence, I was sure, but just to check out my theory I pulled Barney back a few feet from Jesse.

"Stand there," I told Jesse.

"What are we doing?"

"I think Barney heard me."

"Nell, Barney is always knocking me over when he sees me. He likes me."

"So you have one fan, as well," I said. "And you can have two if you stand there."

I knelt down beside an excited Barney. I knew he didn't know what we were doing, but he did know it was some sort of game, and he liked games. I pointed to Jesse, who tapped his foot impatiently.

"I thought we would have dinner together," Jesse called out.

"Be quiet."

I grabbed Barney's face and loudly said, "Get Jesse." Then I pointed to Jesse.

Barney took off, knocking Jesse off his feet in seconds.

"That was amazing," I said. "Let's do that again."

He pulled the dog off him and scrambled to his feet, laughing. "Why?"

"It's funny," was the best reason I could come up with. "Besides, Barney likes it."

I called the dog back to my side, and after he wandered toward a bush, sniffed at some grass, and peed, he walked over to me.

"One more time," I told him. "Go get Jesse."

This time Barney stared at me.

"Jesse," I pointed. "Go get him."

Barney went running over, jumping at Jesse, who managed this time to stay on his feet. Then Barney sat down, revealing his tummy in the unmistakable dog language that roughly translates to "pet me," which Jesse did for a few minutes before he looked up at me.

"Are we done here?" Jesse asked. "I want to go to dinner."

"I guess. I'm a bit hungry too, but we could probably get a snack. Dinner won't be for at least a couple of hours. Susanne said she would cook, and I don't think she's even started yet."

"I'd like to take you out."

"Really?" I smiled. "You want to be alone with me?"

"I have to get cleaned up first."

It seemed like this might be the romantic gesture Eleanor and Carrie thought he'd come to Winston for, but nothing about his actions suggested that Jesse had romance on his mind. I'd been right, I decided. He wanted to go over his conversation with McIntyre and Frank. "We do have a lot to talk about," I said.

Jesse blushed and his tone turned serious. He seemed embarrassed to look at me. "Yeah, we do."

Without another glance my way, he walked toward the house, leaving Barney and me standing there. Whatever he wanted to talk about, it wasn't George's death. Suddenly I wasn't that hungry.

CHAPTER 27

The waiter poured my glass of wine while Jesse stared at me from across the table. He had one of those enigmatic, Mona Lisa smiles, so I wasn't sure whether he was going to propose or arrest me.

"So why are we here?" I eventually asked.

He had taken me to the local Italian restaurant, next to the office building Rita visited earlier. The place oozed romance, with dimmed lights, white tablecloths, roses everywhere, and Dean Martin playing softly in the background.

"I thought it would be nice to get away from the others and have a quiet dinner."

I stared at him.

He laughed. "Seriously. I just wanted to have dinner alone with you."

"So much that you drove up and abandoned your only child?" I said teasingly. Jesse was the best father I'd ever seen, but I did wonder how he managed without his daughter.

"I talk to Allie three times a day, and all she wants to know is what toy I'll bring back," he said a little defensively. "I don't think she even misses me. And why would she? She has my mother wrapped around her little finger."

"I'm just guessing here, but even though you're really into rules and doing things the right way, I'll bet she likes having you around." I smiled, and he nodded and smiled back. "And I know you wouldn't leave her unless you had a really good reason, so what is it?"

He buried his face in the menu and spoke, almost without stopping, about his agonizing decision between the chicken marsala and shrimp with angel-hair pasta. Even though we'd known each other only a few months, I'd already learned that when Jesse talked nonstop he was nervous. I suppose by not giving me a chance to interrupt, he was hoping to keep me from saying something that might make his nerves worse.

"What are you getting?" After five minutes he finally looked up from the menu.

"What are you doing in Winston?"

"Nell, I'm starving and everything looks so good that I can't decide. What are you getting?"

"Pasta primavera. What are you doing in Winston?"

"I thought you might need my help."

"You thought I couldn't take care of myself?"

"I thought . . ." He paused and considered his words. "I knew you could take care of yourself. I just wanted to see you." He paused again. "And when I got here, you had been drugged, so maybe my being here is a good thing."

I leaned back in my chair and crossed my arms, trying to look tough, but I couldn't help smiling. "You left Archers Rest so fast that you didn't even tell your deputies until you were on the road."

"How do you know that?"

"I have people everywhere."

His face turned red and I knew I had him. Unfortunately for me, at just that moment the waiter came over to take our orders. It was the break Jesse had been looking for. Rather than press the issue, I uncharacteristically let him off the hook. I didn't want to be cruel, and even though I was curious, I wasn't sure I wanted to hear what he had to tell me, so instead, as we ate, I told him about my afternoon with the students and later with Rita, as well as my encounter in the woods, and he told me about the conversation he and McIntyre had with Frank.

"He didn't like the guy," Jesse said. "He said George was not to be trusted."

"In what way?"

"He told McIntyre they went hunting together a couple of times, he and George and that Pete guy from the quilt class, and the three of them got separated. They didn't find George again for a couple of hours."

"Where did he go?"

"Apparently George said he got a call from Rita and had to go back to the house."

"I'm stuffed," I said, as I put my fork down for the last time. The food had been so good that I'd eaten more than I needed to. "That's plausible, what George said, isn't it?"

"According to Frank a man who abandons a hunt is not to be trusted. But he made sure to add that George wasn't much of a hunter anyway."

"Based on how he dressed, I don't think he was a natural outdoorsman."

"Maybe not, but Frank is something. He also made it clear that he didn't think too much of Pete. He didn't give a reason, just made it clear that he didn't like the guy.

"I noticed that," I said. "I don't think Pete likes him much either. Kind of makes you wonder why they went hunting together."

"I have a feeling Frank likes being alpha male. Maybe he was trying to prove he's a better man than Pete or George." Jesse gestured toward the waiter. "I want coffee and, knowing you, you probably do too."

"And we can split a tiramisu?"

"I thought you were stuffed."

"I thought you knew me." I laughed.

As we pulled up in front of the inn, Jesse took my hand and stared at it. I waited but he didn't seem in any hurry to say anything, and I wasn't going to fill the space with empty chatter. Though the wait was killing me, it was clear he wanted to say something, and I was determined this time to let him say it.

When he looked at me, he seemed almost scared. "You know what you said earlier about having people everywhere?"

"I meant Carrie and Natalie. They ran into one of your deputies."

"I know who you meant." He took a deep breath. "I saw Carrie earlier in the week, when I was having dinner."

Oh. That was what this was about. The redhead. If he was going to tell me he'd found a new love, I wasn't sure this was a conversation I wanted to have.

"Carrie mentioned it," I told him. "It's no big deal."

He cocked his head to the side the way confused puppies do. "Why isn't it a big deal?"

"I can't speak for you, Jesse. I just mean that if you want to date someone else, obviously you're free to do that. You did tell me that I wasn't the right person for you."

"I never said that."

"You once said I wasn't like your wife. She was more sensible, more restrained, more predictable. More suited to you."

"I know. But you're more . . ." He seemed to be struggling. "You."

"And if you like that, why go out with other women?" I asked.

"My mother fixed me up with a woman she knows from her volunteer work at the church."

I relaxed a little. Blind dates arranged by your mother rarely turn into love matches. At least I assumed they didn't. My mother never set me up on blind dates. She and my father had left for France when I graduated from college, and had been slowly making their way around the world ever since.

"When I saw Carrie, I knew she would tell you and I knew you would read something into it, and so I called to explain, and then you told me what was going on with this place and . . ."

"You got on your white horse and rode up here to save the day?" I leaned in and kissed him on the cheek. "I appreciate that and I'm really glad you're here, even though I can take of myself."

"I knew that." He kissed me on the lips. "I get that, with you and Eleanor and the rest of them. You have things under control. I just want to be available if I can be of assistance."

I kissed him back, and our faces stayed close, just in case the urge to kiss overtook us again. "It's nice to have you around."

"Nell, if I'm uncomfortable with you being so . . ." He searched for a word.

"Exciting?"

"Terrifyingly nosy," he corrected me. "Look, I've only been in love with two women and I lost one. I don't want to lose you, and when you go off on one of your adventures . . ."

"I'm just trying help a friend," I said when I realized he'd buried the lead. "Wait, you're in love with me?"

Even in the darkness of the car, I could see him turn red. "I really like you, Nell."

There it was. He had taken a step forward and then was willing to chew his own leg off to get out of the trap he'd set for himself.

"I like you too," I said.

He stopped for a moment before taking a deep breath. "I don't want to lose you and I get scared when you stick your nose into things."

"Help a friend," I corrected him.

He nodded. "I guess I realized that if I didn't let you be yourself, I would lose you anyway."

"I like that you're protective," I admitted.

"And I like that you're a little unpredictable."

"It doesn't freak you out?"

He brushed his hand on my cheek and let it rest against the back of my neck. "It freaks me out. But this is who you are, and I want to be with you. And if it's not going to scare you too much for me to say this, it might be good for Allie to have a woman as fearless as you in her life."

"Doesn't scare me at all. Nothing scares me," I said grandly.

"I'm aware of that," he said. Then he kissed me again.

CHAPTER 28

I woke up the next morning and smiled. It's amazing what a few good kisses can do for a girl's mood. Then I remembered: George was dead, Bernie was a suspect, and somewhere among the people we had met, I was sure, was a killer.

My grandmother's bed was empty, so I jumped up and readied myself for the day. I left the room and bounded down the stairs, toward the kitchen. I needed lots of coffee to fortify me for the drive to see George and Rita's daughter.

As I walked down the stairs into the entryway, I noticed an ornate silver candlestick on the landing. It must have been moved, and then dropped, by one of the volunteers who had been painting, but I didn't remember it from downstairs. As I picked it up, I heard whispers that stopped me on the way to my all-important caffeine fix. The voice was clearly female, but she was speaking so low that I couldn't determine the identity. Momentarily caught up in the possibility of catching Rita on the phone with the mysterious man from the office building, I moved closer. Tucked against the wall, with the phone against her ear, was my grandmother.

"I miss you too, Oliver," she was saying. "I had no idea I'd miss you this much."

She turned and saw me. I'm not sure who was more embarrassed, but I was the one in the way so I moved quickly toward the kitchen. She stopped me.

"For heaven's sake, Nell, don't make anything of it," Eleanor scolded me once she'd hung up the phone.

"Sorry, Grandma. I didn't mean to overhear, but since I did, I think it's very sweet to see you so happy."

"I'm not the only one. I looked out the window last night and happened to notice you and Jesse lingering in the car. Your conversation about Frank and McIntyre went well?"

"Very well. And your conversation?" I pointed toward the phone.

She smiled a little shyly. "Good. Very good. Now get some breakfast."

As I walked into the kitchen, I realized I had interrupted yet another scene. One of the twins was rubbing a damp cloth against her red T-shirt. "I've gotten some paint on me. A hazard of redecorating, I guess," she said. "So annoying. We've only been here five minutes and I'm already a mess."

I looked closely at the dark spot. It seemed more like grease than the latex paint that was being used on the walls. "I'm not sure water will get that out, Alysse." I took a guess at the name.

"Alice. Don't worry. Not even our mother can tell us apart half the time."

"It must be nice to be so close."

"It is. We would do anything for each other," Alice said. "Though you'll find we are very different in personality once you know us." She swatted at the stain on her shirt and gave up. "I don't want to waste any more time. I'll just leave it and hope I can get it out at home."

After she left I stood at the sink and sipped my coffee. Maybe it had been sitting for a while but it was unusually bitter, so even though I prefer my coffee black, I opened the fridge in search of milk.

I found the milk but I also found the pitcher of lemonade that I hoped was the same batch from a couple of days before. I searched the cabinets for a small storage bowl, poured a cupful into it, and carefully sealed the container. Then I left the coffee behind and brought the container up to my room. I wanted to bring it to Jesse, but I had something more important to do first—to find out why the George and Rita's daughter hadn't bothered to come back after her father's death. I left the container on the dresser and grabbed my car keys.

✄

"Hey there," I called out to Pete as I stepped out of the inn. Pete was walking slowly, grabbing an unhappy-looking Barney by the collar.

"Found him knee-deep in a tangle of vines out in the woods."

"I'm so sorry." I took hold of Barney. "I can't imagine why he keeps doing that. Normally you can't pry him away from my grandmother." I looked back at the house and came up with a reason. "I think he's feeling a little confused by all the activity."

"Nothing for you to do, old boy?" Pete patted Barney's head. "Still, you need to keep him out of there if he's unsupervised. I was doing some hunting this morning and I almost mistook him for a deer."

I crouched down and looked Barney in the eyes. "You've been very bad. From now on you stay with Grandma, you old trouble-maker."

Barney, either because he was nearly deaf or because he was ignoring the scolding, started wagging his tail furiously and licking my face.

"I should get to work," Pete said. "Our goal is to get the entire first floor painted and fixed up as best we can. Are you coming? We can use all the help we can get."

I stood up. "Not right now. I do want to help but I have an errand to run." I jangled my car keys as if it were the universal symbol for errand running.

"Any leads on George's death?"

"None that I'm aware of."

"Well, you be careful. Folks up here are a private bunch. They might give you some trouble."

I winked. "I'm tougher than I look."

"I'll bet you are." He laughed. "Still, if you get into any trouble, go for the knees. You can take down a two-hundred-pound man with a well-placed kick to the back of the knee."

"I'll keep that in mind." I was about to turn away, when I thought of a question. "You knew George pretty well. Didn't you and Frank used to go hunting with him?"

"Just once. And only for an hour or so. George went home. He said something about Rita needing him, but I think that was an excuse. I don't think it was his sport."

"Frank was mad," I said.

He nodded. "Frank likes to act tough but he spent a lot of time at the Olnhausens' house, so I know he liked them. He's not a nice man, certainly not my favorite, but he wouldn't kill George, if that's what you're after."

"Do you have any idea who *would* want to kill him?"

Pete frowned. "Not an idea in the world. Can't imagine it's Rita. A marriage has its ups and downs, but I can't imagine anyone killing over it. Especially when you can just leave." He smiled a sad smile.

"You seem lonely without your wife, if you don't mind me saying."

"I guess I am. My wife and I, we didn't have any kids, so it was just the two of us, a couple of hunting dogs, and whatever stray cat she took to feeding. She didn't work outside the home until a couple of months before she left, so she was always there. I guess I got used to it."

"Have you heard from her?"

"Not a word. Don't expect to. She changed. She was getting these headaches, didn't want to cook or clean anymore. Didn't even want to bake, and she used to love to bake. She got some medication for the headaches, and I thought that would help, but I don't really know. There came a day when she didn't want to be with me anymore," he said. "You would think that after twenty-five years of marriage you could count on a person." He kicked at the dirt for a moment. He seemed like the type of man who was fading from the American landscape: strong, silent, hardworking, but uncomfortable with his emotions.

"I'm sorry, Pete. I really am."

"I perked up for a minute when I met your friend Bernie. I thought she was a nice lady, even with all the marriages she's had, though I guess she preferred George to me."

"Why do you say that?"

"I walked into the house the morning George died, and he was crying. He said Bernie being here had brought back so many memories. He kept saying, 'Where has the time gone?' He was hurting. Then I heard they went on that picnic in the woods. I have to say, I was a bit disappointed in your friend about that. I don't agree with going after a married man."

Barney strained at my grip on his collar. "I better put him in the house," I said.

"And I need to get started on the last coat in the dining room," Pete said. "I need to do a lot of manual labor to work off that lunch the ladies made yesterday. And maybe the one they'll make today, if I'm lucky."

"Good problem to have," I said. "Much better than mine." I looked at my keys and sized up the day I had ahead of me.

CHAPTER 29

The address Carrie had given me wasn't for the daughter's home. It was an office space in a white frame house just off the main street of Saratoga Springs. The town, on the southern tip of the Adirondacks, had been a spa when mineral springs were first developed in the area in the nineteenth century. It retains much of the elegance of that era, making it everything that Winston is not—a thriving community with plenty of tourists and a strong arts population—and exactly the sort of place that could support the kind of bed-and-breakfast/quilt-shop combo that George and Rita had envisioned. Though maybe it was too close to the daughter they didn't seem to get along with.

I parked the car down the street and walked slowly toward the entrance. It finally hit me that I was likely to be the first person to tell this woman that her father had been murdered. It wasn't the sort of news I was anxious to deliver.

In the window was a large, beautifully hand-painted sign that read THE HEALING ARTS, as well as several small paintings, a few clay pots, and a large quilt. There was a happy, casual, handmade look to the entrance that made me smile. I didn't even know Joi, but I already liked her more than I liked her parents.

"Joi Olnhausen?" I asked a large, older woman who stood just inside the door.

"Not me," she said. "Her." She pointed toward a woman of about thirty-five, so much like Rita that I was surprised I hadn't spotted her right away.

"I'm Joi. Not Olnhausen but Percival. Olnhausen's my maiden name."

"I'm Nell Fitzgerald. I need to talk to you about something personal. Is there somewhere we can talk privately?"

Joi looked at me. "I don't keep a lot of secrets and I haven't used Olnhausen for nearly fifteen years, so whatever you have to say can't be that personal."

"It's about your father."

"What about him?"

"Have you spoken to your mother?"

"Not recently. What's this about?"

"I really think you should call your mother."

"I'd rather you told me whatever it is you're trying not to tell me," she said.

I hesitated. It wasn't my place to tell her, but she needed to know. "I have some bad news. He died yesterday."

"That must be why your mother called," the other woman said.

Joi sat down in a desk chair. "What happened?"

"I'm not exactly sure. What we know so far is that he was shot with a hunting rifle."

"Was it an accident?"

I shook my head.

"He was murdered?"

"It looks that way."

"Are you from the Winston Police?" Joi asked. "I heard they moved to Winston."

"No. I'm just a friend . . . An acquaintance." I struggled to find the most accurate description. "I know your parents."

Joi made a weak smile. "Not the warmest people, are they?"

The other woman jumped up. "I'll make some tea for everyone. And I think I have some cookies in back." She directed me toward her chair. "Have a seat, Nell."

I did as I was told and waited for Joi to speak. Though it was my nature to jump in and start talking, I was beginning to learn that it was better to sit back and let the other person lead the conversation. If I asked a lot of questions, I might get the answers I needed, but if I let Joi take the lead, she would tell me what she wanted me to know. Maybe it wouldn't be as much direct information, but what she wanted to tell me, and in what order, would say a lot about her.

Joi sat quietly for a while. There were no tears, but the color had drained from her face. Every few minutes she would gasp slightly, as if she were taking the news in deeper and deeper, feeling the shock each time.

Finally she turned toward me. "My parents and I haven't been close, but you seem to have figured that out or you wouldn't have come."

"Your mother called yesterday," I said, referring to what her office mate had mentioned.

"I didn't call her back. I haven't heard from my parents for nearly three years. Maybe a Christmas card or a gift certificate when my kids had birthdays, but no visits, no calls. Then two months ago my father phoned, and yesterday my mother." She stared off into space. Her face was a younger version of her mother's, but her eyes were soft and kind. I could see George in her eyes.

"You said your dad called." I was hoping to bring her back from the quiet, sad place she had retreated to. "Did he come to visit?" I suddenly remembered the gas station receipt from Saratoga Springs I'd found in Rita's car.

She shook her head. "No. They never came to visit, either of them. I don't even know why he called. He said he just wanted to see how we were. Richard, the kids, and me. I told him we were fine, living our quiet, peaceful life. The kind of life he and my mother hated." She laughed a little. "I told him we just had a huge donation to the arts center and we were going to expand to include kids with disabilities."

"What do you do here?"

"We bring the arts to at-risk children. You know, kids who are getting involved in petty crimes, for example. We work with local artists—there are tons in this area. They teach the kids pottery or painting or woodworking, whatever they can. It gives the kids something to focus on, something to get excited about. We've been doing it for about ten years, my husband and I and a few volunteers. We love it. We've even had a few kids go on to careers in the arts."

"That's really wonderful. It must have made your parents proud of you."

She laughed. "They thought I'd married beneath me and moved to the backwoods. That's what they said on my wedding day. Can you imagine? Richard is a glassblower. He makes the most beautiful bowls and vases." She pointed to a shelf with half a dozen glass objects with art deco shapes and intricate patterns. "Once Richard became established, they came around, I guess. But when I told them we were opening an arts center, to give back to the community, they said we were wasting our lives. Helping people is wasting our lives." She shook her head, as if still unable to believe her parents' words.

"They must have changed their minds," I said after a minute. "You said you got a large donation. Was it over a hundred thousand dollars?"

She took a deep breath. "Why? Are you saying they gave it?"

"I think so. They've made several large donations in the last few months. One was to an organization like yours. I'd have to check, but I think it's a pretty good guess that this was the place."

Joi sat back in her chair, tears rolling down her eyes. "I didn't even bother to call her back," she said.

Mary came back into the room, with tea and cookies. The three of us sat in silence. Mary and I drank our tea. Tears finally came to Joi's face and she buried her head in her hands and cried.

Whatever Rita and George had done to alienate their daughter, she was still their daughter and her grief was painful to watch. Mary and I engaged in one of those "nice weather we're having" conversations to give her as much privacy as we could. After about twenty minutes, Joi gulped down her tea, which had probably gotten cold, and stood up.

"I need to make a call, and then if you don't mind, I wonder if you could drive me to my parent's place. I've never been there and I'm not sure I could find it right now."

"I'm happy to," I said. "Would you like me to call your mother and let her know we're coming?"

"No. I'm not sure she would want me there."

"That can't be true," Mary said.

"You don't know my mother," Joi said quietly.

CHAPTER 30

I was afraid that I would spend the trip to Winston listening to Joi cry, but as we drove, she began telling me about her husband and kids, the work they did at the center, and life in Saratoga Springs. It was hard to believe that someone who looked so much like Rita could be so different from her, but she was everything Rita was not—warm, kind, and open. She didn't ask me who I was or how I knew her parents, and I wasn't anxious to fill her in, so I just listened, hoping that she would eventually stumble onto the topic I was dying to learn about. But she didn't. When we were more than halfway to Winston and she still hadn't brought up her childhood, I ventured in as gently as I could.

"Were you raised in the area?"

"No," she answered. "California mostly. We lived in Napa until I was thirteen; then we moved around a bit. Two years in London, three in New York."

"Sounds glamorous."

"I suppose it does, but it was more lonely than anything. My parents weren't really interested in being parents. They sort of forgot about me a lot."

"Were they in the wine business?"

She looked confused.

"I just thought . . . because you lived in Napa," I explained.

"Oh no. They were in lots of things. They dabbled."

"Like what?"

Joi sighed and looked out the window. "I hope my kids look back on their childhood with happy memories. I think that's why I got into the center. I wanted all the children I could find to look back on their childhoods with happy memories."

I nodded. I could already tell that Joi was wishing she had reconnected with her parents while she had the chance.

"I think your father had regrets," I said, hoping it might lead her to some insights into her parents' marriage.

"I know he did," was her quiet response.

And then she went back to talking about her husband and kids, the weather, the report on CNN of a tornado in the Midwest—anything not to talk about her parents. That was okay, I told myself. She was grieving. Besides, I would have other chances once we were at the inn.

✂

At least I hoped so. The moment we arrived, Joi seemed stunned into silence. She walked around the grounds, checking out the classroom and the shop, before coming back to the car as if she were ready to go home.

"What is this place?"

"It's a bed-and-breakfast," I said. "Your parents bought it."

"It looks like it's falling apart."

"I think they were in the process of remodeling, though I will grant you it hasn't gotten very far. Some of the neighbors have pitched in to help and they're doing a nice job on the inside."

Joi stared at me as if she thought I was lying. "My parents—I mean, my mother lives here?"

"Yes. I don't know if your mom will want to keep it up by herself."

"What do you mean, by herself? Doesn't she have help?"

I shook my head. "They wanted to hold quilt retreats here, and have a shop."

"I don't get it. Why would they buy a place like this?"

"Your mom said they wanted to live out the rest of their lives in peaceful surroundings."

"They were up to something," Joi muttered, then took a step back from the car and, instead of walking toward the house, turned and headed into the woods.

"Who is that?" Jesse was suddenly behind me.

"The daughter."

"She's walking in the wrong direction."

"I think she would disagree with you. I gather she prefers to keep some distance between herself and her mother."

"When did you find out where she lives?"

"Carrie gave me her address yesterday, when I was in town with Rita."

He nodded but he seemed to be biting his lip. "Did you learn anything else?"

"Not really. She said her parents 'dabbled' in several professions, but she wouldn't get specific. I have Natalie and Carrie looking into their backgrounds, so hopefully we'll find something."

He smiled. "Of course you do. You have a larger investigative team than I do."

"You're part of the team, remember? What did you learn this morning?"

"Actually, I do have something to tell you."

Out of the corner of my eye I saw Joi returning from the woods.

"Tell me later."

He nodded.

"I guess it's time to see my mother," she said. "I don't think I can do this alone. Would you come with me?"

"Of course," I said. I wouldn't have missed this mother-daughter reunion for the world.

CHAPTER 31

"Where's Rita?" I asked Bernie, who was hand sewing a tumbling blocks quilt in the living room. Bernie was so engrossed in her sewing she hadn't noticed that Joi and I were standing behind her. After my interruption she finished work on a block and placed it on a pile.

"I'm making a wall hanging for over the fireplace. I love this pattern," she said. "Don't you?"

I did love the pattern, which creates a quilt of three-dimensional blocks, achieved by sewing three diamonds together: two vertical diamonds form the side of the block, and the third is sewn horizontally to make the top. The three-point intersection, what quilters call a y-seam, makes the quilt a popular choice for hand sewing, since sewing by machine would require just as many starts and stops.

"This is Rita's daughter, Joi," I told Bernie.

Bernie had reached her hand out but stopped and seemed on the verge of withdrawing it.

"You are the picture of your mother," Bernie said as if seeing a ghost. "But you're so young. You can't be more than thirty."

"Thirty-five," Joi said. "Though I prefer your guess."

"Do you have brothers and sisters?"

Joi shook her head. "Only child. Do you know where my mother is?"

"I think she's up in her room. I saw her going up the stairs a few minutes ago," Bernie said, her voice still filled with shock. "I'm so sorry about your father, dear. He and I, and your mother, we were friends many years ago."

"Really? My mother must take a lot of comfort in having you here."

Bernie's face started to turn a bright red, so I hurried Joi out of the room and walked with her upstairs to the second floor. We were about to continue up to the third floor when I heard a noise coming from Bernie's room.

"Excuse me a minute." I left Joi standing on the landing and walked as quietly as possible to Bernie's door. It was ajar, but I couldn't see inside. I pushed the door open.

McIntyre looked up at me, completely unruffled by my sudden arrival.

"Nell, so nice to see you again."

I stared at him, dumbfounded, for a minute. "What are you doing here?"

"I'm searching your friend's room."

"Do you have a search warrant?"

He smiled. "No, ma'am, I don't. But I do have permission from the owner of the inn."

Joi was suddenly standing behind me. "What's going on?"

"Another quilter?" McIntyre looked at her. "I heard it was a growing hobby, but you seem to breed like rabbits."

"She's not a quilter. She's the Olnhausens' daughter," I said.

"I am, actually. A quilter, I mean." Joi stepped into the room. "My grandmother taught me."

"Mine too," I said.

"I'm sorry for the loss of your father, ma'am," McIntyre said. "I'm sure it's doubly hard the way he passed, but I want you to know that I'm doing everything I can to bring his killer to justice."

Joi nodded but said nothing. Her eyes were welling up.

"I'm sorry, ladies," he said softly. "I hate to do this, under the circumstances, but I need you to leave. I can't have you in here right now, while I'm searching for evidence."

"Evidence of what?" Joi asked.

"This is Bernie's room," I explained. "He thinks she might have been involved."

Joi turned toward the police chief. "You think that nice woman downstairs might have killed my dad? What the hell is going on here?"

"Please don't curse in my house," I heard Rita say seconds before she appeared in the doorway of Bernie's room.

There was one of the longest periods of silence I'd ever endured. Mother and daughter just stared at each other. McIntyre and I stared at them. The tension was getting to me, so without any particular plan in mind, I decided to break the impasse. But Joi beat me to it.

"Nell came to Saratoga Springs this morning to tell me about dad," she said.

Rita turned her eyes to me, blinking slowly, like a cat deciding whether to pounce. "You pick up daughters *and* dry cleaning. Aren't you handy?"

"You ladies might be more comfortable talking somewhere else," McIntyre jumped in. "I'd skip downstairs if you want privacy. Your neighbors are working on the dining room, and I hear the twins are fixing pasta salad for the group. Might sneak down and get some for myself when I'm done here."

"Maybe we should go upstairs," Rita said to her daughter, who nodded and followed her out of the room.

I was about to go when McIntyre grabbed my arm. "Let 'em go," he said.

I nodded. "You may regret that. If I'm not going with them, then I'm staying here. This," I waved my hand across the room, "is a mistake."

He smiled. "I'm no Sherlock Holmes, miss, but I do find that if the facts lead you somewhere, well, then that's the direction you ought to go. It may make you feel better to know that even your friend Jesse thinks searching Bernie's room is a good idea."

That stopped me. "He does?"

"He suggested it."

Jesse. He could have warned me. I resisted the urge to run outside and confront him, because I didn't want to appear as though I believed Bernie had something to hide.

"Well, you're not going to find anything," I said.

"I already have." McIntyre showed me an evidence bag. Stuffed inside was a blouse I recognized as Bernie's. "It has blood on it. I'd bet it's our victim's."

"But you don't know that."

"Not yet. But give the lab boys a couple of days."

"And if you're wrong, you'll look elsewhere?"

"Nell—I hope you don't mind me calling you Nel— I'm looking everywhere. I'm open to any ideas. If you have one, I'd like to hear it."

I looked at McIntyre. He seemed sincere. I took a deep breath and made a decision. "As long as you're making a trip to the lab, I have something to show you."

McIntyre followed me to my room, where I showed him the container of lemonade and told him how George had drugged me the day of his murder.

"I was going to ask Jesse to get it analyzed, but since he's sharing everything with you anyway, you may as well have it," I said.

"Any idea why George would drug you?" McIntyre asked.

"No. I just know that there's something going on here. Some people say Rita and George were the perfect couple, but they couldn't have been. Rita seemed to have zero interest in the inn. George did everything around here, and she, well . . ." I almost told him about the man in town but thought maybe it was better to save that until I could look into it myself. "They barely spoke to their only child," I said instead. "I don't want to tell you how to do your job but you have to look deeper than Bernie."

He nodded. "Maybe. In the meantime I'll check the shirt *and* the lemonade." He walked toward the door. "You're a bit of an amateur detective, aren't you?"

I folded my arms, getting ready for the inevitable admonishment. "I'm just curious, that's all. And I don't like to see innocent people railroaded."

"Neither do I," he said. "And I assure you it won't happen in this case." He paused for a moment before adding, "My force consists of me, two part-time deputies, and my dog. I could use a smart lady like you. If you learn anything else, you let me know."

"If you're serious," I said, "then there is something else. I honestly don't know if it means anything, but Jesse and I found a dog buried in the woods. I remember reading that hunting dogs were going missing and I thought . . ."

"I'll bring some guys with shovels back from town, and you show me where you found the dog," he said. "There might not be a connection, but as I said, I go where the facts lead me, even if I'm not sure how it all fits."

After he left the room, I spent a few minutes re-evaluating my opinion of Jim McIntyre, not just because he had recognized my investigative skills, but because, though he might be leaning toward her, he hadn't settled on Bernie. That meant he was smart enough to look beyond the obvious. And that was what we had to do if we were going to find the killer.

But first I had to kill Jesse.

CHAPTER 32

I walked around for twenty minutes and couldn't find him. Jesse had been right outside the front door when I brought Joi in. Joi, whom I had completely abandoned. I considered going back inside, but since she hadn't run out of the house crying, I figured she was probably fine.

Susanne followed me out of the inn and waved me over.

"We have to talk later," she said.

"What about?"

"Later." She turned and I saw Helen behind her. Loud enough to be overheard, Susanne said, "Helen is helping us with the quilts today, and we need to get back to it."

I nodded as if I understood, but I didn't. I was about to follow her to the shop when I spotted my target, leaning on the hood of his car, laughing with Eleanor.

"Jesse," I yelled. "If there weren't witnesses, I would strangle you."

Eleanor stood between me and Jesse. She looked like she was about to scold me but then backed down. "This is between the two of you," she said. "I'll leave you to it."

"Don't bother," I told her. "It won't take long. And you'll hear about it anyway."

Though it took him a minute, Jesse seemed to finally catch on that I wasn't kidding. He stood up. "What are you upset about?"

"You told McIntyre to search Bernie's room."

"He didn't need me to give him the idea, Nell."

"But you did give him the idea."

Jesse took a deep breath. "What did he find?"

"Blood," I said. "He found blood on one of Bernie's blouses."

"There has to be a reasonable explanation," Eleanor offered.

"Of course there's a reasonable explanation," I snapped, then thought better of it. Eleanor was, after all, on my side. "I'm sorry. It's just . . . Why would you help McIntyre get more evidence on Bernie?"

"I didn't help him get evidence on Bernie. I discussed the case with him because he's looking for the killer and so are we," Jesse said calmly, almost coldly, in that cop voice that suggested he was being extremely patient with me.

"We're supposed to be leading him away from Bernie," I said. "Not pushing him to find things to use against her."

"Let me ask you something, Nell. If Bernie is the killer, do we cover for her?"

I actually had to think about it, which didn't make me feel too good. "No," I admitted. "If, and this is a purely hypothetical and ridiculous *if*, then no. Whoever killed George has to be found. But Bernie didn't kill George."

"So then if we help McIntyre eliminate Bernie, we help find the killer."

"Why didn't you tell me what you were doing?"

"I didn't realize you were the lead investigator. From now on I'll clear everything through you." The sarcasm was unmistakable.

"You said we were going to work together," I pointed out.

"I was going to tell you once you had the daughter settled in. I told you I had something to tell you, and you asked me to wait, remember?" He cocked his eyebrow at me and waited. I did remember.

"Jesse," I started to say.

He wasn't listening. "Oh, and by the way, partner, thanks for the heads-up on getting the daughter up here." At that he turned and walked toward the house.

"I thought that was a necessary clearing of the air." Eleanor smiled at me after a moment of uncomfortable silence. She reached out and wrapped an arm around me. "We've all been there. Relationships are hard."

"Not for you and Oliver. From the moment you met, all you two have ever done is coo at each other," I said. "I guess Jesse and I aren't soul mates like the two of you."

"We're not soul mates."

"If you're not soul mates . . . ," I started.

"Jesse is a careful man. He follows the rules, not because he's a follower, but because he believes in them. He likes structure. He likes to know where he's going in the morning and where he'll lay his head at night. You could say that's because of his daughter, wanting to provide some stability for her, but my guess is that he's always been that way and always will be." She turned toward me. "You, my dear Nell, are almost his opposite. You love not knowing what's ahead of you. You plunge headfirst into trouble and you enjoy getting yourself out of it. It's why you are an artist. The life is unstable but there are no restrictions."

I'd never thought of myself as an adventurer, an artist looking for a life of no restrictions. I'd thought of myself as a curious, per-

haps meddlesome twenty-six-year-old seeking refuge in my grandmother's house while I figured out my life. Of the two, I definitely
preferred the way Eleanor saw me. It sounded cool and exciting.
In either case, the woman she described was not Jesse's type. I told
Eleanor as much.

"Nonsense. You just have to let go of the image you have of the
man you will love, and if you really want to be with Jesse, then you
have to love him as he is."

"And he has to do the same for me."

"Yes. You both have to let go of the controls a little."

"And then we can be as happy as you and Oliver?"

She shrugged. "I've learned not to get too caught up in minutiae
but to step back and see the bigger picture. Most everything looks
better when you take a step back." she said.

"I think you've said pretty much the same thing about quilting."

She laughed. "I'm a wise woman."

"When do I get to be a wise woman?"

My grandmother grabbed my hand and placed it on hers. "When
your hands look like mine. And even then it's kind of hit or miss."
She patted me on the back and headed toward the shop. "Go find
your young man. It's what you both want."

After standing by the car for a while, hoping Jesse would come looking for me, I headed into the house. The whole thing was a little
foolish, I had to admit. But, then, love was a little foolish. There's
something nutty about a system that requires two people to meet,
and even if they have nothing in common, fall for each other because
of some odd, unexplainable attraction. If it all works, like it clearly
does for Oliver and Eleanor, there's nothing better. But if it doesn't,

then the love can lead to heartbreak—or at least a painfully embarrassing apology.

I would have looked for any reason to postpone it. But when, seconds later, a toaster came flying out the window, narrowly missing my head, I wasn't sure if it was an answered prayer or attempted murder.

CHAPTER 33

Bernie was still alone in the living room, still working on her tumbling blocks quilt. She seemed to want to be alone, to work through her grief over George's death, which was the only explanation I could come up with for why she seemed so calm while the house shook with screams.

"What's going on?" I asked her. "Someone just threw something at me out the window."

Bernie looked up. "Rita."

"I'm not going to just stand here while she throws things at Joi," I said. "I brought that woman up here for reconciliation, not a prize fight."

Bernie stood up. "If you think we should interfere, then we'll pull them apart if we have to."

Several people came out of the dining room, paint rollers still in their hands, offering to help. I pointed out that McIntyre was upstairs and could handle it. But that didn't stop me. Or Bernie. We ran up the stairs, passing one of the twins on her way down.

"Alice," I said. "I thought you were in the dining room."

"The bathroom," she said. "And it's Alysse. Easy mistake."

As she passed I checked again. Though both women were dressed alike, as usual, this twin had the same oil spot on her shirt that I'd seen in the morning on Alice. Or at least that's what she called herself then. I was about to stop her, when I heard screaming. Alice, or Alysse, didn't seem to notice or care. She just kept walking out the door.

Bernie and I reached the second floor, where our rooms were. I wondered if McIntyre had gone back to searching Bernie's room, but there was no time to check. We ran up the stairs to the third floor and Rita's living quarters.

"Is everything okay?" I threw open the door to find Rita and Joi facing each other. Both women had crossed arms, furrowed brows, and tearstains on their cheeks. "I'm sorry to barge in like this." I stumbled on my words. "A toaster went out the window, and then we heard screams."

"I guess we got a bit excited while we were catching up," Rita said calmly. "We were having a discussion."

"We were having a fight," Joi said. "It's what we do when we're in the same room. We fight."

"My daughter and I sometimes disagree," Rita said. "It's really a personal matter."

Joi rolled her eyes. "My father isn't even buried, and my mother is already making plans for the future. I was always a huge disappointment to her. I wouldn't let her control me, wouldn't get in on the family business. But you would think that now we could do something other than yell at each other."

Bernie pushed past me. "Well, you must learn how. George wouldn't want to see the two women he loved most in the world fighting. Now, come downstairs and I'll make some tea, and we'll all have a nice chat."

Out of shock, politeness, or lack of a better idea, Joi and Rita followed Bernie out of the room. I thought it was exceedingly generous of Bernie to offer mediation, considering her own feelings about Rita, but mostly I thought it was a stroke of good luck for me. I stayed behind, hoping no one would notice. No one did. Once I was sure they had gone downstairs, I closed the door and took a look around.

Just as Eleanor had described it, the few photos in the room included only one of a very young Joi and several of a smiling George and Rita. They did seem to be a happy couple, but the photo with Joi seemed strained and uncomfortable. I could almost feel the tension between the three, and Joi must have been no more than five at the time. I could only imagine the resentment and ill feelings that had built up among them in the years since.

I turned my back on the photos and checked the desk for bills, letters, anything that might offer some insight into the pair, but there was nothing that stood out. Aside from an electricity bill, a few business cards for the inn, and the newspaper announcing Susanne's class, the desk drawer was empty.

I walked around, trying to get some sense of George and Rita, but the more I looked, the more the room seemed staged. Though the furniture had a cottage shabby-chic look, on closer inspection it was brand-new. And there wasn't a lot of it. A couch, two chairs, some assorted end tables, a desk, two bland paintings of the local landscape that looked like ones I'd seen in hotels, a few lamps, and a mini fridge. Plus the space that had once held a toaster. I guess Rita and George didn't like walking down two flights of stairs when they felt like an English muffin.

"They'll have to now," I thought as I looked out the window and saw the broken pieces of chrome on the pavement.

The only thing that struck my eye was on a table near the suite's door. It was an ornate candlestick that seemed to be the match for the one I'd found on the landing downstairs. Or maybe it was the same one. I'd left it in the kitchen and forgotten about it.

Whatever they had in the way of personal items must have been in the bedroom. Just as it had been when Eleanor was here, the door to the bedroom was locked. I figured it would be too lucky for me to find a key somewhere in the room but I looked anyway. And just as I suspected—no key. There was something very careful about Rita and George, and it was really getting on my nerves. I went back to the desk in search of a knife or letter opener, but there wasn't one. Probably for the best, I eventually decided. It would be hard to explain scratch marks on the door. I leaned down and peeked through the keyhole and could see a bed, but that was it. Whatever secrets the room held were out of my sight line.

"What are you doing?"

I stood up. I hadn't even heard the door open. "Looking," I said. "What are you doing?"

Jesse walked into the room and closed the door behind me. "Looking for you. I was going to apologize. I don't want us to be angry with each other."

"Apology accepted."

"I haven't actually done it yet."

"You were going to. You just said you were going to," I said. "And I'm sorry too. I should have told you about Joi. I guess I'm just used to you being annoyed at me for interfering. I have to get used to this new you."

"It's a little new for both of us," he said.

"Look, I know I didn't really give you a chance to explain about Bernie. I guess I was upset about the blouse."

Jesse took a step forward. "I want you to know that I considered asking Bernie if we'd find anything in her room."

"Considered," I repeated.

"I can't protect a killer." He put his hand up to stop what he must have imagined, correctly, were the next words out of my mouth. "I'm an officer of the law, whether I'm in Archers Rest or not. And besides, it never occurred to me that McIntyre would find anything."

"I know. That's the hardest part of this whole thing. It's like Bernie is trying to self-destruct."

"We won't let her." He sounded so reassuring that I almost felt convinced. He took another step toward me and the door to Rita's bedroom. "What are you doing?'

"Trying to figure out how to get into that room."

"Is that Rita's bedroom?" Jesse asked. He walked past me and glanced at the lock. "It looks simple enough, but I couldn't get in without damaging the door, and that really is out of bounds. Have you looked for a key?"

"There's nothing."

"Letter opener?'

"Nothing."

"I don't suppose you carry around a lock pick for just such an occasion. All the professional burglars have them."

I smiled. "Not yet, Officer. But it would make a great birthday gift.".

He nodded. "It sounds like you've searched the place, so let's get out of here before Rita finds us." Jesse took my hand and led me to the door to the suite.

"But the answer is in her bedroom. It has to be."

"Then we'll have to look another time."

Reluctantly, I followed him out of the room. As I did I took one more look back. Something in that room nagged at me I just couldn't figure out what it was, and I didn't know if I'd ever get another chance to find out.

CHAPTER 34

By the time Jesse and I walked outside, Chief McIntyre had arrived with several men with shovels, as promised. They followed us to the area where Barney had uncovered the dog's paw, but
there was no paw sticking out from the dirt.

"Somebody could have covered him up again," I offered.

McIntyre nodded. "Maybe. Maybe you have the wrong spot."

"It's obvious the ground has been disturbed, so someone was digging here. Do people hike or hunt through here?" Jesse said.

"Not often," McIntyre replied. "It's pretty remote up here. Not
the best hunting, though some of the locals like it. Once in a while,
you get a hiker whose gone off course, and sometimes lovers come in
here looking for a bit of privacy."

I looked toward the tree where George had been found, covered
by Bernie's beautiful quilt, and I thought of what he and Bernie
might have been doing here only a few days before. A buried dog
seemed like a pretty small mystery compared to what happened
that day.

"It was a pretty shallow grave," I said. "So even covered up, it
shouldn't take too long to find him."

McIntyre's men began digging, going farther and farther until
they had created a hole about three feet deep. But there was no dog.

"I swear it was here," Jesse said.

"Maybe if I got Barney," I suggested. "He found it before. He's been sniffing this whole area."

"But it was here," Jesse said again. "Right here at this spot. I know it seems ridiculous, but I'm used to paying attention at crime scenes and I remember the knot on this tree and the fact that I stood right in this position and saw the murder victim."

"In my experience dead dogs don't move," McIntyre said.

"But . . . ," Jesse started, then stopped. "Maybe I'm wrong," he said reluctantly. "Nell, do you think it was somewhere else?"

I looked around. "I would have said it was here too, but after we saw George, I forgot about the dog," I admitted. "It's just . . . I think Jesse is right about it having been in this spot. Anyway, why would someone just dig a hole and fill it in?"

Jesse turned the corners of his mouth into a slight smile. I nodded back to show that I hadn't just been offering support. I really believed he was right.

McIntyre watched us both, then nodded. "Someone must have unburied him and put him somewhere else."

Jesse turned to me. "Would Pete have done it? He was with us when we found the dog."

"Doesn't make sense," I said. I walked a few feet from the tree and noticed another spot where the leaves seemed out of place and the ground disturbed. "Maybe here," I suggested.

McIntyre crouched down and picked up the leaves. "These are dirtier than the rest. Like someone picked up shovelfuls of dirt and dumped it, leaves and all, right here."

The men began digging in the new spot with a renewed enthusiasm, as Jesse, McIntyre, and I watched from a few feet away. The longer it went on, the more unsure I became. Even if someone had moved a dead dog, what did it have to do with George's death? I was beginning to feel a bit silly for having even brought it up, when one of the men shouted, "Got something."

"It's a hunting dog," McIntyre said after examining the dead animal. "Looks like it's been dead more than a week. But there is good news. It has a collar." He pulled off the collar and held it in front of me.

I read the tag. "Frank's dog. I didn't know his dog was missing."

"Neither did I," McIntyre said. "Two other folks reported missing dogs, Pete and a man who lived down the road, but not Frank."

"Then maybe the dog died and Frank buried him here," I said.

"Not his property," McIntyre pointed out. "You might hike through another man's woods but you don't bury your animals there."

"And he didn't die of natural causes," Jesse said. He was kneeling beside the dog, pointing to a wound on its side.

"Looks like he was shot," McIntyre said. "Boys, get him loaded into a truck, and we'll take him into town."

"Do you think there could be other dogs buried here?" I asked.

"Maybe," Jesse said. "We probably should get Barney to sniff it out."

McIntyre wiped sweat from his large brow. Though he hadn't actually done any physical work, it seemed the police chief was exhausted. "You folks do that and I'll get the local vet to take a look at this dog's remains."

After McIntyre left, Jesse went back to the spot we had originally dug. "I don't mean to sound like a broken record, but that dog was right here."

"Like McIntyre said, somebody moved him," I said.

"It's just weird," he said.

"Everything about this place is weird."

✂

It was getting dark on our way back to the inn, but Jesse didn't seem in much of a hurry. Instead he kept picking up sticks, snapping them in two, and throwing the pieces at the dirt.

"What are you doing?" I asked.

"Thinking." He broke a stick then threw the parts at a tree. "We're missing something."

"The name of the killer."

"Aside from that."

"We're missing the reason why George wanted Bernie to come here. Maybe he was going to leave Rita, maybe not. It's weird how split people are about the kind of couple they were," I said. "And we're missing the connection between a dead dog and George's murder."

"If there is any," Jesse added.

"Right. We're also missing the whole point of the bed-and-breakfast. Joi seems to think it's completely out of character for her parents. And not just her mother. She said her 'parents.'"

"Did she seem surprised to hear that her dad was dead?"

I stopped. "You don't think she had something to do with it?"

"Maybe." Jesse shrugged. "They have a lot of money. She's their only child. She inherits."

"If *both* her parents are dead."

"So she's halfway to her goal."

"You're crazy," I said.

"If you're sure . . ."

"I'm sure. I think I'm sure. She's a nice woman. She wouldn't kill her parents."

As I said the words, I started to run back to the inn just to be absolutely certain I was right.

CHAPTER 35

After what Jesse said, I was half expecting to find another dead body, but instead all the lights of the inn were on, and people from the class and the folks from town who had been helping, as well as at least a dozen others, were wandering in and out of the building. Eleanor was standing with a small group I didn't know, holding coffee and looking a little confused.

"Are they throwing a party?" Jesse asked as we approached the front steps.

"A wake," Eleanor answered. "They've finished with the living room and dining room, and now, apparently, they've invited some friends over to celebrate George's life."

"When did this happen?" I asked.

"It was sort of a spontaneous decision. Joi and Rita suggested it."

"That means they're getting along," I pointed out. "And what about Bernie? She was with them the last time I saw her."

"She thought it was a great idea," Eleanor said, a tone of disapproval in her voice. "I know a man's life ought to be celebrated, but he was murdered. And only two days ago."

"And probably by someone at this party," I added.

"Exactly," she said. "Seems a bit early in the grieving process to be dancing." She pointed toward a young couple on the lawn, swaying to the music, oblivious to anyone around them.

Susanne walked out the door of the inn, holding a glass of wine. "Nell and Jesse, if you're hungry you should go now. The food is disappearing very fast. That lovely woman who owns the bakery brought some cookies, but I think they're already gone."

"You seem to be enjoying yourself," I said. "I don't think I've ever seen you drink before."

She handed me the glass and leaned in. "Don't touch the stuff. It's part of my cover story. I have so much to tell you." She looked around before apparently deciding it was safe to continue. "I noticed one of the twins wandering around and I followed her. Odd, that's what those two women are. Don't twins stop dressing alike after they turn five?"

"You followed her . . . ," I said to get Susanne back on track. She enjoyed tangents, mostly when she was leading to good gossip, and I sensed there was some pretty good gossip coming up.

"Yes," she answered. "She was opening cabinets and drawers in the kitchen. Can you imagine? She turned around and caught me watching her, and I had to come up with a story. So I told her I was looking for wine." She caught her breath. "Then she walked me downstairs to a little wine cellar and grabbed a few bottles. As if she owned the place."

"She knew where it was?" Jesse asked.

"Exactly where it was."

✂

I left Jesse on the porch and walked inside to see how the others were celebrating George's life or, for the one who had killed him, his death. Joi was in the living room in deep conversation with

Bernie. Helen and one of the twins were putting food out in the dining room, and Pete was talking to a pair of men I didn't recognize. Rita was the only person I didn't see at the party. While I was trying to decide where to go first, Susanne came up behind me.

"Nell," she said in a near shout.

"Very subtle," I said as I turned around.

"I don't care. I have to talk to you. I haven't told you the most important thing." Susanne led me into the kitchen, looked around, and though we were alone, must have decided it wasn't safe. She hustled me out a back door.

"You wanted to tell me about something that happened today," I said.

"I almost told Bernie, but then I thought better of it." She took a deep breath. "Helen was having an affair with George."

It took a moment for the words to sink in. "Are you sure?"

"As sure as I can be. Earlier in the day, Helen was cleaning in the kitchen. She seemed to be upset." Susanne looked around, as if she'd heard something, and pulled me a little farther from the house. "So I suggested we take a little walk. Just five minutes."

"Good idea."

"I started talking about my husband and Natalie, and she started talking about Frank and their kids, and then she burst out crying. I just stood there. I figured she was crying about what—well, I'll just say it—what a pain in the you-know-what Frank is."

"But she told you she was crying about George?"

"She told me that she and George loved each other. She said it just like that. That's when I saw you. I suggested she help with the quilting, but she went back into the kitchen."

It reminded me of my conversation with Helen's better half. "Frank stormed out of the house a few hours ago. He told me that

Rita was the widow, not Helen, and he wanted Helen to remember that," I said.

"So he might have known about the affair."

"If it was an affair," I countered. "Maybe they hadn't gotten that far. Maybe George was flirting. Maybe she misunderstood his kindness. I saw the way she looked at him but I didn't notice him looking back."

"Unless he was better at hiding it than she was. Or it didn't mean as much to him."

"Could be. I would think, being married to Frank, she could use a little gentle male attention. Maybe the whole thing was a figment of her imagination."

"Maybe, but the tears were real."

I nodded. "So was Frank's anger."

Behind us the door opened and one of the twins came out holding a bag of garbage.

"Oh," she said. "I didn't expect to see anyone out here."

"We were just chatting about poor George," Susanne said calmly. "It's so upsetting for me, Alysse. I don't know why but I feel so sad, and I hardly knew the man."

"It's a tragedy," Alysse said. "And a double tragedy since you didn't know him. He was one of the kindest people in town. A real gentleman. I always looked forward to crossing his path and I—my sister and I—will miss him."

"He was lucky to have you as a friend," Susanne said sympathetically.

"We were the lucky ones," Alysse replied. She gave a slight, sad smile then walked back in the house, carrying the garbage bag with her.

"That's funny," I said after the twin had left. "She and her sister told me they barely knew the Olnhausens. She, or one of them, said they met Rita at a church function."

"Maybe they did, and then got to know them."

"Rita told me she never went to church."

Susanne shrugged. "Perhaps she's exaggerating their closeness. People sometimes do that after someone dies. Or maybe . . ." Her voice was suddenly excited. "Maybe Alysse was having an affair with George too."

"Busy guy," I said. Then something occurred to me. "How did you know it was Alysse?"

"They both wear gold earrings, but one of them wears pierced and the other wears clip-ons. Once I figured that out, I knew which was which."

"I didn't notice," I said.

"I saw something you didn't." Susanne smiled. "It makes me feel a little like Sherlock Holmes."

I was so impressed by Susanne's powers of observation that I almost forgot something else that had struck me as odd. But as we walked back into the kitchen, I remembered it. "Alysse walked out of the house with a bag of trash but she didn't throw it out. She brought it back into the house with her."

"When she saw us, she must have forgotten."

I nodded but I was sure there was a better answer than that.

CHAPTER 36

I looked for Alysse, but neither she nor her sister seemed to be anywhere around, so I gave up and looked for something to eat. As Susanne had said, the food was going quickly, but I managed to snag a few pieces of cheese, a hunk of French bread, and a brownie. All I was missing was a place to sit and eat.

Bernie and Joi were still in deep conversation in the living room, so I moved close, hoping that Bernie's good manners would overcome a likely desire for privacy, and I was right.

"Nell, sit next to us," Bernie said as she saw me wandering with a full plate and a frustrated look.

I obliged. "Am I interrupting something?" I asked innocently.

Joi shook her head. "Bernie has been telling me about my parents. I feel like I'm hearing about strangers."

"Oh dear," Bernie said. "I was just telling her about high school, the things we did back then."

"Did you know that Bernie and my father were an item?" Joi asked.

"I'd heard something about that," I said. "What's she been telling you?"

"She said they were practically engaged."

I looked at Bernie. That was the first time I'd heard that.

"We were young. We were romantic," Bernie said, blushing. "It was foolish to take it seriously, but you take everything seriously at seventeen."

Joi smiled. "I remember. It's amazing how we think our lives are going to turn out."

"Your father was going to be an actor. I was going to be a dancer." Bernie laughed. "That didn't happen."

"And Rita?" I asked.

"All she wanted was glamour, excitement, and lots of money," Bernie said.

I could see Joi's face fill with sadness. "I guess she got what she wanted," she said, and took a sip of wine.

I looked around the room. It had been cleaned and painted, the hunting lodge feeling was gone, and the drop cloths had been taken off the furniture. It was a significant improvement from earlier in the week but it was still a long way from glamour and excitement. How did someone Joi described as getting everything she wanted end up here?

It was a question that seemed, at least for the moment, not to trouble her daughter.

Joi was more interested in Bernie. "Why did you lose touch with them?" she asked.

I waited. Bernie blinked her eyes slowly, as if thinking of the answer. "Life," she said quietly. "Life just happened." She got up. "Excuse me, dears, but I think I need to lie down for a bit. I don't party into the night the way I used to."

"Unless there's a quilt that has to be finished," I said.

She smiled. "That's different. That's not to be missed." She patted Joi on the head and walked into the entryway, up the stairs, and out of view.

Joi turned to me. "She's the nicest person. I can completely see my dad falling for her."

"But you can't see him falling for your mom," I said, finishing what I assumed was her thought.

"I suppose you never know what goes on between two people," she said.

"Were your parents in love?" It was none of my business, but from the little time I'd had to get to know Joi, I figured she wouldn't mind.

"Desperately," she said. "They couldn't bear to be apart."

I was really walking out of bounds with my next question but I had to ask. "Then why does your mother seem so indifferent to his death?"

Joi seemed to be angry for a flicker of a second, but the look was enough to make it clear that she was Rita's daughter. I thought she was about to tell me off, until she looked away and I slowly realized the anger was directed at her mother. "She must have changed," she said quietly. "My mother used to be terrified that she'd lose my father. Almost irrationally. She was jealous of every woman he spoke to."

"Did she have reason to be? I mean . . ." As the words came out of my mouth, I realized what I was about to say. How do you ask someone if her father, her recently murdered father, had cheated on his wife?

I didn't have to finish the thought. Joi clearly knew what I meant and seemed to take no offense. "I never once saw my father be anything but solicitous toward my mother, but if her feelings for him have changed, then maybe . . ."

When she didn't finish, I looked to where she was looking and saw Rita enter the room with Frank at her side. She seemed a little unsteady on her feet but she came over to Joi and me, smiling. Frank stood there, watching for a moment, then turned and left the room.

"Nell, I can't tell you how much I appreciate your interfering the way you have." Rita stopped and looked suddenly stricken. "Oh dear, I hope that didn't sound mean. I didn't want it to sound mean."

"It didn't." I gestured for her to sit down and she did.

"Joi and Bernie and I had a lovely talk this afternoon, didn't we, Joi?"

"We did. Bernie told me wonderful stories about when she and Mom were small children, about how Grandma taught them how to quilt."

I turned to Rita, surprised. "So you do know how to quilt."

"Heavens, no! I was absolutely the worst at it. My mother got so annoyed with me. She tried to teach me to make a dress, then an apron, then a pillow. Quilting was her last shot at teaching me how to sew." She laughed, and for the first time seemed relaxed. "The next year she tried, and failed, to teach me how to cook."

"But Bernie must have enjoyed it," I said. "She's a wonderful quilter now."

Rita grabbed my hand and held it tight. Her hand was cold but her personality was the warmest it had been since we'd met, so I tried to focus on that. "Bernie took to quilting like she was born to it," she said. "I think my mother wanted to adopt her. I was always such a disappointment to her. I couldn't wait to get out of the house."

"Grandma was wonderful," said Joi, sounding defensive.

Rita nodded. "Everything you are you got from your grandmother," she said. She looked at her daughter. "Thank God you didn't take after me."

✄

Suddenly I felt like an intruder. I excused myself and walked toward the kitchen, hoping to locate Frank, but he was nowhere to be found. Helen was arranging crackers in a circle around the edge of a plate so that each one was equally overlapped by the next. It was pain-

staking, precise, and, to me, silly work, but she appeared to take plea-
sure in it.

"I haven't seen much of Frank this evening," I said, trying to restrain
myself from taking a cracker and completely ruining her display.

"I never know where he goes." She reached into the box and
grabbed another handful of crackers, discarding any that were
slightly chipped.

"You must enjoy doing some things together. After all, you did
take the class as a couple."

She shrugged. "Frank took the class because George asked him
to. At least that's what Frank told me. I took the class because . . ."
She paused. "I took it because I enjoy helping others and George
seemed so concerned about having enough students."

"At least it gives you a chance to take a walk in the woods with
your husband once in a while," I said.

"I don't know what you mean."

"Susanne sends you all out scouting for items. Like she did the
other day . . ."

"The day George was killed? Yes, I suppose we were all out getting embellishments for our quilts. I stayed close to the inn. I don't
like to walk too far. Bad knees." She pointed to her knees as if offering some kind of proof. "I have no idea where Frank walked. He isn't
the type to stay by his wife's side."

"So he wasn't with you?"

"As I've said, I don't know who he was with." She picked up the
plate of crackers, which, despite her hard work, slid into a jumble in
the middle of the plate as she lifted it. "People are hungry," she said,
and walked out of the kitchen.

"Interesting," I said to myself.

"What's interesting?" Joi walked in just as the word came out of
my mouth.

"The characters your parents got to take the class. Not one of them is a quilter."

"They all seem to like it now," she said. "I was talking to the neighbor . . ."

"Pete."

"Yes. He said he's enjoyed himself. He thinks it's a wonderful way for a woman to spend her time."

"He said that?" It was almost word for word what George said the day we arrived.

"Strange, when you consider that he took Susanne's class," Joi added. "He's harmless in an old-fashioned sort of way, I suppose. Not like Frank."

I laughed because, for a second, I thought she was kidding. "Frank's not really a modern guy."

She seemed genuinely surprised by my assessment. "He went on and on about how my mother could do anything. Those words exactly. Just because my dad is gone doesn't mean my mother can't do whatever she needs to do. Sweet, really."

"Which kind was George? Old-fashioned or sweet?"

She smiled. "Both, in his own way. He and my mother were business partners, so I suppose he felt there was no such thing as woman's work."

"What business was that?"

Joi ignored my question and instead grabbed a bottle of wine. "I promised my mother I'd bring her a glass."

"You seem to be getting along."

She nodded. "Bernie helped a lot. Talking about my dad helped."

"Maybe she's realizing what you've accomplished by raising your family and running your own business. As you say, your parents did the same, so maybe she appreciates how hard it is for you."

"Maybe."

"But of course yours is not-for-profit," I tried again, "and they were in business to make money. Real estate, right?"

"What does it matter now?"

She left me standing in the kitchen with no wine, no crackers, and lots of questions.

CHAPTER 37

The next morning I got up early and walked through the house. A few remnants of last night's party still remained—paper cups on the dining room table and a bowl of stale chips next to a half-finished bottle of wine. Unlike my grandmother, I thought there was something very loving about throwing George a farewell party. Even though I hadn't known him well, it seemed to me like the sort of thing he would have liked. I could see Eleanor's point about the timing, however. George was still lying in a morgue, and his killer was still on the loose.

I made myself some coffee and was trying to figure out what to do next when my answer came walking into the kitchen.

"You're up early," Bernie said cheerfully, a little too cheerfully.

"Too much on my mind to sleep, I guess."

"You're trying to get me off the hook for George's murder," she said. Then she kissed me on the cheek. "I feel like a weight has been lifted off my shoulders. You really are a good friend."

"You're not."

She seemed stunned. "What did I do?"

"You haven't told me everything. And if I'm going to help you, then you have to tell me everything that has happened between you and George."

She smiled. "He and I knew each other for more than fifty years."

"Not entirely true, Bernie. You knew him almost fifty years ago. A lot has happened to you both since then," I said. "I think you've gotten caught up in some romantic fairy tale, and it's getting you in a lot of trouble. I adore you, you know that, but if you don't start telling the whole truth, I won't be able to help you."

She nodded. "Let's go for a walk."

The woods were even quieter than the house. Bernie linked her arm in mine as we walked. We talked about the fresh country air, the deer that occasionally crossed our path, and the sound of birds chirping in the early spring morning. I knew if I let her direct the conversation, we'd get nowhere.

"McIntyre found blood on one of your blouses," I finally said.

She nodded. "I knew he was searching the room, so I thought if he were any kind of a good investigator he'd find it."

"He's also going to find out whose blood is on it."

"He will," she said calmly.

"Bernie." I stopped and looked at her. "It's George's blood, isn't it?"

"Yes."

"Which brings me to another question."

"I know it does, Nell, but I promise you I did not kill George."

"It doesn't look good. At least it won't to McIntyre."

"I can see that."

She took a deep breath and seemed almost defeated. She found a large rock nearby and sat. I waited because I could see that whatever she was going to tell me was difficult and I knew, whether she did or not, that she would have to tell the story to McIntyre before this mess was behind her.

"I know everyone thinks I'm foolish for believing in my intuition, but I really had a feeling something was wrong with George."

"I guess you were right about that."

"No." She seemed stressed by the idea that she might have predicted George's death. "No, I didn't see him dying. I saw something. I don't know," she said. "It's like the feeling I have, watching you standing against that tree, that you shouldn't go into the woods. I don't think it's safe."

I looked around. "I don't see anything, Bernie."

She threw up her hands as if she were admitting defeat. "I'm sure you think I'm a silly old woman, Nell, and I've certainly given you reason these last few days, but I had no intention of breaking up someone's marriage or getting myself involved with him. I just, well, I just liked that after all these years he was still carrying a torch for me."

"Did he tell you that?"

She smiled, but it was not a happy smile. "No. Quite the opposite. He went on and on about his marriage to Rita," she said. "That day in the kitchen when you thought you walked in on something, George was on the verge of tears, talking about how much he loved her. I didn't quite know what to say to him."

"So why drag you up here? Why drag any of us up here?"

"That was what the picnic was about. He suggested we go for a walk in the woods for that ridiculous picnic." She looked as if she was about to cry. "Don't judge me. I feel foolish enough as it is. I just wanted to know . . . I guess I'd always wanted to know that he made a mistake by choosing Rita, and I thought maybe once we were alone, talking over old times, he'd admit it. Maybe tell me his life had been hard, that he always has to give in to her. She's not a nice woman."

"I've noticed," I said. "I think everyone's noticed."

"Exactly." Bernie's voice got louder. "I swear to you that if he had told me he'd made a mistake, I would have told him about Johnny, about how happy our marriage was, how close I am to my children and grandchildren, how good my life is. I would have hit him with all of it. I wanted to make him feel like a fool." She started laughing a sad, hollow laugh.

"It didn't happen that way?"

"No. Not at all. He told me that he wanted to be friends again. Me, him, and Rita. The three of us. After all these years, after everything." She stood up. "I was so upset; I just got up and walked away. And that was the last time I ever spoke to him."

I walked over to her and took her hand. As gently as I could, I asked a question. "How did you get the blood on your blouse?"

"As foolish as I felt for having believed that George still cared for me after all these years, I felt even more foolish for having stormed off. It was exactly what I'd done forty-five years ago, only then I didn't give him a chance to explain," she told me. "The more I walked around, the more I thought that with age comes wisdom or at least the realization that storming off doesn't solve anything. I went back. At first I couldn't find him. I thought he had gone, but one tree looks just like another. I walked a little farther and I saw him lying on the ground. When I got close, I could see that he'd been shot. I tried to help him, I swear I did, but he was dead."

"But you didn't go for help?"

"I covered him with the quilt. I knew it would get ruined, but it was my quilt. I thought it would. Keep animals away from him. And then I retraced my steps. I was going back to the inn but . . ." She sighed. "I know how this is going to sound, but I got scared. I started to walk in a different direction, and then I got lost. I doubled back to where George was and I saw you and Jesse discover him. I didn't know what was going on. I just ran back to the inn."

"But you didn't call the police. You went to your room, changed clothes, and hid the blouse, didn't you?"

She nodded. "I knew it would look bad, the way I'd been carrying on about him. And since you had already found him, I knew the police would be there right away. I didn't see anything, so I couldn't help the police. It was stupid, Nell, but I just got scared thinking that everyone would assume I'd killed him."

"But, Bernie, we're your friends. We wouldn't have suspected you."

She raised one eyebrow. "You wouldn't have? With the way I've been carrying on? Honestly, Nell, I would think less of you if you hadn't, for at least a moment, considered me a suspect."

I hugged her. "Then you will be happy to know that I did, at least for a moment. But I'll tell you something—Jesse never did. He even suggested McIntyre search your room because he knew whatever he found there wouldn't point to you as a killer."

She smiled her first relaxed smile of the morning. "He's a good judge of character, Jesse. It's probably why he's so fond of you." She pulled back from me. "You believe me now though?"

"One hundred percent," I said.

"So what do we do?"

"We go over the list of suspects, pore over the evidence, find the killer, and go home."

"That should be easy," she said. "Everyone up here seems to be hiding something."

CHAPTER 38

"What have you two been doing?" Eleanor sounded more worried than angry, but I immediately felt in trouble the way I used to as a child when I'd visit her at Someday Quilts and get caught making a mess of her displays.

"We took a walk," I said.

"And had a nice conversation," Bernie added. She rested her head for a moment on my shoulder. "I could use some breakfast. Is anything cooking?"

"The chief of police is what's cooking," Eleanor scolded. "He's in the kitchen and he wants to talk to you, Bernie Avallone. It seems he has something urgent to discuss."

I grabbed Bernie's arm, and we headed into the kitchen together, with Eleanor just steps behind us. Susanne was pouring coffee, and McIntyre was sitting at the kitchen table, chatting with Jesse about the Winston High School baseball team. Whatever urgency he'd felt about talking to Bernie seemed to have been forgotten.

"So you're back." He smiled when he saw us walk in. "I thought you might have skipped town."

"We have no reason to skip town," I said, still holding Bernie's arm.

"I'm sure you don't, ladies. I just need to talk to Mrs. Avallone." He nodded toward Bernie, who was shaking.

"I haven't done anything," she said quietly.

"I still need to talk to you. Alone." There was a no-nonsense quality to McIntyre's voice that I recognized as the same cop tone Jesse would use whenever he wanted to convey that, although we were friends, he was the law.

Bernie looked to me, and I smiled sympathetically but I didn't see anyway out. Susanne, on the other hand, wasn't having it. She stepped between Bernie and McIntyre.

"Let me tell you something," she said. "Bernie is one of the finest people I know. She not only would never hurt anyone, she would— and she has—gone out of her way to be there for her friends."

"As I imagine they would for her," McIntyre said.

Susanne looked on the verge of either crying or yelling but she did neither. "We're not protecting her. We don't have to. She's a good person who does the right thing. In fact, the only reason she came up here is because that man, George, asked her to."

I waited and prayed that McIntyre didn't make the connection, but it took him only seconds.

"When did George Olnhausen ask you to come up here?" McIntyre turned to Bernie.

"He called me a few days before we came," Bernie stammered.

"Didn't you tell me that the first time the two of you had spoken in more than forty years was when you arrived up here a few days ago?"

Out of the corner of my eye I saw Susanne turn white.

"I just meant . . . ," Bernie started but gave up.

"She was trying to protect Rita from finding out that her husband had looked up an old girlfriend," I said. "Her daughter told me that Rita was the jealous type. She went crazy if another woman even looked at her husband."

"I thought Mrs. Avallone didn't care much for Rita Olnhausen," McIntyre said to me. "I can't imagine why she would try to protect a person she didn't even like."

"Well, then you don't know Bernie. You don't know the kinds of things she would do," Susanne sputtered.

"No, ma'am, I don't. But I'm going to find out."

"Chief, far be it from me to tell you how to do your job, but you're making a mistake you will regret," Eleanor said. "I think that a competent lawman could see that Bernie is just the victim of unfortunate timing. It can't be her fault that someone decided to kill that man the same week she was here."

"I understand your frustration, ma'am." McIntyre leaned forward in his chair. "I believe all of you that Mrs. Avallone is a good person and a good friend. I think you can tell a lot about a person by the company they keep, and this is some of the finest company I've seen in a long time. On the other hand . . ."

"There is no other hand." My grandmother looked about ready to pounce on the police chief, who sat just a few feet away. To his credit he looked mildly embarrassed for having caused such a fuss.

I saw Jesse look over at Eleanor and smile sadly. She seemed to understand that he was telling her it was best to stop arguing and to let the police chief have his way. She backed up a few inches and leaned against the kitchen counter, seeming to accept, as we all had to, what was about to happen.

McIntyre got up. "Mrs. Avallone, I need you to come into town with me."

"Why?" Bernie asked.

Jesse shook his head at her. "He has questions," he said quietly.

"You can ask the questions here," I said, in a last-ditch effort to stop things from going further.

"If it's about the blood on my blouse, I can explain," Bernie said.

"Yes, ma'am, it is. And a few other things," McIntyre told her. "If you don't mind, I'll drive you to the station myself."

"Are you arresting her?" I asked.

"Not right now." He turned toward Bernie, blocking me. "If you don't mind, ma'am."

"I'll get my purse," Bernie said meekly, and disappeared out of the room.

McIntyre walked over to me. "I'm just going where the evidence takes me," he said almost apologetically. "You can call over to the station in a couple of hours, and I'll let you know what the next step will be."

"She didn't do it."

"I'm aware that you all think so," he said, and walked out of the kitchen.

We were all silent for a minute until Susanne said quietly, "Bernie told me about the call last night. She said she had talked to you about it, Nell."

"She did."

"She said she wanted to be honest about everything. I just assumed she told him the truth about talking to George."

"Of course you did, dear," Eleanor said. "She'll clear it up. Not to worry."

"We need to help Bernie," I said, stating what everyone was obviously thinking.

"How do we do that?" Susanne asked. "I'll do anything to help Bernie. I really will."

Tears started rolling down her face, leaving us all to assure her, again, that Bernie had gotten herself into this mess by lying to McIntyre in the first place.

Jesse got up. "I think we could all use a cup of tea," he said. I watched him squeeze Eleanor's hand. "And then we need to put our heads together and come up with a strategy and perhaps the name of a good lawyer."

I turned to him. "What other things? McIntyre said he wanted to talk about the blood and other things."

"A witness. I don't know who."

"A witness to what?" Eleanor moved past me and was practically on top of Jesse.

"I don't know exactly," Jesse admitted, "but I assume he means a witness to the murder."

CHAPTER 39

There was nothing that could be done in town. That was what everyone said. I fought it and lost. Standing outside the police station wouldn't help. Eleanor kept saying that the truth was the most direct way out of this mess.

"Then what do we do?" I asked.

"We find the killer," Jesse said.

"Who do we think it is?" Eleanor asked. "Could it be a stranger?"

"If it's a stranger, then we're cooked," I admitted. "But this place isn't easy to get to from town. There's only one road leading here and a car would have passed by the inn."

"What about a hiker?" Susanne asked.

"No one from outside this inn could have known George was going to be in the woods that day," Jesse told her. "And McIntyre has said, and I agree, that given George's height, the shooting wasn't in error. George even had his wallet on him, so it wasn't a robbery. I really think it was someone here."

"That leaves Rita, the students in Susanne's class, or one of us," I added.

"I think we can safely eliminate us," Eleanor scolded me.

"I'm just trying to think like McIntyre," I said.

"Then what would he do?" Susanne asked.

"What he has been doing—talking to each of the students alone," I said. "It's what we have to do. Problem is, with the class canceled and the main floor pretty much cleaned and painted, I don't think any of them will be back."

"So we have to go to them or get them back." Jesse finished my thought.

I was frustrated and scared. I kept thinking that Bernie was at the police station explaining her psychic gifts and her belief that George had been pining for her. I could only imagine how that would go over with a man like Chief McIntyre.

Susanne seemed past her frustration and excited about a new idea. "I'll call each of them and suggest we work on a group quilt, something that can be used at George's funeral," she said. "I'll tell them it's a tradition among quilters."

"It is?" Jesse asked, surprised.

"It was, and they wouldn't know if it weren't. Women have often made quilts using pieces of the deceased's clothing as a way to preserve their memory or draped their coffin with a favorite quilt. And in pioneer times, sometimes when a woman was mourning a lost child, or husband, other women would bring her fabric to piece as a way of occupying her thoughts while she grieved."

"It hasn't been done too often in the last century, except maybe in the AIDS quilt," my grandmother added. "Though it's a nice idea."

"We'll get them back in the classroom and start talking about George and see if it leads us to our killer," Susanne said.

She looked to me for approval. "I like it," I said. "But I don't think our killer is just going to announce himself."

Susanne looked at me with confidence. "Leave it to me."

"That leaves Rita and Joi," Eleanor said. "We can hardly ask them to work on the quilt."

Under normal circumstances she was right. But these weren't normal circumstances. We were desperate. "Why not?" I asked. But I didn't wait for an answer.

I took the steps up to the third floor two at a time. I was determined to come up with a reason why Rita should join us by the time I reached her door. But I didn't have to. Just as I was about to knock, Joi surprised me by opening the door to Rita's suite.

As soon as she did, my determination left me and I felt, suddenly, that my suggestion was out of line. "I'm coming to see if you want any breakfast," I said instead.

"My mother's not hungry right now, but I guess I should come down and get something."

"I also wanted to let you know that we're asking the students to help us make a memorial quilt for the funeral. The class and this inn were George's dream, and we thought . . ." I was scrambling.

I felt bad that my words made Joi cry, not just because I'd made her cry—I assumed that, given the situation, she was crying a lot these days—but because my words were insincere. We weren't honoring her dad. We were trying to reveal the killer, even if that person was her mother.

Joi finally composed herself. "I can't think of anything nicer. It's really one of the reasons I quilt. It's such a caring community, you know? And to think after all the neighbors have done for my mother, to do something so personal . . ." She couldn't continue.

An hour later the students were back in the classroom, ready to help with this latest project. On the first day they'd held back, having been pushed or persuaded or forced to take a class they didn't want to take.

Now they were excited. Pete and the twins were helping one another pick out fabrics. Frank was telling stories about George, to help those of us who didn't know him well. Even Helen, who had been so against continuing the class after George's death, was enthusiastic about our latest endeavor. But this, as she pointed out, wasn't for entertainment. It was to help others. And that made it okay. Though neither Joi nor Rita had joined us yet, we were all anxious to get started.

"So this is a tradition?" Pete asked "I think that's nice."

"It's a lovely one," one of the twins said. "We were going to suggest it but didn't think it was our place."

Susanne nodded. "Jesse and Eleanor are joining us. We're lucky to have Eleanor since she's so experienced. And Jesse . . ."

"Has no idea what he's doing," Jesse finished for her.

Frank laughed. "You've been sucked in like the rest of us. But you'll like it."

Helen sighed at her husband's words in a manner that was nearly impossible to ignore, but Frank seemed to manage it.

"What do we do, boss?" Pete asked.

I could see that Susanne was thinking. "We'll each make a block," she said finally. "Sort of a journal quilt. We'll each draw or piece or embellish a swatch of fabric in a way that reminds us of George. When we're done, we'll sew the blocks together."

The students needed no further explanation. They each picked up a square of black flannel and began sorting through fabrics. I watched as Jesse positioned himself near Pete, my grandmother stood between Frank and Helen, and I took the twins.

"I'm not sure what to do," I said honestly. "I barely knew him."

One of the twins was sketching the inn onto a piece of muslin. She looked up at me, wrinkling her nose. Her hair covered her earrings, so I couldn't use Susanne's method of identification. Instead I guessed.

"Alysse, you must have the same problem."

She nodded. I'd guessed right. "It is hard to think of what represents him. I'm going to do the inn. I understand this place was his dream."

"That's an amazing idea." I glanced at her sketch again and marveled at her accuracy. "You're quite an artist," I said. "I don't think I could do as good a job of getting the inn right even if I were looking at it while I sketched."

She blushed. "I have a good memory, I suppose."

"That might come in handy. Especially if you remember anything that happened on the day of the murder. Maybe you were in the woods . . ."

"I wasn't." Her response was quick. "I stayed near the classroom. So did my sister."

Alice leaned in. She had been paying close attention to my conversation with Alysse.

"That's true," she said. "We spent the whole afternoon together. We spend most of our time together."

"So you might have both seen something."

They looked at each other and then at me, but neither of them said anything.

"So you don't remember anything? Anything that might help the police?"

"You're worried about your friend, Bernie," Alice said. "I heard McIntyre arrested her."

"Not arrested. Questioned. He asked her to go to the station for questioning."

"Of course." Alysse glared at her sister. "We don't like to gossip, as it causes pain. We're very good at keeping confidences."

"But if those confidences could lead to the killer."

"They couldn't."

"So you saw nothing?" I tried again. I was going around in circles.

Alysse and Alice exchanged glances; then Alysse nodded. Alice whispered to me, "We saw Helen go into the woods."

"It was either the day of the murder or the day after. We can't remember. There was so much going on."

"She said she couldn't walk into the woods," I said. "She said she had bad knees."

Alysse shrugged an "I don't care if you believe me" shrug. "She was a little slow. Maybe she was in pain. But she walked into those woods. I'd swear to it."

"Did you tell McIntyre?"

The sisters shook their heads in unison. "We don't like to gossip and we don't know if it means anything," Alysse said.

I let them get back to their quilts and looked around the room. Jesse nodded to me as if he had learned something. Then Eleanor did the same thing. I looked toward Susanne and she looked back at me, smiling.

I wondered if it was possible that we had found the killer that easily.

CHAPTER 40

We hadn't.

When we broke for lunch, we walked together to the inn. Everyone was feeling excited about their small part in George's memorial quilt, and the creativity of it had boosted everyone's mood. But when we walked in, Joi and Rita were waiting in the dining room.

"I didn't think I had much to offer, sewing-wise," Rita said. "But I have this."

She pulled a deep blue men's shirt out of a bag and handed it to Susanne. "This was George's favorite shirt. I bought it for him in London, and he wore it out but he never wanted to get rid of it. Joi tells me that memorial quilts often contain the clothing of the person, the deceased. Maybe you can use this."

Susanne was holding back tears, as we all were. I could see that I wasn't the only one who felt guilty, at least for the moment, for thinking that Rita had murdered George.

"It's very kind of you to offer it," Susanne said. "I hope we're not upsetting you or your daughter by making this quilt."

Rita waved off the suggestion. "George would have been surprised to see so many people interested in honoring him. He didn't have much faith in people."

Joi put her arm around her mother. Looking at the two of them, it seemed as if the reunion had succeeded. Whatever rancor had existed between them seemed to have completely disappeared, and there was nothing but love there now.

"I should put together some lunch," Helen said, and headed toward the kitchen, with the twins following closely behind.

I saw one of the sisters nudge the other one, but her twin shook it off. Frank and Pete went outside to see if they could assess what work might be needed on the exterior of the house, while my group made a not-too-subtle run for my bedroom. Only Susanne had the good sense, and manners, to stay talking with Rita and Joi. I squeezed Susanne's hand, and she nodded in understanding. But then she glared at me, making clear that if any discussion about our suspects started without her, there would be another murder on the property.

✂

When I got up to the room, I realized that no one else was willing to wait.

"I suspect all of them," Eleanor announced as I walked in the door.

"They didn't all do it," Jesse pointed out. "We have to find the right one."

"Let's take them one at a time. Or in my case, two." I told everyone about my conversation with the twins.

"They could be lying," Eleanor suggested. "Trying to set Helen up."

"But what would be their motive?" Jesse asked.

"I don't know, but they've lied about how they know Rita and George," I said.

"Has anyone asked Rita how she knows them?" Susanne asked as she walked in.

It was so obvious, so simple, that it hadn't occurred to me. "I will, right after lunch," I said. I turned to Eleanor. "Why don't you like any of them?"

"You can tell a lot about a person by the way they express themselves in their art," she said. "Helen's quilt was careful, well-thought out, very structured."

"A little controlling," Susanne offered.

"Exactly. If she's our killer, it was planned. Her husband, on the other hand . . ."

"Is too hot tempered to plan a killing," Jesse finished the thought, "which means that if he killed George, it was probably a spontaneous act."

"Everything about that mess of a quilt he is making seems to suggest spontaneity to the point of recklessness," Eleanor agreed.

"He seems very fond of Rita," I pointed out.

"She seems fond of him." Susanne waited for a moment before she continued. "When I was chatting with Rita and Joi, Frank came into the room with a cup of tea for her. He didn't say anything in particular, just asked how she was. But there was a look between them."

"I wonder where she was when George was killed," Eleanor said. "I just don't see how we can reasonably ask her."

"We'll have to find a way," I said. I turned to Jesse. "What about Pete? You were standing next to him."

He shrugged. "I didn't get much from him. He's always very nice. Maybe too nice."

Considering the source, I had to laugh.

We couldn't spend the whole lunch hour in my room. It would look too odd. Besides, I was hungry. Susanne went down first, Jesse followed, then Eleanor, and finally me. As I passed the dining room, I saw Rita still sitting there but Joi wasn't around.

"Are you okay?"

Rita looked up. She seemed tired. "Fine," she said. "They're making lunch. Joi is getting me something. She insists that I eat."

I sat next to her. I wanted to ask her about the day of the murder without seeming to ask her about it. I wasn't thrilled with myself that I was thinking of the investigation when Rita seemed so alone, but I had to think of Bernie.

"You were so in love," I started, as gently as I could. "It must have been a terrible shock."

"It wasn't the way I thought things would turn out."

"Did you get the news from McIntyre?"

She hesitated but then nodded. "I was upstairs, resting. George was so helpful to me. He adored me."

I took a deep breath but plunged in anyway. "I happened to be looking in the window that morning and it seemed as if you were having a fight."

Nothing. Not a smile, not an angry look. She just stared ahead. "We weren't," she said firmly.

Just as she finished speaking, Joi walked into the room with a plate of food. "There are cold cuts in the kitchen if you're hungry, Nell," she said, an unmistakable look of suspicion in her eyes.

"I was just keeping your mom company," I offered.

Surprisingly Rita looked up at her daughter and nodded. "It's amazing to see how many people are worried about me."

Once in the kitchen, I grabbed a sandwich and Jesse. "I really think we should go check on Bernie. He's had her all morning."

"We can ask, but he's probably not going to tell us anything."

"But we can ask," I said insistently.

"Not every cop is as weak willed as I am, giving you information every time you bat your eyelashes."

I batted my eyelashes.

He rolled his eyes but he was smiling. "He'll probably show you everything he has in the case file."

CHAPTER 41

Jesse was right. McIntyre wouldn't let us see Bernie. He did tell us that Maria had brought bread and chicken salad over from the bakery, as well as two large double-chocolate brownies, so even though she was being held, Bernie was well fed. That was beside the point, I told myself. I wanted my friend to be released.

"We got the autopsy reports on George and the dog," McIntyre added, I think to distract me from my insistence on seeing Bernie.

"You did an autopsy on the dog?" I wasn't sure I'd heard correctly.

"We're not so interested in what caused the dog's death," McIntyre smiled, "but whether there is evidence in him that might aid the investigation into George Olnhausen's death."

"What did you find?" Jesse asked.

"What we assumed. George was shot right through the heart with a hunting rifle. Probably died instantly."

"And the dog?"

"Pretty much the same thing with the dog. I mean, not through the heart but dead-on."

"With George, how far away was the gun?"

"The medical examiner said it was intermediate range, on account of the powder stippling on the skin."

"Which means?" I asked.

"The gun wasn't up against George, but it was less than a yard or two away," Jesse said. "It left abrasions caused by unburned grains of powder hitting the skin."

"No way any of it could be an accident?" I asked.

"None. Standing that close, you know what you're aiming at."

"And the bullets?" Jesse asked. "Were they the same for George and the dog?"

McIntyre nodded. "A match. The gun that killed the dog was used to kill George."

Jesse looked over to me. "Nell figured as much," he said.

"Then why are you holding Bernie?" I asked. "That dog was dead before we got here. You can't possibly be thinking Bernie had motive to kill it."

"Doesn't mean that she didn't use the same gun," McIntyre said. Then he held up his hand as I opened my mouth. "I know what you're going to say—that it's a bit far-fetched. And maybe it is, maybe it isn't. But I am going to investigate this my way."

"Meanwhile the real killer is wandering through your town," I pointed out.

I could see Jesse shaking his head at me but I didn't pay attention. If cops don't want their mistakes pointed out to them, then they shouldn't make them in front of me. McIntyre didn't take offense. He just smiled. He was in the driver's seat and I was only an annoying backseat driver.

"By the way," McIntyre said, "we got the result for your lemonade. A mild liquid sedative, that's all. Nothing that could have done you any harm."

"Just put me to sleep."

"It can't have anything to do with the case," he added, "because . . ." Then he closed his mouth and turned toward the holding cell.

"Because Bernie didn't do it?" I asked. "You can't dismiss something like that so easily."

"She's right, Chief. If that's all you have . . . ," Jesse started; then he paused and I could see his expression grow serious. "Unless your witness told you something."

"I'll drive Mrs. Avallone back to the inn when she and I are done talking. Won't be long now." He paused and looked at us. "I do appreciate the advice though. It's nice when we're all working together."

It seemed we were pretty much at an impasse, but I was heartened to know that the killer had used the same gun for the dog. It had to be someone from the area, and if the gun was the one that had been above the mantle at the Patchwork Bed-and-Breakfast, it had to be someone with access to the house in the last few days. That removed any possibility of a stranger and meant that, in all likelihood, our killer was back at the inn making a memorial quilt.

✂

"If someone is saying that they saw Bernie kill George, then that person is lying," I said to Jesse as we walked out of the police station. "And if we get the name of that person, then we have our killer."

"Assuming that's what the witness is saying. Maybe they saw Bernie with George earlier or saw her walking from the woods with blood on her blouse. There's something nagging at McIntyre or else he would have let Bernie go."

"But if Bernie told him the truth—" I stopped.

Jesse was about to open the car door but looked up at me instead. "You don't think Bernie is telling him the truth."

"Shh."

"Why?"

"Shh," I said again. This time I said it louder, which made the whole point of shushing him seem kind of silly.

"Nell." Jesse tried, and failed, to get my attention. It was elsewhere.

I watched as a familiar figure walked across the street and in the direction of the office building Rita had visited just two days before. When I was sure it wouldn't look too conspicuous, I grabbed Jesse's hand and pulled him toward the building.

"What are we doing?" Jesse whispered to me.

"Following that man," I said. "That's the man I saw with Rita when I drove her to town."

He entered the office building, and so did we, about ten feet behind him. The elevator doors were about to close, but the man saw us and pressed the Open button. We jumped in and stood there, not sure what to do next.

"What floor?" he asked.

I saw that the button for the sixth floor was lit so I said, "Six."

"I guess we're all going there." He smiled the bland smile strangers give each other in polite but disinterested acknowledgement. He was a nice-looking man, well dressed and neat. He looked like he took good care of himself. I could see Rita being attracted to him, if indeed she was. For all I knew, he could be her bookie.

When he saw me glancing at him, he nodded. I nodded. Jesse nodded. Then we waited. It seemed to take an inordinately long time to reach the sixth floor, but when we did, I still hadn't come up with a plan. The man gestured to let us off first, an unfortunate situation since it meant we would have to find somewhere to go. Thankfully, Jesse's shoelace had become untied, so he stopped just outside the elevator to tie it. The man walked down the hall and into the last office on the left.

"Did you see which office he went into?" Jesse asked me when he was done with his shoe.

Then it hit me. "You did that on purpose. You stepped on your lace and untied it." I looked down at his gym shoes.

He smiled, clearly enjoying how impressed I was. "Let's find out who he is."

CHAPTER 42

W e walked quickly toward the last office on the left. It had a light wood door with JASON NOREIKA, MD, stenciled on it.

"We can go to the library and look him up on the Internet, find out more about him," Jesse suggested.

"Or we just go in and ask. That way we can find out how he knows Rita."

"We have no jurisdiction. We can't just ask for a list of the man's patients, or his lovers."

"Why not?"

I opened the door and walked into a small, neatly decorated office with about a half dozen padded chairs in its waiting room, a few generic paintings of flowers on the walls, and a small nurse's station up front. Jesse was two steps behind me but was clearly letting me take the lead.

"Can I help you?" the nurse asked.

I looked around for something that might be helpful. Nothing.

"I'm here to see Dr. Noreika. I understand he's a wonderful dentist." I took a stab at it but figured I was wrong.

"Are you sure you're in the right office?"

"Dr. Noreika. Jason Noreika. This is his office?"

"He's not a dentist. He's a cardiologist," she said.

"Oh." I turned to Jesse. "Honey, I must have written the wrong name down."

"You must have," he said, an amused expression crossing his face.

I turned back to the nurse. "Rita Olnhausen recommended him."

"Mrs. Olnhausen? She told you he was a dentist?"

"Maybe I confused her dentist with her cardiologist. She is Dr. Noreika's patient, right?"

"We don't give out that information."

"Of course not. She did say his staff was very discreet. In fact, she's had nothing but the nicest things to say about all of you. You're Karen," I said, reading it off her name tag. "She told me you've been so kind."

I was running out of things to say so I paused, hoping the nurse would jump in. Thankfully, she did.

She smiled. "That's nice to hear. I try to give our patients the best care possible. Especially patients like Mrs. Olnhausen."

I leaned in. "Especially now," I said in a dramatic whisper.

The nurse gave me a knowing smile. "It's just so sad. Her husband passing like that. So . . ." I watched her struggling for the right word until I couldn't take it anymore.

"Suddenly," I said to finish her thought.

She nodded. "They were so in love. Please make sure she's taking care of herself. She's so delicate, poor thing."

The door to the office opened and a heavyset man walked in. "Mr. Walker," the nurse said, "the doctor will be with you in a minute."

It was our cue to leave. We hadn't solved the murder, but I felt that at least one mystery was unraveling. And maybe that would lead to the rest.

✄

"You don't know that it means anything," Jesse cautioned as we drove back to the inn.

"She has a cardiologist," I said it louder, as if that made it more important.

"So she has high blood pressure or an irregular heartbeat."

"It means something. I have a feeling." As I spoke I realized I probably sounded a lot like Bernie, talking about her psychic gifts, and if I did, then Jesse would take me as seriously as I took Bernie.

"Lots of people see cardiologists. I'm going to need one too, if I keep hanging out with you." He laughed, but he could see that I did not find any humor in the situation. His tone softened. "Nell, not everything means something. You're going to find, if you keeping sticking your nose where it doesn't belong, that lots of leads go absolutely nowhere. And this is probably one of them."

"But she lied about it."

"She didn't lie about it. She just didn't tell you where she was going."

"But why not tell me? Especially when she insisted I drive her to town. Why not just say she had a doctor's appointment? By going out of her way *not* to tell me, she made it a bigger deal than a simple check-up. Which means it was a big deal.

"Maybe she's cautious."

I sneered at him for effect. It was fun to talk over the clues with Jesse, even if he didn't think they were actually clues. "She had me drop her off at the police station, and then she walked back. She didn't even want me to see what building she walked into. That's not cautious. It's hiding something."

"So she's private."

"It's more than that. It is. Trust me."

He reached his hand across to my leg and gave it a quick squeeze. "I do."

And just for good measure, I added, "And I'm not sticking my nose where it doesn't belong. I'm helping a friend."

He nodded. "She's lucky to have you." For a second I felt that I'd won, but he wouldn't let me. "And you are sticking your very cute nose where it doesn't really belong."

"Well, then so are you."

"I got in with the wrong crowd." He sighed dramatically. "Quilters."

CHAPTER 43

When we got back to the inn, we didn't have time to tell the others about our news. Shouting was coming from inside the classroom and the sound of furniture being moved or, possibly, thrown. Jesse jumped out of the car and ran inside, with me right behind him.

Frank had apparently just punched Pete in the nose, and Eleanor was standing in front of Pete so he didn't hit back. Helen was crying, Susanne was trying to calm everyone down, and the twins were standing to the side with smug looks on their faces.

"What is going on here?" Jesse shouted as he walked in the classroom.

"We're just clearing the air," Pete said.

"Well, clear it with a little less violence." Jesse grabbed Frank's arm just as he was about to swing it.

"If McIntyre hasn't deputized you, then stay out of it," Frank yelled at him.

"What happened?" I asked, but no one was paying attention to me.

Pete tried to move around Eleanor but couldn't do it. "Stop it, now," she said. "You need to let it go."

"Please!" Susanne's voice was straining. She looked stricken and hurt. "This is a quilt class."

"He is not a man of honor," Frank shouted.

"You're not even a man," Pete spit back.

"You killed my dog," Frank yelled back.

"I did not."

"Why else would he have been buried on your land?"

"Why would I kill your dog? You're the one that's always hunting on my property. You probably shot the dumb thing yourself."

Frank kicked at Jesse to get away, and nearly did it, but Jesse wrapped his arm around Frank's neck, pulling him back and subduing him. It would have been an impressive feat, except Jesse was thirty years younger than Frank. Eleanor was more inspiring. Pete was a large man at least ten years younger than she, but she was not about to let him get around her. After a few minutes of standoff, we were all getting a little tired, and I figured it was about to blow over; then Pete made one more attempt to break free.

He darted around Eleanor and made a grab for Frank, who kicked at him. I ran between the two men, which was a little stupid since Jesse stepped on my foot as he tried to move Frank farther back.

I turned to Helen. "Can't you tell your husband to stop?"

She wiped her tears away. "Stop, Frank. You look foolish," she said flatly, as if she knew her words would have no impact.

And she was right. Frank pulled and pushed at Jesse, while Pete was barely being held back by my grandmother. Susanne and the twins seemed to have given up and were just watching to see what happened next.

"Someone's going to end up in the hospital," I said to them. "And it may well be Jesse and Eleanor."

At that my grandmother put one hand on Pete's chest, the other on Frank's. "That's enough!" Eleanor shouted in her sternest grandmother voice. "I am ashamed of both of you. I really am."

Frank took one last kick in Pete's direction, but Jesse had moved him out of striking distance. Pete grunted for a moment more, but the fight was losing steam. Eleanor looked from one man to the other, with a withering gaze that suggested they were sad excuses for human beings. It had been aimed at me a few times, deservedly so, and I'd promised myself I would learn it. No one was immune to its effects, not even these two. Eventually both men relaxed their stances, and Jesse cautiously let Frank go.

Pete looked to my grandmother and said quietly, "I'm sorry. Got out of hand, that's all."

We all looked to Frank and waited. I was sure he would bolt without saying a word, but he nodded. "It's been a tough few days," he said. He reached down to the floor and picked up a set of keys that had fallen out of his pocket.

"Then shake hands." If I knew Eleanor, she would not be satisfied until they'd agreed to play nice and share their toys.

We all watched and waited. I could see Jesse ready to grab Frank again if it became necessary, but amazingly, after a few grumbles and a little hesitation, the men shook hands.

As the ruckus died down, Helen cleared her workspace, put her quilt to the side, and said something about needing to get home. The twins put their found objects in plastic bags, folded up their fabrics, and also started for the exit.

"Remember, tomorrow is our last day," Susanne said. "We need to finish our squares and sew them together to present to Rita. So, please, let's try to remember why we're doing this."

Pete and Frank stood at the door, but Frank stepped aside and let Pete pass. Helen rolled her eyes at her husband, glanced quickly toward the rest of us, and left. The twins simply left without saying a word. Minutes after the fight, only our group was left, staring at each other, mystified but relieved.

"So who is going to tell us what happened?" Jesse asked.

CHAPTER 44

"It was the craziest thing," Eleanor started. "We were all making our quilts and chatting."

"I finally felt like I was teaching this retreat for a reason," Susanne said. "You know, that it was finally something more than as a ruse to get Bernie up here. I felt like everyone was working together on a common cause."

"It's a wonderful class, Susanne," Eleanor told her. "You can see that everyone is very involved in what they are making. You'll have to put together something like it at the shop. I think my customers would really enjoy making a journal quilt. They're all the rage at shows these days."

"I would love to, Eleanor. Maybe once a week."

"You would get a lot of interest," Eleanor said. "It could be an on-going thing. I know I would take it and I'm sure Carrie and Natalie would too. Wouldn't it be wonderful for her to make a few journal quilts for a happy occasion, like the new baby?"

Eleanor and Susanne began to talk excitedly about all the pos-sibilities for journal quilts, and how the class could attract new stu-dents who wanted to make an art quilt but were too intimidated to take on a large project. Jesse shot me a look, and I could tell that he was about to burst out laughing. Quilting always came first with this crowd, ahead of fistfights and murder investigations.

"So, if we have the upcoming Someday Quilts class schedule figured out," I said, fighting back the giggles myself, "maybe you guys can tell us how this bar fight broke out in a quilt class?"

They looked at each other, confused, and then Eleanor stepped forward.

"It was odd. About twenty minutes ago, Rita and Joi popped in with some items that belonged to George. I said something to Helen about how nice it must be for Rita to have her daughter around because she seemed to depend so much on George and might be lost without him."

"It was an innocent enough thing to say," Susanne interjected. "But Helen took it as some kind of insult. She said something about George having given his life to that woman . . ."

"Which made Frank snap at her." Eleanor took back the story. "And then Pete told Frank not to yell at Helen, and Frank said he could talk to his wife any way he liked, which made Helen cry."

"And that's what they fought over?" I asked.

"Not exactly," Eleanor said. "Pete said a real man doesn't make a public spectacle of his marriage, and Frank said Pete was hardly an expert since his wife was so miserable that she left."

"He didn't say exactly that," Susanne stopped her. "He said, 'If anyone knows how miserable your wife was, it's me.'"

"Then Pete swung at Frank, Frank swung at Pete," Eleanor added, "and that's where you came in."

"The way you guys held them back was pretty impressive," I said.

Eleanor shook off the compliment. "Children. That's what they were. Overgrown children."

"True," Jesse said, "it's not what you expect to see in middle-aged men."

"From the first day, they made it pretty clear that they didn't like each other," I said. "Maybe, after five days in the same room, it had to come to blows."

"But over Helen?" Susanne shook her head. "How many men does that woman have?"

"More than she needs, apparently," my grandmother said, and bent down and started picking up the pieces of fabric and embellishments that had fallen on the floor. There were quite a lot, so we all pitched in and tried to straighten the mess out.

"What did Rita bring of George's?" I asked as we were making piles.

"A pin from a Grateful Dead concert, a few mementos from their trips, a pair of cuff links with stars on them, and some ribbons he'd won in high school track," Susanne told me.

I found the ribbons, the pin, and several items that seemed to come from exotic locales. But I couldn't find the cuff links.

"They have to be here," Eleanor said. "They just got knocked off the table."

Even though we had already cleaned the room, the four of us searched again. We found dust and spiders but no cuff links.

"We can't tell Rita we lost something precious of her husband's!" Susanne sounded alarmed. "We have to find them."

"A lot of things have gone missing here," I pointed out. "Have you noticed? The old quilts, the collage . . ."

Susanne nodded. "But some of them came back. Like my postcards."

"These will too." Eleanor wrapped her arm around Susanne's shoulders. "We'll find them."

For another hour we searched the classroom and the area around it, with no luck. Since there was nothing we could do, Jesse and I left the others and walked outside to look at the setting sun. The sky was a wonderful soft blue streaked with just a touch of pink, and I thought that I should learn to hand dye my own fabrics so I could re-create the effect for a quilt, maybe one that represented the growing closeness between Jesse and me.

Soon Eleanor and Susanne admitted defeat and headed toward the inn. Jesse and I decided to take a walk. It might have turned into a romantic evening stroll, but moments later Barney came bounding out of the inn, running in circles and dragging his leash behind him.

"He's been cooped up all day," Eleanor shouted to us. "Take him for a walk."

Instead of letting him head toward the woods, Jesse and I, after considerable persuasion and numerous tugs on his leash, got him to walk in the direction of the dirt road that leads from the inn to the larger road into town.

"Plenty of things to sniff here, my friend," I said to him.

Barney was unconvinced and would only halfheartedly direct his nose toward a flower or the base of a tree before walking on, head hung low. It was unlike Barney to complain—he was always happy simply to be included—and I could tell Jesse was softening to the idea of letting Barney have his own way.

"What's the big deal with the woods?" Jesse asked.

"I don't want some hunter mistaking him for a deer," I explained. "And I especially don't want to risk him digging up another dog."

I tried to boost Barney's excitement with a round of "Get Jesse!" but after one attempt, he lost interest. We walked a little farther, but Barney kept veering off the road and into a ditch that ran alongside and led to a small creek. Eventually we gave up trying to pull him back and just followed him. At one point I was explaining to Jesse that I thought Joi's reunion with her mother had gone a little too smoothly, and he was accusing me of finding suspicious behavior in everyone, when I noticed that he had slipped his hand into mine. It was nice, and I hoped Barney wouldn't suddenly want to head back to the inn and spoil it.

But only a few steps later, something else did. Jesse saw it first, something stuck in the mud between the grass and the creek. He dug for a moment before uncovering a rifle.

"Do you think it's the murder weapon?" I asked.

"Probably not. But it might be loaded, and that's dangerous. Let's go back to the inn and call McIntyre. He can come and properly catalogue it."

"Can't we just check it?"

Jesse turned toward me. "Assuming for a second that our touching this gun wouldn't contaminate possible evidence of a homicide, if you got a better look would you even recognize it as the gun from above the mantle?"

I had to admit that I wouldn't. I grabbed Barney by the collar and pulled him back toward the road and the inn. It was further proof, I hoped, that Bernie wasn't involved, though I wasn't yet sure how it would prove it. I just felt that since the gun was disposed of on the road that led away from the inn and toward town, it was probably stashed there by one of the students who drove past the spot on their way to and from class, which meant Helen, Frank, or the twins.

I was pretty sure McIntyre was thinking the same thing when he arrived, with Bernie in the passenger seat. That is, until I saw Bernie. She looked exhausted, but more than anything she looked scared.

Whatever happened in that police station, it hadn't been enough to get Bernie off the hook.

CHAPTER 45

While McIntyre bagged the gun, Jesse, Bernie, and I waited in the kitchen. Eleanor and Susanne had gone out to dinner, leaving us a note promising to bring back food. The house was almost in darkness when we arrived. Though I assumed Joi and Rita were upstairs, I didn't bother to look. First I wanted to know about the gun.

"I'll run a check on the gun against the bullet we found in George," McIntyre said once he had finished collecting the evidence.

"And you have to find out if it's the gun from above the mantle," I added.

"No, ma'am, that I don't have to do. I know it is."

"Did Rita ID it?" Jesse asked.

McIntyre shook his head. "Didn't need to. I don't know the Olnhausens well, but I had a few dealings with Mr. Gervais, the man who used to own this house. This was his gun."

"You're sure?" Jesse looked at the rifle, wrapped carefully in plastic and tagged with an evidence number and McIntyre's signature.

"A hundred percent. Gervais was a crazy old man. He convinced himself that he had a fortune in the house, and once in a while, when some unlucky soul would wander onto his property, he'd take a shot at him." McIntyre smiled almost nostalgically, as if he were remembering better days. "He never killed anyone or even got close to hitting them. He was a terrible shot." He laughed. "But I took this gun away from him about five times. I'd recognize it anywhere."

"I heard about him," I said. "His nephew inherited the place and tore it apart looking for the fortune. I hear he didn't find anything."

McIntyre rolled his eyes. "My guess is that somewhere in the deep recesses of this house is a photo of his first love or a ticket to the world's fair or something that meant everything to Gervais but wouldn't sell on eBay for a nickel."

I tried to get McIntyre to give me the name of the witness, or at least tell me if he was finished questioning Bernie, but all he did was smile that friendly smile and say things like, "I'm just going where the evidence leads me." And after McIntyre left, Bernie retreated to her room and was unwilling to answer any more questions, even from Jesse and me.

"It's just a polite way of saying it's none of your business," Jesse said when I complained about McIntyre.

"I get that. But how can it be none of my business? How am I supposed to solve the case if I don't have all the facts?"

Given the reaction that got from Jesse, I might as well have told the world's funniest joke. When he saw that he was only infuriating me, he laughed harder, then stopped, leaned forward, and kissed me. "We'll get to the truth. But tonight it looks like we have the house to ourselves. Any thoughts on what we might do?"

"Yeah. Let's find Rita and Joi. Her car was in the driveway, so they didn't go anywhere. They must be upstairs."

"You sure that's who you want to spend your evening with?"

"Yeah, I'm sure." I kissed his cheek.

We walked up the three flights of stairs and were almost at the top when Rita's door opened and she and Joi walked out.

"Is something wrong?" Rita asked.

"I just wanted to check on you. To see how you're feeling," I said. That wasn't true, of course. I had a few questions for her—about Bernie, about the twins, and about the last time she saw that gun.

"I'm fine. Joi and I were just chatting." She turned toward her daughter, who nodded in confirmation.

"Bernie's back," I said.

"From where?"

"The police station. McIntyre was questioning her about George's death."

Rita looked confused.

"Hadn't you heard?" Jesse asked. "I thought the others were talking about it today."

She moved her head slowly from side to side. "I wasn't paying attention."

She looked at Joi, who nodded encouragingly at her, as if she were hoping Rita would say or do something. Rita seemed at first to resist; then she took a deep breath, walked passed her daughter, me, and Jesse, and down the stairs. We followed her as she stopped on the second floor and turned toward Bernie's room. I couldn't tell if she was angry, so I wasn't sure if I should stop her. The last thing Bernie needed, after a day with the police, was an angry widow making accusations.

But Rita's knock on Bernie's door was gentle. If she was angry, she was doing a masterful job of hiding it.

Bernie answered the door, buttoning the last button of her pajama top as she did. "Rita. Is everything all right?"

"The police brought you into the station," Rita said matter-of-factly, almost as if Bernie wasn't aware of it.

"McIntyre was trying to clear up a few things."

"He can't possibly think that you had anything to do with it."

"I lied to him about something," Bernie said.

"I know. You lied about George calling you and asking you to come up."

Bernie looked toward me, and I shook my head. She turned back to Rita. "How do you know that?"

"George told me."

I moved toward Rita. "When?"

Rita looked at me. I could tell she was wondering why I felt it was my business, but she answered anyway. "The day he called. At first we thought you would come up to help, like the others, but when Susanne gave him a list of the names, so we could have rooms ready, yours wasn't on it. Then George suggested he just call you directly. I didn't think it was a good idea but he insisted, and George was usually right about these things, so I went along."

"Why did he call Bernie?" I asked.

"He did it for me. I wanted to see her."

"Then why didn't you call me yourself?" Bernie stood back from the door, which Rita, Jesse, Joi, and I took as an invitation to enter. Bernie and Rita sat on the twin beds that were next to each other, Jesse stood near the window, Joi took the only chair, and I leaned against the desk. When everyone was in place, Rita finally answered.

"You wouldn't have talked to me. You've hated me for too many years to accept a call from me."

Bernie didn't say anything, so Rita went on.

"And I really needed to talk to you," she said.

"Because you're sick," I blurted out.

Rita just stared at me. "You are the strangest girl I have ever met," she said. "How do you know something like that?"

"I guessed," I lied. There was no way I was going to reveal how

I found out, and since no one actually told me that Rita was sick, in a sense I was telling the truth. "You're so fragile," I said, instead of going into a longer, and more accurate, explanation.

She nodded and seemed to accept my answer.

"What's wrong with you?" Bernie reached out and took Rita's hand. All the animosity Bernie had felt when we first arrived, only six days ago, seemed to fall away after George died. And now, with this latest news, she'd gone even further, offering compassion and perhaps even friendship. Standing there, I wondered if I had Bernie's capacity for kindness.

"She has a heart condition," Joi said, when Rita didn't answer the question. "I've been begging her to tell you since I found out yesterday."

"It's a minor inconvenience." Rita looked to her daughter, a stern look crossing her face before softening to a smile.

Joi wasn't having it. "She needs a heart transplant, which she's not going to get."

Bernie looked from mother to daughter and back again. "Why not?"

"It's too late, and I don't deserve it. I've not been a good person. If anyone knows that, it's you, Bernie."

Bernie took a deep breath as if she were taking it all in. "Are you on a transplant list?"

"She's not," Joi said strongly. It was clear that she'd had this conversation with her mother, which probably explained why a reunion that began with a flying toaster had turned out so peacefully.

Rita put up her hands as if to stop the discussion. "I don't want to be, and I'm not qualified to be. I just want to live the rest of my life in peace, and to die in peace, and maybe God will be merciful and let me spend eternity with my beloved George." A tear rolled down her cheek. "I know you think I'm callous for not having grieved for him more, but all I can think of is that I'll be with him soon, which is selfish, I know. But he used to say that he didn't want to outlive me. And I guess I made sure that he didn't."

"What do you mean?" I asked.

"Well, he was shot in the heart, wasn't he? Who do you think is responsible for that?"

CHAPTER 46

"I'm not a very nice person," Rita said again, and out of politeness we all pretended to disagree. "I've done a lot of things in my life I'm ashamed of. I've hurt people to make money, so I could have things." She waved her arm around Bernie's bedroom, a barely decorated room in her broken-down inn.

She seemed so deflated that I felt guilty for having disliked her, but she had made it so easy. I wondered if it was an act, a way of protecting herself from getting too close to anyone. If it was, and my powers of observation were even close to what I thought they were, I should have seen through it. It made me wonder what else I had missed.

The others were clearly not thinking about my observational skills. They were waiting for Rita to explain her remark about George. Yet there was something in her body language that made me think she didn't see her words as needing further explanation. I saw Jesse shift his weight slightly, and I knew that he had given up waiting.

"Why are you responsible for George's death?" he asked quietly.

She looked toward him. "You're a nice young man," she said. "I understand you care for Nell." He nodded. "You're lucky. Nell is a good person who uses that intrusive personality of hers to help other people. I can see why you love her." She smiled at me and I smiled back. "If you love someone, you want to please them, like George wanted to please me. And little by little he became like me. He wanted money. He wanted things. We lived for that. We cared about ourselves, and now look what it's cost us. My heart is failing from lack of use, and his . . ." Tears welled up in her eyes. "His is gone."

"You're not responsible," I said quietly. My dislike for Rita, and the way Bernie had felt about her, made me want her to be the killer, but it was clear that she had neither the motive nor the strength.

Rita looked up at me. "You are so nice to me. All of you. You wouldn't be if you knew what I did for a living."

"I don't think that's true. Whatever you did . . . ," I started. "We already know you didn't inherit this place from your father, and it doesn't matter."

"No, I didn't. My father never had a dime in his pocket. We just said that because people can be so curious about money." She looked at me but there was no accusation in it. "George and I had various businesses," she went on. "We never did anything illegal, but we cut a lot of corners. We set up an Alzheimer's foundation and gave only a percent or two to research and kept the rest for ourselves. We ran a business that was supposed to help people in foreclosure, but we were really buying their houses out from under them and selling them at huge profits." She gasped for breath. "George was charming, and I was all business. People trusted us. And we thought . . ." She stopped. It seemed she couldn't bring herself to admit any more.

Joi finished for her. "They thought they deserved to have whatever material possessions they wanted, no matter who got hurt. They wanted me to help with their schemes. It tore us apart."

"I wanted the kind of security I didn't have growing up. I thought if I gave that to Joi, she would have everything." Rita sighed. "And in the end all I really did was hurt my only child and my oldest friend."

"So you were going to cheat me out of money?" Bernie looked as if she were trying to keep up with a story she could hardly believe. "Nell thought, when we first arrived, that you believed I'd inherited some money from my first husband and that you needed it."

Rita waved her hand to dismiss the idea. "We have money. We have more money than we'll ever need. More money than Joi will ever need, and she'll do good things with it." She smiled at her daughter, who was softly crying. "I didn't want to cheat you out of money, Bernie. I already cheated you out of George."

We'd heard the others walking up the stairs but were all too riveted by Rita's story to pay attention. When I finally looked toward Bernie's open door, I saw my grandmother and Susanne crammed into the room's entrance, trying to be inconspicuous, without any success.

"It was a long time ago, Rita."

Bernie had come all this way and been through so much to find out what really happened forty-five years ago. And yet, as she was about to find out, it seemed clear that she didn't really want to know.

Rita must have sensed her hesitation, but having come this far she was going to tell the whole story. She looked toward Eleanor and Susanne at the door and motioned them to come in. They crowded around us, looking for someone to fill them in on all they had missed, but that would have to wait.

"How did you cheat her out of George?" I asked.

Rita collected herself and went back to her story. "When we were young we were best friends, Bernie and I. But I always envied the courage she had. She left the area to go to college. She wanted something bigger for herself. I used to think she had a gift for seeing the future. She seemed so certain of it."

I glanced over at Bernie, who was blushing.

"I wasn't so sure of myself back then," Rita continued. "I guess that came later. All I knew was that I wanted a good man to take care of me, someone as unlike my father as I could find. Someone with ambition and dreams. To me that someone was George."

"But he was Bernie's boyfriend," Joi said. "I never knew that until last night. He always said you were the only woman he'd ever dated."

"I made him say that. I was so jealous of Bernie that I wanted to erase her from our memories."

"But if he chose to be with you over Bernie," I cut in, "what's to be jealous about?"

"He didn't. At least not at first. Bernie was away at college. He was lonely. I missed her, too. We used to steal whiskey from his parents' liquor cabinet, cheap stuff, and drink together and talk. One night when we both had too much . . ." She stopped and took another breath. She buried her head in her hands and we all waited. For a moment I wondered if she was too ill to go on, but then she lifted her head and started again. "That's a lie. That's the lie I told him so many times that I began to believe it. One night when he had too much to drink, I pushed myself on him. He was eighteen. He didn't need a lot of persuading, but, still, it was my idea."

"And you got pregnant," Bernie said.

Joi let out a gasp. "You had another baby?"

"No."

"But, Mom," Joi said, "that was ten years before I was born."

"I wasn't pregnant." Rita looked at her daughter and then at the rest of us, "I just told Bernie that I was. I went to visit her at school and I made up this whole elaborate lie. I told her I hadn't said anything to George and I didn't know if I should. I told her my father would beat me if he found out I was going to have a baby out of wedlock."

Bernie nodded. "He would have," she said quietly.

"Probably. But there was no baby."

I looked at Bernie, who had let go of Rita's hand and was shaking her head in disbelief. "What did George say when you talked to him?" I asked her.

"I didn't," Bernie said. "I mean, I asked him if anything had gone on with Rita and he admitted it. I didn't ask about the baby because, well, what Rita just said. She told me he didn't know." She sighed. "I don't think it really matters. He'd betrayed me, baby or no baby. That was enough. I went back to school and met Johnny, and then we got married. I heard things about Rita and George from my mother from time to time, things she'd heard in the neighborhood, but I didn't want to know. I didn't want to hear about their growing family or their great life, so I shut out as much as I could. I just assumed there was a baby until I met Joi and realized she was so young."

Joi stood up. She looked as if she was about to storm out but couldn't quite leave. "You trapped Dad into marrying you?"

Rita shook her head slowly. "The one decent thing I did in my whole life was to tell George the truth. After Bernie confronted him, he came to me and we talked. I told him about the lie, and I fully expected he would leave, but he didn't. I'm not sure why. I knew he loved Bernie and I guess he figured it would be too late to win her back, so he stayed."

Bernie gasped, as if she were out of breath. Then, slowly, she leaned toward Rita and took both her hands, holding them in her own. "If he loved me," she said, enunciating each word, "he would have called your night together a mistake. He would have come after me, fought for me, done something to win me back. But he just let me go. Because he wanted to be with you." The way she spoke, it felt to me that Bernie wasn't just saying it to Rita; she was finally realizing the truth herself.

Bernie stood up, pulling Rita up with her. The two old friends stared at each other for a moment, then fell into a long hug. When they let go, Rita turned to her daughter.

"Can you get my sleeping aid?"

Joi nodded and left the room. A few minutes later she returned with a glass filled with a pale yellow liquid.

"Is that lemonade?" I asked.

Joi nodded. "My mother puts a liquid sedative in it. She has trouble sleeping. And she has trouble swallowing pills."

"Did George know that?" I asked Rita.

Rita shook her head. "He thought if I took a sedative I wouldn't wake up, so I put it in lemonade. He hated lemonade, so I knew he'd never catch on. I didn't want to worry him. We never fought, so there was no reason to start over something so small."

I shifted uncomfortably, unsure if this was the time to point out that that wasn't exactly true. After a moment I decided it was. "I saw you and George through the window," I said. "It seemed like you were fighting."

"I was upset and scared. I thought I would die before I'd made things right. George was trying to calm me down, but I think it scared him too."

I thought of that day in the kitchen and how George told me things were harder than he thought they would be. I realized now, he wasn't talking about running an inn. He was talking about the possibility of losing Rita.

Rita turned back to Bernie, and the two women sat on the bed telling us stories of their childhood antics. The tears of a few minutes before were replaced with loud laughter.

"She got what she came for," Eleanor whispered to me. "Now we can all go home."

"No," I whispered back. "Not with George's killer still out there."

CHAPTER 47

Rita was exhausted from finally having told her story, so Joi took her up to bed. Bernie, too, was tired, and after a few minutes of talking, it was clear that the others also needed sleep.

But not me. I went downstairs to the sitting room. The scene in Bernie's room kept playing in my head, as did everything that had happened in the last few days. It hadn't even been a week since we'd left Archers Rest, and yet I felt like I'd been gone from there for a lifetime. I wanted to go home. Even though most of my closest friends were asleep upstairs, I felt far away from much of what mattered to me—Someday Quilts, my grandmother's house by the Hudson River, Jitters coffee shop, and the feeling that everything makes sense. Here, in this rambling old house with sad people who lived sad lives, nothing seemed to.

But as much as I wanted to go home, I knew that if we didn't find the killer, if a cloud still hung over Bernie's head, I would never feel at ease. It annoyed me that I couldn't be more like Rita—a thought I'd never imagined I would have. She could make her peace without having the answers. I doubted I ever could.

I sat in the darkened room, looking at the freshly painted walls, and the empty spot above the fireplace where the gun had been.

I went over the clues in my mind. There was the gun, the dead dog shot with the same kind of bullets that had killed George, the seam ripper with the red mark that I'd found by the murder scene, and the witness McIntyre wouldn't share with us. And there was still so much that Rita hadn't explained. Maybe all of it pointed to the killer. Maybe none of it did.

If Rita was telling the truth, and in my heart I knew she was, she had no reason to kill George. But neither did anyone else. Except Bernie. Finding out the truth tonight did nothing to eliminate her motive. My mind kept going back to what McIntyre was probably thinking, and it didn't reassure me.

There were still a lot of unanswered questions, but for tonight, anyway, I knew I had to stop reaching for them. As Oliver had said before I'd left Archers Rest, I had to look beyond the obvious. And to do that I needed to stop trying so hard. Instead I just sat and stared and thought about all that was wasted in being afraid of the truth. George had loved Rita for all these years, but she was so certain she had been second choice that she'd never really trusted it. And Bernie had walked away from her chance to find out the truth and spent more than forty years wondering what might have been. It was a lesson I knew I was learning; not to be afraid of the truth. In fact, I found myself obsessed with it, though somehow it was just outside my grasp.

I stretched out on the couch and stared up at the ceiling. Not really wanting to sleep, but without the energy to go upstairs to bed, I closed my eyes and drifted off.

There was the sound of a door opening slowly, or maybe a window. Or maybe it was closing. I couldn't be sure. I lay still and listened, but there was no more noise. I closed my eyes and was waiting to fall asleep again when I heard a creak—the creak a floorboard makes when someone walks across it. Someone was up and, by the look of the sky outside the window, it was just before dawn, the part of the night that seems the darkest and most menacing. I decided I'd dreamt the noise and lay back down, turning sideways, with my head facing the back of the couch, to block out the light. But as much as I tried to ignore it, I was cold. And not just cold. there was a breeze against my legs.

I forced myself off the couch. My stupor reminded me of the day I had been drugged, though I knew that wasn't the case this time. I walked to the inn's front door. It was locked. I looked around the entryway and the living room. Everything looked just as it had a few hours before.

I made a sweep of the living room. I thought I saw something move outside the window but I couldn't be sure. My heart racing, I went to the front door, opened it, and looked out. There was nothing, but just as I was about to close the door, I saw it. A flash of light from the woods. I could either do the sensible thing, bolt the door and go upstairs, or I could be stupid and walk toward the woods and find out what it was. I chose stupid.

I grabbed my shoes and headed out the door. The light was still there, just at the edge of the woods, but I couldn't see its source.

"This is how people die in horror movies," I whispered to myself as I walked.

But just as I got close to the light, it went away. I stood in the darkness unsure of whether to go forward or go back. I took ten steps forward but it was pointless. Even with stars in the sky, I couldn't see much once I was in the woods. Afraid of getting lost, I retreated.

I went back to the B-and-B, more than grateful that I hadn't encountered something I couldn't handle. Once safely inside, I closed the door, locked it securely, and just for good measure checked the hall closet, under the couch, and inside an ugly armoire.

I was about to go back to the couch when I noticed, in the corner of the room, where it led to the dining area, an open window.

I couldn't swear to it but I didn't think the window had been open the night before. I walked closer and checked the windowsill. There was a thick layer of dust on each side but the center of the sill was nearly clean, as if something had brushed against it. Like the leg of a murderer as he climbed in the window to kill us all.

"That's enough," I said to myself out loud. "Either go back to bed or get up."

I stood weighing my options for a minute but realized that as long as I was thinking, I was already up.

If my imagination was going to go wild, then it needed caffeine. I went back to the open window, looked outside of it once more. Seeing nothing but feeling the definite chill of an April morning, I closed the window and headed toward the kitchen, already making a list of questions for Rita.

But when I opened the kitchen door, I had an entirely new question to ask.

"What the hell are you doing here?"

CHAPTER 48

"I don't care for profanity," was the answer.

"I don't care what you care for, Alysse or Alice, whichever one you are. It's five thirty in the morning."

"I'm an early riser," she said. "What are you doing up anyway?"

"I'm an early riser too."

"No, you're not. The house is always very quiet at this time of day." She sounded smug for just a moment but must have realized she'd only made things worse for herself.

"You've been in this house before when you weren't supposed to be," I said.

"That's ridiculous." On the floor was a paper bag that I wouldn't have noticed if she hadn't been trying to keep me from noticing it by moving her leg in front of it.

"What's in the bag?"

She turned white, then red. "I don't know what you're talking about."

I reached over and grabbed the bag. Inside was an old, ugly clock, the kind that normally sits on a mantelpiece. It was wooden, with two bulldogs flanking the clock face. Each of the bulldogs was wearing a bowler and holding a cane. At the foot of the bulldog on the right was a smaller dog on a leash.

"What is this?" I asked.

"A clock."

"I've figured that out. Why are you taking it?"

"I'm not taking it."

"You're breaking into the house at dawn to surprise Rita with this clock? You're going to have to come up with a better story than that."

"I don't have to come up with any story," she said. Her words were defiant but her voice was shaking. "You may fancy yourself some kind of real-life Nancy Drew, but you are not a police officer."

"I am." Jesse walked into the kitchen. He was wearing pajama bottoms and an old T-shirt, and looked very sexy and very sleepy. He also looked surprised to find company in the kitchen.

"What are you doing up?" I asked.

"Allie. She had a bad dream. She called the inn's phone. Woke Joi up, and she came and woke me up." He looked at our visitor. "Which twin are you?"

"I don't have to tell you."

"I'll call McIntyre," he said grumpily. "It's too early in the morning for twenty questions. He can arrest you for breaking and entering . . ."

"And stealing." I held up the clock.

Jesse made a face. "Really? I guess there's no accounting for taste. Still, it's a pretty good list of crimes. You'll probably get three to five years."

The twin's lip began to quiver. "Wait."

Jesse leaned against the kitchen counter. "If you're going to confess to the murder, then I need coffee."

"I was just about to make it," I said. I looked at the twin. "But she's not going to confess to the murder. She didn't do it."

Jesse nodded. "I knew it couldn't be that easy. Worth a try though."

✂

Ten minutes later Jesse and I were sitting at the kitchen table, waiting for the captured twin to stop sobbing and tell her story.

"You're hunting for treasure," I said when I got tired of waiting.

She looked at me through wet eyes but said nothing.

"I couldn't figure out why one of you was always in the house but it makes sense. You heard about the crazy guy who used to own the place and the rumor about his treasure, so you and your sister took the class so you could get inside the inn. That's probably why you dress alike, so you can be in two places at once."

I looked to her for confirmation but got none. Jesse leaned back in his chair and motioned for me to continue.

"You've been going through the place when you were supposed to be out searching for things to embellish your quilts or helping with the renovation." I was proud of myself for figuring it out. "George changed the locks when he heard noises, so you must have needed an excuse to get in every day and leave a window open. And since today is the last day of class, it's your last chance to have a good reason for being in the house, so you wanted to make the most of the opportunity to steal everything you could."

"That's a lie," the twin shouted.

"What's going on?" Joi walked into the dining room with Rita steps behind her.

"It looks like everyone got up early today," Rita said.

"Rita, how do you know the twins?" I asked.

The twin started to speak, but I held my hand up to stop her. "I want to hear it from Rita," I said.

Rita shrugged. "This one, or the other one, showed up the day before the quilt retreat and said she'd seen the ad in the paper. She wanted to know if the class would be held in the inn. When

George told her it would be in a separate building on the property, but lunch would be served at the inn, she signed up herself and her sister."

"So what?" the twin asked me.

I turned back to her. "What's a log cabin?"

"It's a wooden house. Why?"

"You're not a quilter," Jesse said. "Even I know that a log cabin is a quilt with strips around a center square."

"You know that?" I asked.

He shrugged. "You pick up a few things when you date a quilter. And that's not the point. She lied about being a quilter. She is a treasure hunter."

"That's a horrible thing to call me," she said as she jumped up and ran from the house.

Rita watched her go. "That was dramatic."

I turned to Jesse. "So what do we do now?"

"Call McIntyre and let him arrest her for breaking and entering and attempting to steal a really ugly clock."

"That'll teach her to call me a liar," I said.

"How do know he shouldn't arrest her for murder?"

"Because when George was killed in the woods, they were searching the house. I thought it was weird that they kept their found objects in a plastic bag, but it makes sense if they didn't go out looking for embellishments during class time."

"You think they brought them from home."

I nodded. "After the first day they knew that Susanne would send them out for leaves and twigs and other things. And on the first day one of them made sketches while the other searched. It's why the sketches were so alike despite their having such different quilting styles."

"But what if George found them stealing?" Jesse asked.

"Then they would have killed him in the house. That is, if George cared that they were taking things from the house . . ."

"And he wouldn't have," Rita interjected.

"Exactly. George might have wanted the objects back, like the quilts, but I don't think he would have pressed charges. And if he had . . ."

Jesse nodded. "He would have called McIntyre from the house right then. He wouldn't have left the thieves to wander around while he went on a picnic."

"I just don't see either of them being killers," Rita said.

"Neither do I, but, then, that's the case with everyone here," I admitted.

Rita walked over to me and took my hand in hers. "I feel that I've gotten Bernie into this mess and I don't know how to get her out of it. If I hadn't wanted to make things right with Joi . . ."

Now it all made sense. At least the part that didn't include the murder. "This house isn't for you," I said. "Not the classes, not the quilt shop. You're creating something to give to your daughter for her charity."

Joi looked at her mother. "What are you talking about?"

Rita shook her head at me. The softness of the last twelve hours was momentarily replaced by the impatience I'd first witnessed in her. "I should have assumed that you would blurt out my secret," she said. Then she turned toward her daughter. "Your father and I wanted everything to be done for you," she said. "He was so worried I'd be gone before we got everything in place that he rushed to get Bernie and the others up here before we were really ready. He wanted to bring you here as well."

"He even drove to Saratoga Springs once to tell you," I said to Joi.

"How do you know that?" Rita looked at me.

"The gas receipt in your car. It makes sense that he would do that. But he changed his mind."

"I begged him not to. I thought Joi would feel as if we were mocking her life if we presented her with a broken-down inn. I even changed my mind at one point and put it on the market, but I knew this was the last thing I could do for you. I just wanted it all to be perfect, and it's all turned out such a mess."

"Why would you do all this?" Joi was in tears.

"It's your dream to have a place like this."

Joi looked around.

"Well, not like this," Rita continued. "Better than this. We were running out of time, and I wanted so much to have it nice for you. I thought that with Eleanor's help I might at least get the shop ready."

Mother and daughter held each other, and I felt suddenly as if I were in the way. I nodded to Jesse, and he and I went to the kitchen to get coffee. We were so close to finding the rest of the secrets but I, too, was running out of time and I still had so many unanswered questions. But now that I knew why the twins were in the house, I was sure of at least one thing.

CHAPTER 49

"The bullets don't match the gun from the inn," I said before McIntyre had a chance to speak.

Jesse had called him and told him about the twins' escapades. In the sort of police work that can only happen in a small town, McIntyre had called the sisters and asked them to make sure to come to the inn to clear up what he had called "the confusion" about the missing objects, which they'd agreed to do. One of them even made a feeble joke about coming back to the scene of the crime. Then McIntyre drove over to the inn, bringing pumpkin doughnuts from Maria's bakery.

"Well, Chief?" I waited. "The bullets don't match, do they?"

"How does she know that?" McIntyre looked to Jesse for the answer.

Jesse just shrugged. "It's like a magic trick. If she tells you, it spoils the fun."

"I think the twins have been stealing items from the house to check their value," I explained. "They probably stole the gun, and when they realized that you thought it was the murder weapon, they ditched it."

"So the killer didn't need to have access to the house, just a gun. Any gun," Jesse said.

"That doesn't eliminate anyone in the county," McIntyre told him.

I took a breath. "Or anyone here."

"So who did it?" McIntyre asked.

"I don't know," I admitted. "But you know something I don't. The identity of the witness."

"I guess, since you've gotten this far, it might help if I told you everything. I promised the witness I'd keep it confidential so I'm trusting you both to be discreet."

Jesse and I promised that we'd keep it to ourselves, though I wasn't so sure I would keep that promise, especially since that person was responsible for getting Bernie hauled into the police station.

"It's Mrs. Ackerman," he said.

"Helen?"

He nodded. "She said she was out in the woods and she saw Mrs. Avallone."

"Doing what?" Jesse moved closer to me, as if he were protecting me from bad news that was about to come.

"According to her statement, she saw her bent over the body."

I paused for a moment to consider whether Bernie had told McIntyre the whole story, but even if she hadn't, it had to be told. "She may have seen Bernie bent over the body," I said. "But when Bernie left George at the picnic site, he was alive," I stressed. "She realized she had something more to say, so she went back. When she got there, he was already dead. If Helen saw Bernie, then she saw her discover George, not kill him."

McIntyre seemed to have an additional piece of information. After a moment's hesitation, he shared it: "There was a gun next to her."

I walked out of the kitchen and into the living room. Joi, still overwhelmed with gratitude at her parents' generosity, was there with Rita, who, clearly unaccustomed to being seen as kind, seemed slightly uncomfortable but happy. I was intruding, but I figured at this point Rita was used to it from me.

"You're friends with Helen and Frank," I said.

She looked up at me. I could feel her about to tell me, once again, how odd I was but, thankfully, she refrained. "Yes. I suppose."

"How are Helen's knees?"

"Terrible. She has arthritis and can't walk very far without being in terrible pain. Why?"

"Just asking."

She nodded. "I suppose you have your reasons."

Now that we were this close, it was frustrating to wait for the students to arrive. I walked to the classroom, thinking I might pass the time finishing my block for George. I had been working on an abstract piece that would represent the inn, but now I wanted to incorporate his love for Rita and Joi in the piece. That meant a lot of work, but I was too distracted. Instead I looked at the other blocks.

Frank had drawn a man and woman holding hands. The woman, with short blonde hair, was clearly Rita, but the man was nondescript. It was an amateurish drawing but it was very touching—assuming the man was George. Next to it was Helen's block, with a very neat appliqué of a bird in flight. At the bottom of the block, on what I guessed was meant to represent the earth, was a crisscross of fabric pieces that reminded me of barbed wire. Maybe it was her way of saying that George was freed from the burdens of life. Pete's wasn't nearly so emotional. It was a simple drawing of two houses with some trees between them and a caption, "A Good Neighbor. A Good Man." At the last table, the twins' quilts were nearly finished. One was the detailed drawing of the inn, and the other, two hands clasped together. One hand had a large diamond on it, so I figured that was meant to be Rita. The other quilts were abstract, and I knew they belonged to Eleanor, Jesse, and Susanne. Like me, they didn't know enough about George to offer much insight, but their quilts were made with considerable care and attention, and that was lovely in itself.

I loved the idea of journal quilting, even though this was only my second attempt. To make a small quilt, without any concern for durability or even beauty, but one that represented a thought—that was something I could really embrace.

When we arrived, the plan had been to make three quilts: one for the world around us, one for our lives as they are now, and one for our future dreams. We'd only made the first before "our lives as they are now" became a murder investigation. As I sat in the empty classroom, I thought about what I would have made, not just for the second quilt, but, more importantly, for the third. What did I want for the future?

Out loud I said, "I want the truth."

I had learned from Bernie and Rita that you pay a terrible price for holding back the whole truth. Maybe there was a truth about my own life that I hadn't been willing to face.

I took a piece of white felt and laid it down at a workstation. I took paints and colored the felt a soft blue and drew a sketch of the truth that scared me the most.

"You're early."

As I was finishing my sketch, I heard someone walk in behind me, but I was too busy to look up. When I did, I saw Helen holding a tote bag.

"I've been trying to work out a few things," I said.

She nodded. "It's nice to have a bit of peace and quiet."

She took the items out of her tote bag and lined them up at her workstation—a photograph of George outside of the inn, some pastels, scissors, several needles, and a book of poems. I picked up the book.

"You love poetry," I said.

"I always have but I never had the time to read it. Frank isn't a fan of such things, but maybe the grandchildren would like them. It would be nice to share my interests with someone."

"Where is Frank?"

"He came with me but decided to go into the woods before class starts. If that man has twenty minutes free, he either wants to flirt with someone or kill something."

She looked down at her table and rearranged the scissors and needles so all her items were lined up from smallest to largest. As she did I noticed something on the scissors.

"What is that?" I put my finger on the red mark.

"Nail polish. It identifies the scissors as mine. That way they don't walk out with someone else in the class."

"Good idea. You should have a seam ripper too."

She looked at her things then checked the tote bag. "I think I gave it to Frank. He's always forgetting to bring his supplies. And what he manages to remember falls out of his pockets."

I took a step back. "I'll let you get some work in. It's going to be a while before the others show up, and I should probably get some breakfast."

"You do that, Nell. You look so tired. I think you've been trying too hard to solve George's murder. I would think if you're going to get yourself involved, you have to look at it logically. Who has the most to gain? And who had the time to do it?"

"I suppose." I wanted so much to ask her about seeing Bernie in the woods, but I couldn't betray my promise not to. Not if I expected any more information from McIntyre. Instead I took a different tack. "You were very fond of George, weren't you?"

"He seemed to be a nice man," she said calmly. "Of course, I didn't know him that well."

It was clear that she was a liar, but whether she was lying to me, to Susanne, to McIntyre, or to all of us, and why, was beyond me at the moment.

I cleaned up my space a little, I left my unfinished future quilt on the table and walked out of the classroom.

CHAPTER 50

Joi and Rita were sitting on the porch, enjoying each other and the morning air. Maybe it was only because I knew how sick Rita was that she suddenly looked so fragile, but I felt a concern and affection for her that startled me.

"My grandchildren are coming up to see me," she said as I walked up the porch steps.

"That's wonderful."

Joi smiled at her mother. "My husband is bringing them up tomorrow. They'll stay for Dad's funeral, and we're going to spend the week. My husband is wonderful with his hands, so if anyone can take this from a dilapidated old Victorian house to a beautiful inn and school, it's him. And maybe some of the neighbors will keep helping."

"I'm glad for you both." As I said it, Eleanor walked out with Barney just behind her. Barney ran down the steps and sniffed at the trees for a moment, then sat on the lawn.

"I think he's finally put the woods behind him," she said.

"Or he's gotten too lazy to bother."

"Either way he'll be easy to find," Eleanor said.

"Where's Jesse?"

"He's in the shower. He'll be down in fifteen minutes." Eleanor smiled. "You two can't bear to be separated. Two minutes ago he asked me where you were. It's nice to be in love, isn't it?'

"I wouldn't know. Jesse told me he 'really likes me.' "

"And what do you feel?"

I thought about my future quilt: a sketch of me and Jesse and his daughter, Allie, with the Main Street of Archers Rest in the background. "I'm scared. His life is so fully formed and mine is so . . . not. If I love him, maybe I'll find myself fitting into his plan, when I really need to make my own."

"You can be no one other than who you are, Nell. It seems to me that Jesse has figured that out. As soon as you do, you'll be okay." Eleanor nodded toward the dog. "I'll leave him in your capable hands. I need a cup of tea."

As soon as Eleanor walked back into the inn, Barney stood up. He looked for a moment as if he was going to follow my grandmother, but instead he turned and ran toward the woods.

"Oh, that nut," I said. I ran down the steps after him.

"I'll help you," Joi called out, and the two of us headed into the woods to find Barney.

"Barney," I called out as we headed toward the spot where I thought I'd seen him digging in the past. I knew he wouldn't hear me—his deafness was nearly complete—but I didn't know what else to do.

The woods seemed darker than ever before. The sky wasn't overcast, and it was very early in the day—not yet eight in the morning—but I felt myself getting confused, as though the light was fading and I was being trapped.

"I'll check over there." Joi pointed to another path. Before I had a chance to respond, she was gone.

"Be careful," I shouted after her.

There could be traps, or rabid animals, I worried, and somewhere among the trees Frank was wandering with a gun. I stood for a moment, hoping Joi could take care of herself, and then I wondered if I could.

"Barney," I yelled. There was rustling and I thought I heard something else. "Barney," I said again.

I turned in the direction of the sound and realized that I was walking toward more darkness, but at least now I had figured out the reason. There were evergreens throughout the woods and in this section they were particularly dense. Just knowing why made me breath a little easier. It even looked a little familiar.

"I've seen this before," I said to myself as I noticed a slightly mounded area of dark earth.

And then I knew. Seconds before my biggest concern was a missing dog, but now that I knew the truth, I could feel the blood drain from my face. I'd been wrong. I'd been wrong about everything.

CHAPTER 51

Just as I was about to turn and run, I saw Barney sniffing at a nearby tree. When he saw me, he came over and licked my face.

"We're leaving, sweetie," I said. "Grandma will be mad if you keep her waiting."

But he didn't want to leave. Once he'd sniffed at the dark mound of earth, he wouldn't let me pull him away. He started to dig. I tried to pull him off the hole but I couldn't. In just a minute, his digging had revealed the thing I knew was there but I'd dreaded seeing: a woman's hand.

"We have to go now," I told the confused dog. He pulled away from my grip. "Now!" I shouted.

Then I heard a shot.

"You and that dog are exactly the same," I heard. "Stubborn. Too stubborn to live."

Another shot. I pulled Barney toward a tree. "Run," I whispered to him. "Get Jesse."

Barney licked my face as if he was trying to play, but I put my hands on his jowls so we locked eyes.

"Get Jesse," I said again, then let him go.

For a second he seemed confused; then suddenly he took off toward the edge of the woods. And away from Pete, and me.

I ran the opposite way, hoping the noises going in two different directions would confuse Pete. I saw that I was heading toward the hiking path that would take me toward Pete's house, and that was the last place I wanted to go. I turned right and ran through the trees.

When I couldn't run anymore, I crouched behind the largest tree I could find and tried to steady my breathing. It's startling how loud breathing can be when you're trying to be quiet. My hands were shaking and I didn't know how long my legs would hold, but my life depended on it. The thought made my hands shake more.

I listened. There was nothing but the sounds of a few birds. I knew it was probably pointless but I took my cell phone out of my pocket. There was one bar, so I took a chance and dialed Jesse. Just as it started to ring, the call was dropped. No signal, only the quiet of country life that my grandmother had been extolling a few days before. I wrapped my fingers around the phone, just in case.

I heard leaves rustle. I tried to think. Was it thirty or forty feet away? Did I have time to run or should I just hope for the best and stay hidden behind the tree? I thought about every action movie I'd ever seen, trying to figure out an escape plan, but nothing came to me. All I could think of was my unfinished journal quilt—the one that was supposed to depict my life as I hoped it would become.

My heart was pounding. I looked around for a possible escape route. I wasn't sure my feet would move even if I wanted them to, so I waited. More noise. But this wasn't birds. This was something else. Footsteps. I held my breath and prayed they would move in the other direction.

Then nothing. The noise, the footsteps, had stopped. I realized I'd been standing in tangled vines and my ankle was itching. I tried to ignore it and concentrate on the footsteps. I'd have plenty of time to scratch my ankle once I got out of this. If I got out of this.

The footsteps started up again and for a moment moved toward me. I held my breath. Then, just when they seemed on top of me, they stopped and seemed to move in the other direction.

"Keep going," I thought. "Just let me get out of here and I will never again stick my nose where it doesn't belong. I will live a long life making quilts and drawing pictures and staying out of trouble."

The footsteps were gone. Definitely gone. I stood up, took a deep breath, and ran as fast as I could in the opposite direction. I didn't care that tree branches were slapping me across the face as I ran. I didn't care that my feet kept getting stuck in mud. Or that I had bitten so hard into my lip that it was beginning to bleed. I just wanted to get out of the woods and back to the inn as fast as I could.

I was heading toward the edge of the woods when my cell phone rang. The sound was so startling that I nearly dropped it.

"Nell?" I heard Jesse's worried voice on the other end.

"Jesse," I whispered. "I'm near where we found the body. I'm in trouble. I'm heading toward the inn."

"I'm coming to get you," he said. "And Nell, I . . ."

The signal was lost, and with it Jesse's comforting voice. My heart sank.

"Don't let that be the last time I talk to him," I silently prayed.

Then I saw the gun.

"Jesse's on his way right now," I called out as defiantly as I could, but even I could hear the fear in my voice.

"Well, he's going to be too late," was the response.

I looked at his face. The gentle man who had become a friend, and who I'd thought might be a nice match for Bernie, was George's killer—and was ready to kill me.

The gun was pointed directly at me. I made a choice. I turned and ran back toward the trees. I'd taken ten steps when I heard a loud sound.

After that all I could feel was pain.

I fell to the ground. I could feel Pete getting closer. In seconds he was standing over me with his gun pointed directly at me.

"Your first quilt," I said. "It was a grave."

"I didn't mean to do that. Susanne was right about forgetting yourself when you make one of those quilts. I thought you had figured it out, that day in the classroom. I was scared. But you didn't." He laughed a little. "It was reckless of me but it was funny too. You think you're so smart, and you didn't see it."

"I see it now."

"I know." There was sadness in his voice. I hoped it would translate into a reluctance to shoot me. "I tried to keep you out of here, but you wouldn't listen. I don't understand why you just couldn't mind your own business."

The gun was getting closer to my face.

It was stupid, but it was all I could think of. I kicked his knee as hard as I could. I expected the rifle to go off, but instead Pete stumbled, dropping the gun.

"What the hell?" he said, as startled as I was.

I jumped up and grabbed the gun. I could feel a searing pain in my shoulder and I knew the wetness I felt against my skin was blood, but I was the one with a weapon. That was all that mattered.

I took the butt of the gun and hit him. Pete fell back for a moment but came after me. I knew I wouldn't have time to run.

"Go ahead and shoot that thing," Pete taunted. Whatever kindness there was in him was buried under desperation. "You need to know what you're doing with a rifle and, trust me, city kid, you don't."

He started to get up. I pointed the rifle at him, awkwardly, wincing at the pain that shot up my arm.

"Do you really want to take that chance?" I yelled.

Pete nodded. "Yeah, Nell, I think I do."

I tried to remember everything Frank had taught me. Then I pulled the trigger.

"Damn!" Pete fell to the ground in what seemed like slow motion, gripping his right leg.

My whole body began to shake and I found the rifle slipping from my arm. I held it at my side, watching Pete writhe in pain.

"Great shot."

I turned and saw Jesse, Frank, and McIntyre running toward me, led by Barney.

"Thanks, Frank," I said, and handed him the rifle. Jesse grabbed me and I collapsed in his arms.

"I'll get an ambulance," Frank said, and ran from the scene while Jesse wrapped his arms protectively around me.

McIntyre stepped over to Pete. "This is probably pretty obvious, but you're under arrest for the attempted murder of Nell Fitzgerald."

"And the murder of George Olnhausen," I said.

McIntyre nodded toward me, then turned his attention back to Pete. "That too. Now, if you will just tell me why you did it."

Pete scowled at him but said nothing.

"I know why," I said. "His wife's body is buried twenty feet from where we found George."

McIntyre turned back to Pete. "You killed Siobhan?"

Pete grimaced. "I'm not saying anything. If you want answers, you'll have to ask the busybody from out of town."

McIntyre looked at me. "I will, Pete. Thanks for the advice. It's nice when we're all working together." He reached down and handcuffed Pete's hands.

CHAPTER 52

My shoulder wasn't as bad as the initial pain had led to me to believe. The bullet had gone right through, and once the doctor had patched me up at the hospital and given me a very welcome pain reliever, Jesse took me back to the inn.

"And you're going straight to bed," he said.

But much to Jesse's annoyance, that didn't happen. As soon as our car pulled up, McIntyre stepped forward to thank me for my help, and then my grandmother, Bernie, and all the students from Susanne's class ran out to greet me. Joi and her mother were on the porch but came down to welcome me. Barney, who had his nose in a flower bed, looked up and came running, pushing past the others.

"You solved the case," I said as he jumped all over me. "If you hadn't insisted on digging in those spots, we wouldn't have found out what happened."

"That's probably why Pete killed Frank's dog," McIntyre said. "If he was hunting on the property with Frank, he probably sniffed at the body and started digging. Pete didn't bury her very deep."

"Barney must have discovered the body that day," I said. "And when Bernie left, George went looking for her. I think he must have left the picnic basket but taken the quilt because it was too nice to just leave it there."

"That's why George wasn't where I left him," Bernie said. "I thought I'd walked back to the wrong tree."

"While he was looking for you, he probably found Barney, and what Barney was digging up, and went looking for help."

"And found Pete instead," Jesse said. "All this time Barney's been going back into the woods, looking for that spot. He was trying to uncover a murderer." Jesse stroked Barney's head. "I guess you've been hanging out with these detectives long enough to want in on a case."

"He nearly got Nell killed," my grandmother said. "I don't know what I would have done . . ."

I reached out and hugged her with my good arm. "I'm fine. And Barney didn't almost get me killed. He saved my life. He ran to get Jesse."

"It's true," Jesse said. "Barney found McIntyre and me and brought us right to her."

"How did you get there?" I asked Frank.

"I heard shots. Then I heard you yell out. I knew if you kept wandering in the woods you'd get yourself in trouble, so I came to help."

I hugged him. "You're a difficult man to like," I said, "but you're a good man."

He laughed. "A lot of people feel that way about me. Including my wife."

I looked at Helen, who was standing the farthest from me of any of the students. Even the twins had crowded around.

"Your wife doesn't feel that way, Frank," I said. "She tried to set you up for a murder rap."

"That's ridiculous," Helen protested, as Frank turned to her, confusion spreading across his face.

I shook my head. "She told Susanne that she and George were in love. That was nonsense, but if anyone thought you believed it, it would be a motive for a hot-tempered guy like you to shoot him. Plus you seemed to be so fond of Rita. That might look like an affair, too."

"He was my pharmacist," Rita said. "He knew what medications I was on. He knew I was sick."

"I figured that out, but it took me a while," I admitted. "You also knew about Pete's wife and her headaches. And, I'm assuming, her unhappiness."

"Pete wanted things his way. We all do," Frank acknowledged. "But he was particularly rigid. When Siobhan, his wife . . . when she got a job and started to come into town a lot, he didn't care for that. She used to confide in me because she knew I had a professional obligation to keep it to myself. We don't have any therapists in Winston, so it's me or the bartender at McGrudy's."

"And then you heard she'd left Pete."

He nodded. "I was happy for her. I thought there couldn't be an unhappier wife in the county." He looked toward Helen. "I guess I was wrong."

"But why kill her?" Joi asked. "Hasn't he heard of divorce?"

"He told me that his place was a dream he'd worked all his life for. And if they divorced, I guess he figured she'd get half," I said.

"I don't see why you're accusing me of doing anything wrong. Pete's marital troubles have nothing to do with me," Helen said.

"You gave your seam ripper to Frank after George was killed. Frank must have dropped it in the woods when he went hunting. It probably fell out of a hole in his pocket. You got lucky that if fell out so close to the murder scene."

"No, she didn't," Frank said. "She knew I hunted in that area. And in the days after George's death she's been giving me things to hold. Earrings, her spare car key, that seam ripper. She must have figured something would fall out in the woods. I guess that explains why I kept finding a hole in every pair of pants I put on."

"I knew Frank was innocent when I realized, the seam ripper had to have been dropped there after the murder, because if had been there when we found George's body, I'm sure McIntyre would have found it." I looked toward McIntyre and smiled. "He's a very good cop. If I'd believed that at the beginning, I wouldn't have almost fallen for Helen's scheme to frame Frank."

"If not for you, I might have thought it was Bernie," McIntyre said.

I turned back to Frank. "And Helen made a point of telling me that you were alone in the woods on the day of the murder. In fact, Helen went out of her way each time I saw her to point me in your direction."

Helen made grunting noises but didn't move or deny it.

"I was thrown off the track when the twins told me that she had walked into the woods, but she couldn't have."

Helen glared at the twins, who ignored her and looked toward me.

"Pete told us he saw her, but didn't want to get in the middle of it, because he and Frank didn't get along as it was," one of them said. "So we agreed to say something."

"We thought we were doing the right thing," the other added.

"There is one thing that doesn't make sense," Jesse said to Helen. "If you didn't go to the woods, how did you know about Bernie being bent over the body?"

Helen shrugged and seemed to give up her protestations. "Pete told me." Her voice was hard, as if she was being treated unfairly and was the real victim. "After his fight with Frank, I called to thank him. I'd never had a man defend my honor before." She glared at her husband. "Pete told me that I was a real lady. And then he told me that he'd seen Bernie in the woods, bending over George. He asked for my advice, something my husband never did. He didn't want to cause any problems for Bernie, but he felt the police should know, so I promised to tell McIntyre. I guess he was using me, like he did the twins." She sighed heavily. "I obviously had no idea he'd killed George."

"He set you up to frame Bernie," I said, "and you used it to set up Frank. The items Frank dropped in the woods would point to you, but any investigation by the police would uncover your severe arthritis. You couldn't possibly walk that far into the woods with your bad knees. McIntyre would assume you were covering for someone. And it would be perfectly reasonable for him to assume that person was Frank."

Frank took a deep breath. "I had no idea you were so miserable," he said to his wife.

"Of course you didn't, because you never think of my needs. George did everything for Rita and you did nothing for me."

"So you set me up for murder?" Not that I blamed him, but the tone of Frank's voice had gone from disbelief to hatred. I watched as Jesse moved closer in case it crossed over into something physical. But Frank made no move toward Helen. He just yelled at her for having made him a suspect.

"That," Helen screamed, "is what I have put up with! That temper. Yelling at me if dinner is late. Yelling at me if the children were acting up. I want some quiet time in my old age. I've been good to you and instead of appreciating what you have you yell at me and go running after women like Rita and Susanne, who couldn't be bothered with you." She was now in near hysterics.

McIntyre walked over to her and put his arms around her. "I'll get a deputy to drive you home, Helen."

"I don't want to go to jail," she sobbed.

"You interfered with a police investigation, but I think we can look past that. You just go home and get some rest."

She nodded and let herself be led away by McIntyre's deputy.

We all stood in silence, watching for a further explosion from Frank. But he seemed to deflate.

"I deserved it," he said quietly, his anger changed into disbelief. He turned to Rita. "Even knowing what you and George were going through with your illness, I envied you. The way you loved each other. I should have been to Helen what George was to you."

"We all have regrets," Rita said. "I guess the trick is to make your peace with them and move on."

"Who would have guessed that she was so devious?" one twin said to the other after Helen had gone.

"Pot calling the kettle," I said. "One of you is guilty of breaking and entering this morning."

They shrugged in unison. "But only one of us. And you don't know which one."

"The one with the pierced ears," I said. Since Susanne had pointed out the small difference between the sisters, it was easy for me to check when I saw the one in the kitchen with her hair behind her ears. "Which one is that, Susanne?"

"Alice," she said.

"Then McIntyre you can arrest Alice for stealing."

"But we were only taking what was ours," Alysse said.

"Nothing in that house is yours," Jesse pointed out. "And you knew that or you wouldn't have been sneaking around."

Alysse looked sheepish. "Maybe not legally ours," she acknowledged. "But we took care of Mr. Gervais. We visited him once a week and brought him his groceries and anything he needed. In return he promised us this." She reached into her purse and took out a piece of paper. When she handed it to me, I saw that it was a drawing of two plus signs.

Alice added, "When he gave us this drawing, he said it would provide us with financial security."

"He wouldn't tell us what it meant," Alice explained. "He thought if he told us, we would take it, and then we wouldn't come to visit him anymore."

I studied the sketch. "It reminds me of something," I said, "but I don't know what." I held it up so the others could see.

"A double cross," my grandmother offered.

"That's what we thought," Alysse said, "but the double cross quilt George showed us is worth just a few hundred dollars."

"Maybe it means he double crossed you," McIntyre said. "You ladies helped him and got squat in return. And he told you in the form of a puzzle, which was just like the old coot. He loved riddles and games."

"We're going to jail for nothing!" Alysse began to cry.

Rita stood up and walked over to the twins. "You're not going to jail. I won't press charges. Nothing you took means anything to me, and if you were promised something, then you had every right to it."

A week ago I couldn't have imagined Rita making such a statement and, looking at the tears forming in Joi's eyes, it was clear that she wouldn't have, either. But it was also obvious that she was proud of her mother.

"But we didn't get anything," Alice said, joining her sister in tears. "And we brought everything back." She ran to her car and began frantically taking items from the trunk. The three quilts, a candlestick that matched the one I'd found on the stairs, the ugly collage, and a dozen other items.

"You can have everything back," Alysse said. "We weren't going to keep anything that didn't rightfully belong to us. We were just waiting for the right time to sneak these things back into the house."

"That's what I was doing with the clock," Alice said. "I was bringing it back. I swear."

"One of you stood in the woods and signaled," I suddenly realized. "Why?"

"In case a light went on or the door opened. If Alice was in the house, searching, I'd signal her to get out."

"You took my postcards too," Susanne blurted out.

"But when we realized they had nothing to do with the house, we returned them. We were just looking for that." She pointed to the sketch.

I studied the two plus signs again, and started laughing. "You said Mr. Gervais liked puzzles?"

"He loved them," McIntyre said.

Suddenly, I remembered. I whispered in Jesse's ear, and he smiled and then went running toward the house. When he came back, he was winded from the climb up three flights of stairs, but he had the two landscape paintings from Rita's room.

"Is this what you wanted?" he asked.

"I knew something struck me when I was in Rita's room," I said. "I was just so focused on finding evidence against her that I didn't look closely at anything that didn't seem to matter. But I know I studied this painter in art class." I looked at the nearly illegible signature, and confirmed it. "They are both by Patrick Cross. I didn't recognize it at first. He's not that well known, and I think he's terrible, but after he died two years ago, his paintings went up in value. They're maybe worth two hundred thousand dollars."

The twins were too shocked to cry anymore, and they just stood staring at the painting that Jesse held. Rita whispered to her daughter and then turned to the ladies.

"When my husband and I bought this place from Mr. Gervais's nephew, we bought everything in it. He didn't see the value in those paintings, and obviously neither did we. But, then, they didn't really belong to us. They belong to you two."

Alice and Alysse looked at her. "We can have them?" they asked almost in unison.

"Don't be sure that money will bring you what you want," Rita warned. "You have something far more important, because you have each other."

It was a lovely sentiment, and one the twins obviously agreed with, because they hugged each other, and then Rita, for a long time. For a moment I thought they might leave the paintings. But I was wrong. They took them gingerly from Jesse's hands and held them as if they were newborn children.

"What are you going to do with the money?" I asked.

They laughed. "I don't know," Alysse said. "We were so focused on getting it that we never considered what we'd do with it. But we will finish George's quilt and we'll help you, Rita, in whatever way you need."

"And you don't have to promise us a fortune. We'll keep coming to help," Alice added.

"Well, Nell, it looks like you've solved all the mysteries of this old place," Rita said.

"Not all of them," I said. "What's in your bedroom?"

She laughed.

CHAPTER 53

The next morning Jesse put my suitcase in his car. "Do you want to go back with me or Eleanor?"

I pointed to my suitcase. "I guess I'm going back with you."

He put his arm around me, and I winced and pulled back. I tried to position myself so I was in his arms but not in pain. I bent my knees a little and moved slightly to the left so that my shoulder didn't touch his arm. It wasn't a perfect solution, but at least we were holding each other.

"When you get better, I am going to yell at you for a really long time," he whispered.

I looked up at him. "Looking forward to it."

"Nell, I love you," he said. "I know I should have said it before . . ."

I kissed him. "I love you too. And, look, I know there's a way things are supposed to go: we date, get married, have kids. And that would all be wonderful. I just don't want . . ."

"To end up like Helen." He finished my thought.

"I just don't want to follow the pattern someone else creates for me. I want a life I create for myself."

"Do you want me in it?" There was tentativeness in his voice, and it broke my heart that he felt he even had to ask the question.

I reached into my purse and pulled out my unfinished future quilt. "I was going to give this to you when it was done." I handed him the sketch I'd made of us with his daughter. "This is the future I want."

Jesse didn't say anything. He just held me for a long time, and this time I didn't feel any pain in my shoulder.

Just as we finally let go of each other, Bernie walked out of the house with Joi on one side and Rita on the other.

Rita was still holding the memorial quilt we had made for George. After the excitement of the arrest died down, Frank and the twins stayed to help Eleanor, Susanne, and Jesse finish the quilt. With my bad arm, I couldn't do much in the way of sewing, but I did stay up to offer support. We left out Pete's block, but there were still the eight blocks we had created in class, plus a block Bernie made, with three colors wrapped together to symbolize Rita, George, and herself. With our nine blocks, we made a three-by-three arrangement, and we cut up George's favorite shirt to use for the sashing. What had started off as a way to get a bunch of suspects together in the same room had taken on great meaning for us, and I was glad everyone had spent the night piecing and quilting it. It was clear how much it meant to Rita.

"Susanne wants to head home to her grandson," I told Bernie, when I saw her, "so you better get packed up if you're going with her."

Bernie nodded. "I think I'm going to stay a few days," she said. "I can help Rita and Joi around here, and we have a lot of catching up to do."

Rita walked over to me and took my hand. "Thank you. You gave me everything I could want. I'd never known the kind of friendship you all have. Maybe I should have joined a quilt group." She smiled. "I've been so touched by the way you all help each other. And by the way you've helped me. I wish George were here to see this, but somehow his death made it all possible." She shook her head. "And I'll see him again soon."

"Mom," Joi said quietly. "Not too soon. I need to spend time with you, too."

Rita nodded. She reached into the pocket of her cardigan and pulled out a black-and-white photo. "Nell, you asked what was behind my locked door." She handed me the photo. "All my valuables were there. I was worried about having strangers in the house, so I put everything of importance in the room and locked it."

I looked at the photo. It was a young and smiling trio: Rita, George, and Bernie.

"She has tons of photos," Bernie said, "of Joi, of us as kids. And two quilts her mother made. It will take us a week just to look at them all."

Rita smiled at her old friend. Behind her I could see Susanne come out of the house with her suitcase. Like me, she stopped when she saw what would have seemed impossible a week before: the two old friends holding each other.

Susanne walked over and hugged Bernie. "I'm so glad it all worked out."

"Why didn't you call me an old fool for holding on to such a silly idea for all these years?"

"I don't know why I didn't think of it." Susanne laughed.

Bernie turned to me. "I don't think all these years I was wondering why I had lost George to Rita. I think I was wondering why I'd lost Rita. She was my best friend. I've missed her terribly."

"It's nice to have an old friend to rely on," I said, as I looked at the two women.

Bernie took my hand. "And it's nice to have a new friend to rely on, as well."

I could feel tears coming down my face but I didn't stop them. After wanting for an entire week to go home, I couldn't bring myself to leave so I just stood there while Bernie and Joi helped Rita back into the house.

"Honestly, Nell," Eleanor said as she walked down the steps, with Barney at her side. "It's bad enough that you have only one good arm. Now you're crying. We have a shop to get back to and quilts to make. You can't help if you're completely worthless."

"Completely worthless?" I said in mock alarm. "I did manage to solve a murder and learn to long-arm quilt."

She smiled. "You do remember it's Friday, don't you? We should be back in Archers Rest by this afternoon. And I assume we're having a quilt meeting tonight."

"I'll make sure we're ready. But no gossip. We're going to have to talk about quilting for at least five minutes," I said sternly.

As we got in our cars to leave, I sensed that everyone, including Barney, was laughing at such a ridiculous idea.

Clare O'Donohue

ISBN 978-0-452-28979-6

ISBN 978-0-452-29558-2

Available wherever books are sold.

Plume
A member of Penguin Group (USA) Inc.
www.penguin.com